UNDER HER
INFLUENCE

By the Author

Romance Novels

Mergers & Acquisitions

Climbing the Ladder

A Swedish Christmas Fairy Tale

Second Chances

Going Up

Lost at Sea

The Startling Inaccuracy of the First Impression

Fitting In

Detour to Love

Under Her Influence

The Flight Series

Flight SQA016 (Ylva Publishing)

Grounded (Ylva Publishing)

Journey's End

The Remember Me Series

Bring Holly Home

Keep Holly Close

The Around the World Series

The Road Ahead

The Big Uneasy

Mystery Novels

Huntress

Death Before Dessert

UNDER HER INFLUENCE

by

Amanda Radley

2021

UNDER HER INFLUENCE

ISBN 13: 978-1-63555-963-7

THIS TRADE PAPERBACK ORIGINAL IS PUBLISHED BY
BOLD STROKES BOOKS, INC.
P.O. BOX 249
VALLEY FALLS, NY 12185

FIRST EDITION: JUNE 2021

CREDITS
EDITOR: RUTH STERNGLANTZ
PRODUCTION DESIGN: STACIA SEAMAN
COVER DESIGN BY TAMMY SEIDICK

Acknowledgments

Thank you to the wonderful team at Bold Strokes Books for helping me to bring this story to life. Special thanks to my editor Ruth for her words of wisdom.

For the readers.

Chapter One

B eth Fraser stalked towards the main entrance to Fraser Park.
    "Good morning, Miss Fraser," the security guard greeted
as he opened up the gate to allow her past.

She mumbled a greeting in return, distracted by the overflowing
rubbish bin she saw just beyond one of the visitor entrance turnstiles.
Pausing, she turned to see who was on duty at the front of the park.
Thomas McCourt caught her eye and hurried to approach her,
obviously noticing his boss and her irritated glare.

Beth didn't say a word and simply pointed to the bin.

"I'll deal with it right away," Thomas replied.

Beth slowly continued her walk through the entrance plaza,
checking other details as she went. She wasn't afraid to admit that
her attention to detail was extraordinary. Her well-trained staff did
their best to keep up with her high standards, but Beth was known
for being able to see any manner of minute issue at a hundred paces.
Being the co-owner of a multi-million-pound theme park and one of
Scotland's top tourist destinations meant unrelenting standards and
expectations.

She paused by the park dedication plaque and reached over into
the flower bed to prevent a stray plant leaf from obscuring the text.
One of the grounds team hurried over. "Let me do that for you, Miss
Fraser," she offered.

Beth took a step back and watched the employee gently
encourage the leaf to stay underneath the signage rather than

continue its growth over it. It was unlikely that many guests actively stopped to read the story of the park's history, all too eager to get into the theme park and enjoy the food, rides, and sights.

Which was a shame as the story was a good one and told of strong female entrepreneurs going back over a century. Fraser Park had been established by Agnes Fraser, Beth's great-grandmother, in 1911. Agnes Fraser had been blessed with a husband with a lot of land, a lot of money, and no idea what to do with either. As a child, Agnes had experienced the growing popularity of public gardens as places to visit, employment laws making it possible for many people across social classes to discover the concept of leisure time.

Fraser Park had been filled with all manner of greenery, from woodland to rose gardens, all lined with neat paths and wooden benches. When Beth's grandmother, Lillian, had taken over in 1946, she set about creating an environment not just of relaxation but one of fun. She took inspiration from amusement parks that had been popping up around the world and started to introduce new elements such as a wooden roller coaster and a large Ferris wheel. Lillian Fraser had a knack for the theme park industry long before it truly existed.

Nowadays, Fraser Park was part of a resort which included an award-winning theme park, a nature reserve, historic gardens, two hotels, and the start of a water park.

It was a large venture that Beth felt the pressure of running every single day. Never more so than when her brother decided to, yet again, go off and do his own thing without asking or even informing her.

Remembering the reason for her hurry, she abandoned her spur of the moment inspection of the arrival plaza and headed towards the first building on the left, seemingly a row of brick-built farmers' cottages. Beyond the facade of the homes lay the offices of Fraser Park, where a small management team worked away. And where she would no doubt find her brother.

Frustration welled up inside her. It wasn't the first time that Cameron had gone off on a whim and done something without informing anyone, and it wasn't the first time she had asked him not to do such things.

She reminded herself that he wasn't being malevolent—he was just eager and forgetful, a disastrous combination. She entered the building through the side door and immediately slipped from the magical world of the theme park to the cold reality of the office.

Beth nodded a greeting to Angela at reception before going straight upstairs to the managerial offices. Cameron's office door was closed, and she could hear him laughing inside. She narrowed her eyes; her brother was about to get a sharp reminder of the chain of command at Fraser Park.

She pushed the door open and was shocked to see a projectile flying straight for her face. The screwed-up piece of paper landed on her chest before falling harmlessly to the floor.

In front of her, Cameron and Fraser Park's general manager, Peter Wilkins, stared at her with wide eyes as they wondered what her reaction would be.

She folded her arms.

"Sorry, sis," Cameron said jovially. He stood up from his crouched position and removed the small basketball hoop that had been stuck to the back of the door.

Beth looked around the door to see a mountain of balls of paper. They'd clearly been playing for a while.

"You're forty-two," she told him.

"So are you," her twin brother replied.

"I'm not the one playing games," she shot back, already feeling the ever-present throbbing vein in her forehead start to make itself known. Not for the first time, she wondered how on earth she could be related to the man-child in front of her.

At least Peter had the good sense to look concerned at her arrival.

"Why is there a fifty percent off deal running in the *Herald* this week?" Beth demanded, eager to get back on track.

Cameron plucked an orange from the fruit bowl on the edge of his desk, sat down, put his feet up, and started to peel the fruit. "They offered me this great deal."

"We talk about things like this," Beth reminded him.

Peter stood awkwardly in the room, and Beth turned to him. "I'm sure you have something better to be doing?"

He took all of two seconds to make his escape. Beth knew that her reputation preceded her. It wasn't what she wanted, but someone had to put Cameron in his place, and she was the only person who could. If Cameron was left in charge, the park would be bankrupt in a week. And the damn man would still be grinning.

"Honestly, Beth, it was a great deal." Cameron sat up straight and started sorting through the piles of paper on his desk. "I have an invoice here. Somewhere."

"I don't care how good the deal was—you need to talk to me. We have other promotions happening at the moment and no way to track the success of what you're doing. Not to mention the front gate doesn't know what to do with these new vouchers."

Beth watched as Cameron stood and went to the pile of scrunched-up paper that had been used as makeshift basketballs. He unfolded a couple to read them. Beth shook her head in despair.

"Cam? Are you listening to me?"

Cameron continued hunting through the pieces of paper. "Wait a sec—it's here somewhere."

Beth rubbed her forehead to try to massage away the pounding behind her eyes. Her brother didn't mean to be a thorn in her side, she knew that. It was just that he had always been encouraged to be a dreamer while she had been the practical one. It wasn't done with any malice, just an amplification of their natural personality traits. Which had been irritating but manageable when they were kids.

Now they were adults and attempting to co-operate a large business together. Cameron's disorder and snap decisions drove Beth to distraction on an almost daily basis.

Of course, it had gotten worse seven years ago. After the death of his beloved wife that had rocked the family, Cam had become even more…Cam. If such a thing was possible. The steadying factor in his life was gone, and now Cam roamed from thing to thing like a kitten chasing reflected lights across a floor.

"Cam?" She tried again.

He unfolded a piece of paper and handed it to her.

She took it and looked at the contents with a frown. It wasn't the invoice as she had been expecting.

"What's this?"

Cameron returned to his orange. "It's an email I received from a company. We can increase our Twitter following by ten thousand."

"Tell me you didn't," she warned.

He popped a segment of orange in his mouth and shook his head. "I was going to run it by you first."

"Then how come it's a makeshift basketball?"

"I must have gotten my piles of paper mixed up." He frowned at his messy desk.

Beth scrunched up the junk email and put it in the bin where it belonged.

"Please, don't sign off on anything promotional without talking to me about it first, okay?" Beth stared at him, hoping that this time would be the time when that message would finally sink in.

He nodded. "I promise, sis."

CHAPTER TWO

Jemma Johnson walked into the hotel lobby and lifted her magenta aviator sunglasses up to get a better look at the space. The castle-like exterior gave way to a modern, airy lobby with light and tasteful design touches that reminded the guest they were in Scotland.

The high ceiling and large windows let in a lot of natural light, which Jemma knew would help immensely when filming the hotel tour she had planned for later that week. She adjusted the large camera bag over her shoulder and pulled her pink hard-shell suitcase over to the check-in desk.

"Morning, I'm checking in," she greeted the receptionist.

"Good morning, may I take your name?"

"Her name is Jemma Johnson," a male voice replied from behind her. She turned to see a cheerful man approaching her with a lopsided grin. He held out his hand. "I'm Cameron Fraser—we spoke on the phone."

Ah, the owner, Jemma reminded herself. She shook his hand. "Nice to meet you."

"Likewise, my children love your YouTube channel," Cameron replied. "My youngest informed me yesterday that she wants to be a YouTuber when she grows up."

Jemma smiled. She'd heard that a thousand times before. People watched her social media feeds and wanted to be a part of the influencer industry. She couldn't blame them but suspected none of them knew the amount of work it entailed.

"I told her to wait and see," Cameron continued. "Between you and me, I think she just wants to eat ice cream all day and tell other people how delicious it is."

Jemma laughed. "It is delicious, but it can be hard work when you have to taste every single flavour."

"You'll have your work cut out for you here, then," he said.

"I'm really looking forward to it," she replied.

It was true. Fraser Park had been on Jemma's to-do list for years. She remembered seeing the advertisements on television when she was a child and had begged her parents to consider a trip to Scotland to visit the resort. Unfortunately, they weren't big fans of theme parks, or going out in general, and Scotland was a long way from their London home. Still, it was the overall reluctance to see and do things that had galvanised her desire to travel and see the world.

Cameron walked behind the reception desk and started tapping away at the keyboard. "I have you booked into our Cavendish Room, great views of the resort. You can even see the evening fireworks if you choose to stay in. We have you booked in for five nights. Obviously, you're welcome to stay longer. Just let me know, and I'll be happy to extend your stay, on the house, of course."

When Jemma had sat down to plan out her days, she'd been surprised by how big the resort was and how much was on offer. Five days sounded like a long time, but she needed to see and film everything. Every ride, every restaurant, every menu, every show. Having hundreds of thousands of followers meant enormous pressure to experience everything. The Fraser Resort website was out of date, and Jemma was sure that there was more to see and do than she currently knew of.

"I think I have my schedule planned out," she said. "I should be able to get everything done in that time, but it might depend on the weather."

Cameron leant heavily on the reception counter. "The Scottish weather can be problematic," he admitted. "Why my family couldn't choose to build the park in Spain, I'll never know."

Jemma chuckled. She already liked Cameron Fraser. He

appeared to be charming and easy-going and not at all what she expected the owner of a busy resort to be like. When she visited places, she was often guided around by a person from marketing, the upper levels of management being far too busy to deal with the likes of a social media influencer. Most of them didn't know who she was or what she did, anyway.

"Let me show you to your room," he offered. He came back around the desk and picked up her suitcase. "Do you have any questions for me?"

"What's your favourite snack?" Jemma asked.

Cameron laughed. "I have to pick just one?"

"Yep."

They walked towards the elevator, and Cameron pressed the call button.

"I'd have to say the doughnut ice cream sundae," he said. "It's pure gluttony, so I don't have one too often, but if I was visiting as a guest, then that's what I'd have."

Jemma recalled seeing the sundae appear on a few Instagram posts. It was very pretty and definitely something she could get some online traction from. "Sounds great—I'll check it out."

In truth, it was probably already on her list. She'd spent nearly three weeks preparing for her trip to Fraser Park. She'd quickly learned that planning was key if she wanted to get enough usable photographs and footage during a trip. Lighting, weather, location, crowd levels, and more all had to be taken into account.

"Do you have any filming restrictions, on the rides for example?" she asked as they stepped into the elevator.

Cameron selected the top floor and shook his head. "No, you're free to film anywhere. On the thrill rides, we ask that people wear a GoPro or something similar rather than hold their phone."

Jemma patted her equipment bag. "I brought my GoPro and the harness."

He looked at the bag and chuckled. "Did you bring the kitchen sink?"

"Almost," she confessed. "I have my main DSLR with my primary lens, my fisheye lens, and my telescopic lens. I have my old DSLR, which for some reason is much better in low light. I have three replacement battery packs for each camera. I have my GoPro too. Extra memory cards and chargers for all. I also have my tripod and my monopod—"

"Monopod?"

"A camera support with a single leg," she explained.

"Then it would fall over."

"Well, you still hold it. It steadies the camera. Good for awkward spots where a tripod might not fit."

Cameron grinned. "It's a whole new world to me. Sounds like you need a lot of equipment for this social media lark. I'll tell my daughter to save her pocket money."

"She should! It doesn't come cheap. And this is just camera equipment—you also need a good quality phone, data package, laptop, software…"

Cameron blinked. "So you're a one-woman production company?"

"That's me." Jemma smiled. "It's worth it, though. I get to travel around the world, see all kinds of things, and share it with my followers."

"Well, I'm just glad you could take time out of your schedule to come and see us," he said.

"I'm glad you asked. I've always wanted to come and see this place but never got around to visiting."

The elevator doors opened, and he led the way down the hallway. The grey carpet complemented the white woodwork, and the comfortable look was completed with a grey and blue tartan wallpaper. Pictures hung on the walls between the doors to the rooms. Some were artwork, and some were old photographs of Fraser Park over the years.

Jemma had stayed in more hotels than she could ever hope to count, but Fraser Hall, one of the two on-site hotels, was already floating to the top of her all-time favourites. While it was clearly a luxury resort, graded four stars by the Scottish tourism board, it was also comfortable and unpretentious. Expensive hotels easily fell into stuffy territory with guests feeling out of their depth and almost unwelcome in the opulent surroundings. Fraser Hall was effortlessly warm. Jemma felt she could kick off her shoes and stroll through the corridors admiring the art without hesitation.

Cameron stopped by room 4020 and swiped a key card against a discreet black panel. A green light illuminated, and he opened the door, standing aside for Jemma to enter. She walked into the room and was pleased to see the comfy decor continued inside. Everything looked clean and modern, spacious and inviting. And, best of all, there were large windows and plenty of lights in the room. Lighting was always at the forefront of Jemma's mind; it was the single most important element when it came to filming and photography.

Cameron placed the suitcase on a luggage rack set up by the window.

"Breakfast is between six and ten, and the park opens at eight. The reserve opens at nine." He placed a business card by the phone. "You can call me or email me if you have any questions, or obviously you can ring down to reception, and they'll be more than happy to help."

"Could I grab some time with you at some point for an interview?" Jemma asked. She rarely had such access to the people at the top and knew it would be a unique opportunity to bring such content to her channel and her followers.

"Absolutely." Cameron sounded enthused by the idea. "Drop me an email, and we'll get something in the schedule. Is there anything else you need?"

Jemma shook her head. "No, I think that's everything. Thank you so much."

"Not a problem, I hope you have a great stay." He paused by the door. "And tell all your followers how wonderful it is here, obviously." He winked at her, a cheeky grin adorning his boyish features.

"Obviously." She laughed.

Cameron left, and Jemma let out a deep sigh. She was exhausted. Her own bed was nothing but a distant memory. Before arriving at Fraser Park, she had visited both Edinburgh and Glasgow, before that she had returned from a spur-of-the-moment trip to New York, and before that she had attended a series of Pride festivals across the United Kingdom. She loved the Pride festivals, even though they weren't technically on brand for her channel. Her channel was mainly about travel and food. Of course Jemma added in the odd reference to her sexuality, but there were other—far better—channels that focused on LGBTQ+ matters.

It was just the way it worked out sometimes. Trip after trip sounded glamorous, but it was actually tiring. But without endless travel, her travel channel wouldn't be much of a success. The algorithms of Instagram and YouTube were hard mistresses to appease. They needed constant attention and an endless supply of new content.

The algorithms were second only to her audience. She loved her fans and knew she'd be nothing without them, but the relentless schedule, lack of sleep, no real place to call home, and never seeing her family were draining. On top of all that, recording and posting every day meant she had to be camera-ready at all times, and even when she was, there were still people who had a negative comment or two to post about her looks that day. Some people were never pleased and quite happy to post public messages to that effect.

She unzipped her case and dug through her hastily packed belongings for her make-up bag. After turning all the lights on in the room, including all the lamps, she entered the bathroom and did the same. She peered in the mirror at her reflection.

"Not *too* bad," she mused to herself. She had touched up her appearance once already at the train station on the way over. She unfolded the make-up bag and set to work preparing herself for filming. After fifteen minutes, she was as happy as she was likely to get and closed the bag up again. She put it back in her suitcase and placed the suitcase by the door.

Next, she opened her camera bag and picked up her state of the art DSLR, attached her standard lens, and checked that the memory card and battery were ready to go. She hid her bulky camera bag under the bed—viewers didn't need to know just how much stuff she carted around on a daily basis.

She took one final look at herself in the mirror before picking up the room key card and opening the door. She pulled her case across the threshold and closed the door behind her. She prepared the camera to begin filming herself before hitting the record button.

"Hi, guys! It's Jem, and we're here at Fraser Park in Scotland! I am *so* excited to show you around this place. It's somewhere I've wanted to visit my entire life, and now I'm here. I'm honestly so excited."

In the distance a door opened, and Jemma lowered the camera and waited for the guest to disappear. She sucked in a deep breath and reaffixed her smile before lifting the camera to eye level again.

"We're staying at Fraser Hall, one of the two hotels on-site at this resort. Disclaimer—I'm being hosted by the lovely people here, so I'm not paying for my room or my park entrance fees, but I will be paying for my food and any other extras. I'll be sure to let you know what's included and what I'm paying out of pocket for. But, as always, you can rely on me to give you an honest review. Speaking of which, let's start with my room."

Jemma swiped the card and opened the door. "Oh, wow, this is gorgeous," she said, pretending it was the first time she had laid eyes on the room. She changed the camera settings away from selfie mode and started to show off the room.

As with all of her hotel tours, she made her way around the space showing the view, the bed, the television, and any amenities. She showed the bathroom, pausing as she always did to wave to the camera in the mirror. When she was done, she lay on the bed and turned the camera to face her again.

"So, that's the room tour—what do you think? Drop any comments down below. I'd love to know your thoughts. Stay tuned because I'll be showing you everything Fraser Park has to offer—the food, the rides, the shows! Everything. If you've been, and you have some suggestions on what I absolutely have to see or eat, then leave that in the comments below as well. And remember, have a perfect day!"

She hit the pause button and took a deep breath. After a few seconds she smiled brightly again and hit record on the camera and filmed her outro a second time. She'd learned a long time ago that it was always a good idea to film the end of the video twice, just in case her tiredness was starting to show during the first take.

Satisfied that she had what she needed, she switched the camera off and heaved herself up from the bed. If she stayed on the sinfully comfortable linens any longer, there was a good chance that she'd fall asleep.

She pulled her camera bag out from underneath the bed and started to unpack her equipment. The first thing she did was unwrap her charging cables and plug them into an extension lead that she then plugged into a power socket above the desk. One of the things Jemma looked for in hotels was plug sockets—considering she needed everything to be fully charged to do her job, they were a requirement wherever she stayed. Fraser Hall did well with a selection of plugs and USB sockets. Jemma didn't think she'd need to unplug a lamp, and that was rare.

Once her phone and all her cameras were on charge, she opened her laptop and accessed the Wi-Fi. She opened her metrics dashboard to see how her channels were getting along. She'd been keeping up with comments and replies while on the train over but knew there would be more by now.

Social media never stopped. Channel owners who engaged with their audiences were rewarded with higher search positions and more space in the highly coveted *also watched* sections of platforms. While the technical algorithms that made all the decisions were closely guarded secrets, it was obvious to all that on all platforms, engagement was the number one way to get to the top and stay there.

That meant not only garnering replies to her content, but also replying to *those* replies. It was time-consuming, but it was how Jemma had quickly grown her YouTube, Instagram, and personal blog following from a handful of fans to literally hundreds of thousands of people around the world in just a few years.

It took forty minutes to catch up on all the comments and perform the general maintenance that she needed to do to keep her channels healthy.

She looked at her watch and calculated what time it was globally. Her frequent trips to America had boosted her social media numbers with users from that part of the world, which meant posting in the mid-afternoon UK time was the best time to capture the biggest percentage of her audience.

So she had a couple of hours before it would be time to announce to her followers where she was. If she got some room service for lunch, she could edit the hotel room tour and prepare that for going live that evening. While it was uploading, she could send an update to her Instagram account to announce she had arrived at Fraser Park and then reply to the messages that came in afterwards.

Plan in mind, she sought out a room service menu and prepared to spend a few hours editing and preparing. If she was lucky, she might get to see the park around dinnertime. Gone were the days where she'd throw her suitcase down and head straight out to have fun. Now it was room service and hours of editing and prep work. The supposed glamourous life of an influencer, she thought. If only they all knew.

CHAPTER THREE

B eth hung up the phone and ran her fingers through her hair. She then winced, realising that she'd been touching her hair a lot, and it must now surely look a mess. It was just one of those days. Everything that could go wrong had done so.

First there was the problem with one of the food deliveries, which had meant the temporary closure of one of the most popular restaurants in one of the themed lands. This meant enormous queues had formed at the other two restaurants nearest. Crowd management was everything in a theme park, and closures inevitably meant lines. Lines were undesirable and always bad for business.

After she'd dealt with that as best she could, she was back to coping with the front gate and the flood of vouchers that were coming in as a result of Cameron's last-minute decision. Annoyingly, the promotion had been a success, and plenty of guests were turning up. It didn't help that the vouchers were now stacking up on her desk while she decided what to do with them and how to process them in the computer system. Not to mention that every new shift of staff in the ticket booths had to be advised of the new policy.

In between there were the usual meetings, emails, and phone calls that filled her days. It wasn't as if she hadn't tried to lighten the load. As the business grew, Beth had frequently hired more people to take on the work. It just seemed that the work accumulated faster than the staff. And no matter how many people she employed, there were some things that could only be handled by the top. That meant by her or her brother, which essentially meant her.

Beth's thoughts were interrupted by the sound of small but heavy footsteps clomping up the stairs. She checked her watch and was surprised to find that it was already four o'clock.

Abigail entered her office first, charging towards Beth with open arms.

"Aunty Beth!" Abigail called out with glee as she barrelled into the hug.

Beth pressed a kiss into her hair and pulled her close. "Hello, darling, how was school?"

Luke walked into the office and offered a wave. At fourteen he was too old to be hugging his aunt these days. Beth would just have to make do with eleven-year-old Abigail's enthusiastic cuddles.

"It was good—I didn't get any homework today," Abigail said, pulling away from the hug and flopping in her usual place on the sofa.

"Was that the reason it was a good day?" Beth asked.

Abigail shrugged. Luke sat beside her.

"I got maths, English, *and* history homework," he grumbled.

Beth winced in sympathy. As much as she complained about being an adult sometimes, she wouldn't ever want to go back to the days of school homework. She was about to offer commiserations when her phone rang.

The children sat quietly whispering to one another while she was on the phone with facilities, organising the best time to shut off the water to fix an aging pipe by the Glass House Restaurant. It was a familiar scene—the kids would arrive at the park after school and either call in on Beth or their father, more often than not, Beth. They would patiently wait for her to finish up her work, and if time permitted, she would spend an hour or so with them before Cameron took them home. Sometimes they stayed longer and ate dinner in the park as a treat.

It was a good arrangement. Cameron was up early to get the kids ready for school, so he took the first shift at the park. Beth arrived mid to late morning and started her own shift, working into the evening until after the park closed.

Despite being focused on the call, she could tell the children were up to something. The intense whispering and the furtive glances in her direction could only mean that they wished to ask her a question. Probably a question they assumed she'd say no to.

When she was done with her call, she hung up and turned her chair to face them.

"What's with all the whispering?" she asked.

Luke elbowed Abigail to encourage her to go first. Beth smothered a smile. She couldn't help but remember when Abigail was smaller and Luke would speak on her behalf when the surrounding adults had no idea what her gibberish meant. Now that he was older, he had developed the unfortunate social skill of embarrassment and preferred to throw Abigail under any potentially humiliating buses they might encounter.

"Will you go on the Runaway Express with us?" Abigail blurted, practically bouncing with excitement.

Beth rolled her eyes. "I really don't see the fascination with that ride—it's over fifty years old."

"It's so cool," Luke piped up, unable to stop himself.

"It's the best ride in the park," Abigail announced.

"I thought you said that was the gliders?" Beth queried.

"She changed her mind," Luke replied.

Beth suspected her mind had been changed for her. Abigail was still young and easily manipulated. And Luke was the right age to take full advantage of that.

"Please?" Abigail begged.

It wasn't that Beth didn't like the Runaway Express—she'd spent large portions of her childhood on the wooden roller coaster. It was just that once she was out of the office, it took her a few hours to get back, and she was swamped with things to do. The more she thought about her workload, the more she realised that any time off was absolutely impossible.

"I'm sorry," she said. "You'll have to ask your father."

Luke looked resigned, but Abigail merely turned her pout up to full.

"Please, Aunty Beth! It's always better with you!"

Beth doubted that very much. Of the two of them, Cameron

was undoubtedly the more fun. But she enjoyed the compliment for a couple of moments before sadly shaking her head.

"I'm sorry, I'm just too busy. I have things that are already late and simply have to be done today."

Abigail opened her mouth to complain, but Luke placed a warning hand on her forearm and shook his head. Beth wondered when he had grown up so much. It seemed like just the other month he was too short to ride the log flume.

"Will you call me before bed?" Abigail asked, changing track.

Beth looked at her watch and calculated Abigail's usual bedtime, the time Cameron would actually remember to send her to bed, and the meeting with the American architect she had scheduled for that evening.

"I'll try my best, but I am very busy and sometimes—"

"Things overrun," Abigail finished the sentence on autopilot.

Cameron stepped into the room. "I know those voices," he cried playfully.

"Daddy!" Abigail jumped up and ran into her father's arms. "Daddy, will you come on the Runaway Express with us?"

"Only if I get to sit in the front row," Cameron replied. "Let's leave Aunty Beth to her work."

Beth waved them goodbye and watched them leave. Part of her wanted to slam her pen down and go and spend some time with her family, but she knew the work would still be waiting for her when she got back.

A stabbing pain in her chest caused her to take a sharp intake of breath. It had been happening more and more lately. Stress, the doctor said. Although why she had taken an hour out of her working day for someone to tell her the bloody obvious she didn't know. Of course she was stressed.

Unless medical science had progressed to a point where an injection could magically make her brother understand how to read a spreadsheet, or enable the investors to grasp the long-term plan rather than focusing on short-term gains, then doctors were useless to her.

Right now, things were more pressured than ever. Next to the park was a large building site that would one day become a state-of-the-art water park, one of a very small number in Scotland. But the project hadn't gone to plan, and more and more money needed to be secured.

While the resort as a whole was doing very well, the additional expansion and necessary investment capital were a constant pressure on Beth's nerves. For the first time in the resort's history, an unsympathetic board of directors watched their every move. Beth's fault, and something she keenly felt.

Beth shook her head to shake the thoughts away. She found herself spending more and more time worrying about the new board lately. All that could really be done was to ensure the resort continued to run like a well-oiled machine. Not always an easy task, considering parts of it were over a hundred years old.

"Beth?"

She looked up to the doorway to see the marketing manager, Carrie. She was holding a handful of vouchers. "What code are we putting these through in the system?"

Beth blew out a long breath.

CHAPTER FOUR

Jemma swiped her park ticket at the turnstiles and was cheerfully greeted and welcomed by a member of staff. It had only been a ten-minute walk to Fraser Park through some of the most beautiful gardens she had ever seen, and now she was somehow at the entrance to the theme park.

She knew her hotel was nearby—she had views of the park from her room and other locations in the hotel—but just how close it was had taken her by surprise and was a definite positive.

The entrance to the park was themed to look like a Scottish village. Buildings surrounded the large square and were themed to look like cottages, shops, a pub, and a blacksmith's. In the middle was a grassy area with paths and a bandstand in the centre.

Jemma was a big fan of theming. She loved being transported to other times or locations by clever design. Theme parks all over the world utilised different levels of theming—some were very good at it, and some not so much. So far, Fraser Park was doing very well. A few steps into the park, and she felt as if she was in a nineteenth century village, despite the jaunty music playing through speakers tastefully hidden behind planters and atop lampposts.

Members of staff were all in period costume with a modern twist, and the smell of popcorn and candy floss drifted through the air. Some things were universal, no matter where Jemma was in the world; theme parks selling snacks was one of them. And her channel ate it up.

Well over a million people had tuned in to watch Jemma eat and review snacks. Her father didn't quite understand what she did, so he told people she ate food for a living. Her parents' elderly neighbours thought she was a taste tester in an experimental kitchen.

Jemma didn't correct him, or them. Being an influencer was a hard thing to explain. Very few people understood how you could make money from visiting places and eating food.

She looked down at her park map to familiarise herself with her surroundings. She wasn't filming her first arrival yet—that would come tomorrow. Today she would look around and get a feel for the place before returning the next day and filming as if she had never been there before.

She didn't like being dishonest with her viewers, but at the end of the day, she was creating an entertainment show, and for that to be as slick as it could be, she needed to be prepared. If she didn't scope out a location prior to filming, there was a chance she'd get lost, miss a key sight, focus too much on her wayfinding, and forget about what she was saying. The alternative was to admit that she had been there the day before, but then her audience would feel as if they had missed out on something.

The small white lie was the perfect middle ground. It allowed Jemma to prepare, then overact a little when filming. Everyone was happy.

It had taken extensive research to find the right balance for her channel. She watched hundreds of other content creators and trialled many different approaches with her own viewers. Now she had the perfect balance—something she was proud of, her audience enjoyed, and that attracted a constant supply of new subscribers.

Positivity was Jemma's watchword. *Life with Jem* wasn't just a travel channel, it was a lifestyle. Jemma worked hard to make sure that every video and photograph she uploaded showed the very best side of things. Her message was always about being kind, and if Jemma ever felt negative, then she most certainly didn't let that show on her channel. Sure, sometimes it required more than one take to get things right, but Jemma didn't mind. It was the message that was important.

She'd already spent a lot of time looking at the map and familiarising herself with what Fraser Park had to offer. If she was going to see everything in her short time there, she needed to be prepared. But often maps were out of date or not to scale, and Jemma liked to have a little look around. Not to mention that it was nice to be off camera for a while.

She strolled through the village square and up the main road that led to the other areas of the park. Some theme parks had very distinctive lands, while some simply offered a slight amount of theming around key attractions. Fraser Park was in the latter camp—no futuristic world butted up against princesses. Everything was frozen in a simpler time, classic and classy with hints of China around the new triple-inversion steel roller coaster that resembled two warring dragons.

Jemma preferred this style. Some parks bit off more than they could chew with multiple lands all needing to be kept on theme while being situated next to each other. It was impossible to keep the view and the music separate, so there was always some strange blurring of realities when the festive perma-Christmas land was within sight of the Old West complete with gunshots firing on the soundtrack loop.

A cart selling churros, a rarity in Britain, caught her eye, and she couldn't help but pick one up. She took a bite of the crunchy-yet-soft treat, enjoying the warm goodness and the way the grains of sugar stuck to her lips.

The one problem with her job was that her diet was undeniably terrible. When she was playing tourist at a location, she ate every bad thing she could find because that was what people wanted to see. They wanted to see the ludicrously big doughnut, the greasy burger with far too many toppings to fit in the bun, and the playful twists on old classics. And so Jemma ate them all and reviewed them. When she was off-site and doing other things for her channel, she exercised like crazy and lived on salad.

Unfortunately, junk food was maddingly addictive, and every time she set foot into a theme park, the smell of deliciously terrible food got her mouth watering within moments.

Chewing on her churro, she strolled through the park, taking in the sights and sounds. She looked at the menus outside of restaurants to check that the dishes she planned to eat were still available and checked out little details that she suspected other vloggers might have missed.

Jemma was keenly aware that she wasn't the first influencer visiting Fraser Park. Many had come before her and many would visit after, although she didn't know if they were hosted trips at the request of the owner as hers was.

Her own audience would watch her, but if she wanted to get traction beyond her existing viewers, then she needed to offer more than her competitors.

Sometimes those details could be as small as a quiet place to watch a parade, or a little-known spot for a photo opportunity. Sometimes it required a full blow-by-blow plan for how to get as much as possible accomplished in a single day.

Thankfully Fraser Park was big but not unwieldy. There was plenty to see and do, but not so much that visitors had an eager air about them. She'd visited many places where mothers had plans that would make an army general proud, and they also held a glint in their eye that meant they would happily elbow you to the side if you put them a minute off their schedule.

The churro was finished as quickly as the impulse to buy it had arrived. She threw the wrapper in the nearby bin and realised she was by one of the park's older rides, a water-based dark ride. Dark rides became popular in the 1960s when most theme parks came to the realisation that rides for all the family, including the baby and grandmother, were required. Floating cars that drifted slowly around a scene were relatively cheap to construct, and they started to pop up everywhere.

The Sleepy Glen was a classic and had been entertaining guests for many years. It was also a ride that Jemma was a little concerned about filming. Getting usable footage inside a dark environment was extremely tricky and often required more than one attempt. Modern cameras were incredible, but few managed to focus on subjects that went from light to dark quickly, especially when the user was moving in a ride vehicle that bobbed along in water and had no access to stabilisation equipment.

The short queue was what finally persuaded her. A quick scan of the interior of the ride with her iPhone would be enough to figure out how many run-throughs, or how much editing, documenting the ride would require.

She got into the queue, appreciating the theming of woodland creatures and fairies as she went. The continuous nature of the ride meant that in no time she was at the front of the queue and informing the costumed team member that she was a party of one and would like a front row seat, if possible. Jemma had rarely encountered a member of staff not happy to meet her requests. She knew they received a lot that were far stranger and delivered with much less of a smile than she offered. A little kindness went a long way, especially when someone was working hard to ensure guests were having a good time.

Jemma had never had a job like that, or done anything that would be considered a real job. At fifteen she realised that money could be made passively for work she had already done. Rather than attending a place of work and being paid per hour, she could be paid for something she created again and again, as long as people wished to consume whatever it was she had made.

By sixteen her dad had allowed her into the scary world of YouTube, and a few months later she added Twitter to her portfolio. It wasn't long after that she received her first payment. Three dollars and change. When she converted it into pounds it sounded even worse than it had done in dollars. But Jemma was excited, and she had the social media bug.

She'd produced some terrible videos, but someone somewhere in the world had watched them. She could see the potential, and now she was consistently earning six figures a year. A good six figures, still nothing like the millions some of her fellow influencers earned, but she was happy and knew she was extremely lucky to be in the situation she was in.

She boarded the boatlike vehicle, unlocked her phone, and started to play with the settings.

"Excuse me," an imperious voice bellowed from the dockside. Jemma looked up. "Yes?"

The woman wasn't in a themed costume, but she didn't look like a guest either. She was dressed in a trouser suit and looked completely out of place, for the ride and the whole park. Despite her firm tone, Jemma couldn't help but be transfixed by the beautiful woman staring down at her.

"You can't film here," the woman told her in a whisper, so the other guests couldn't hear her.

"Oh, I have permission from the owner," Jemma explained. She flashed a smile and hoped that would smooth over the misunderstanding.

The members of staff looked hesitant about whether or not to start the ride, and the boats were backing up.

"Oh, really?" The woman sounded unconvinced.

"Yes, I spoke with him this afternoon. Cameron Fraser. I'm Jemma Johnson—I'm touring the park." Jemma couldn't remember a time when she had ever had to explain her presence in a location. The customer was always right, and no one wanted to create a scene. But this woman seemed to not have read that memo and looked to be seething at Jemma's words. Either she was having a really bad day, or she wasn't cut out for customer-facing roles.

In Jemma's opinion, this just made her more attractive.

"Launch the boat," the woman commanded to one of staff before turning sharply on her heel and marching through a door to the backstage area.

Jemma bit her lip, wondering if she was allowed to film or not.

A friendly looking fairy looked down at her. "Go ahead and film—it's fine," she said with a smile that Jemma was more used to seeing in a leisure resort.

The boat was launched, trundling along a large rubber conveyor belt before splashing down lightly into the water and starting to bob along. The theming was beautiful, and the music boomed through hidden speakers, but Jemma couldn't help but wonder who the woman had been. If she worked for the park, then she assumed she'd find out soon enough. Jemma smiled to herself. She was looking forward to that.

❖

Beth marched across the car park towards her brother's car. She'd only just managed to catch up with him before he took the children home. She realised she could have called him, but she was so incensed at being caught on the back foot again that this required a face-to-face conversation.

"Who the hell is Jemma Johnson?" Beth demanded when she was in earshot.

The children were in the back of the car, headphones on and phones in hand and completely unaware of her presence. Cameron was unplugging the charging cable from his vehicle.

"Oh, damn, I forgot," he said, looking genuinely apologetic.

"Who is she?" Beth pressed.

"She's an influencer," Cameron explained, closing the charging-point cap on the car. He leaned back on the vehicle and looked at her. "I'm sorry, I completely forgot to tell you that I'd invited her to stay."

"What on earth is an influencer?" Beth asked.

Cameron rolled his eyes in the same way he did when she asked who a singer was, or who an actor was. "It's someone on social media with a large following. You know, like Instagram. Which is a social media site for photos and videos."

"I know what Instagram is," Beth complained. It was half true. She'd heard of Instagram, but she wasn't entirely sure what it was. Beth didn't really use any social media at all. She had a Facebook account but had long ago forgotten her password. Twitter seemed to be the realm of celebrities and politicians, which sounded like zero fun. All in all, she just didn't have time to be documenting her lunch online for people to see and comment on. Nor did she see the point.

"Well, she has a YouTube channel and an Instagram channel,

both called *Life with Jem*. She travels the world and records what she sees, does, eats, that kind of thing."

Beth blinked. "And people watch that?"

Cameron laughed. "They really do. She stayed at a certain American theme park whose name we do not speak, and within three days of uploading a hotel tour of where she was staying on-site, she had racked up over a quarter of a million views."

Beth's mind raced at the numbers. "As in…?"

"As in the video was watched a quarter of a million times. Even if you assume that some people will watch it twice, that's still over two hundred thousand individual views. In three days. But it doesn't just happen when she's in the place we never speak of. She went on all the roller coasters at a park in Sweden and got over three hundred thousand views. She went to Japan when a park there was opening a new ride and recorded her experience and got half a million views. Her channel is closing in on a million subscribers."

Beth had to admit she was impressed that Cameron had done his research. This wasn't like his ridiculous scheme to advertise in schools, or on the sides of buses.

"The kids love her and watch her channel all the time. Or her Insta stories."

Beth held up her hand. She was only just discovering what a channel was—she didn't need to know what a *story* was. That seemed to be like running before she could walk.

"So you've invited her to stay?" Beth asked, trying to get a grip on how this influencer thing worked.

"Yep. Basically, she travels around and sees different things. Sometimes she'll choose—like, she'll decide to go to Edinburgh Zoo one day—but sometimes she'll be hosted."

"Hosted?"

"Yes, that's internet speak for we pay for her to stay. She'll tell her viewers that she's hosted, and they'll know that we asked her to come and stay and comped something. In this case she's at the Hall for a week with entrance to the park and the reserve. She'll tell her viewers what costs extra and what the prices are."

Beth shook her head to refocus herself on the point at hand.

Clearly, she had a lot to learn about this new visitor, but she would have preferred to have done so *before* she arrived.

"Why am I only finding out about all this now?" she demanded.

Cameron looked contrite. "I'm sorry, really. I didn't even think about it. I asked her on a whim—Abigail asked me to ask her. I didn't think she'd say yes, but she did, and I booked everything in and then forgot all about it. It was only when my phone notification came in that I remembered her arriving today."

Beth pinched the bridge of her nose. "Could you possibly, when you're scheduling a notification for something, schedule a second one to tell me about whatever it is you're off doing on your own?"

Cameron quickly nodded. "Absolutely. I'll do my best."

Beth knew she could sigh or even cry as much as she liked, but Cameron would never change. He was forgetful, always had been. When they were growing up, Grandmother Lillian had always held Beth to a higher standard. She seemed to quickly grasp that Cameron was forgetful and that would never change, and she somehow took all that pressure and piled it on to Beth instead.

It had always been up to her to ensure they were home on time from school or that there were no schedule conflicts in either of their diaries. It was a task that Beth had taken on without a second thought. Nowadays she wished she could have a moment where she could just be responsible for her own things and not her brother's as well. Unfortunately their lives were just too intertwined for that to ever be the case.

"Oh, before I forget…" Cameron added, as if suddenly recalling something.

"Yes?"

"Tom Coulter called me—he was called down to London for a meeting."

Beth's eyes widened. "Oh, was he now?"

"Yep. That's weird that one of our investors was called to meet with our other investors without our knowledge, right?" Cameron asked, sounding confident but seeming a little unsure.

"It is weird," Beth agreed. "Why did Tom tell you and not me?"

Cameron shrugged. Beth knew the answer, of course. Cameron

was more approachable and friendly to everyone he met. People gravitated towards him, and he made friends everywhere he went. If someone had news to tell the twins, they'd almost always tell Cameron. It grated on her, but she could at least reap the benefits of his laid-back attitude in some ways.

"I wonder why they wanted to talk to him," Beth mused.

Cameron shrugged again. "We'll worry about it when we need to."

Beth barked a laugh. "I'll worry about it now, thank you very much."

Cameron pushed off the car and pressed a kiss to her cheek. "Don't spend too much time worrying about it, sis." He walked around the car and opened the driver's door. "I'll see you in the morning. Don't forget to call Abigail before bed."

"I'll try. I have a meeting with—" She looked at her watch and realised she would soon be late for that meeting. "I have to go."

He nodded and waved a goodbye as she turned and hurried back to the park offices. She needed to prepare for a meeting that was starting in ten minutes, deal with Cameron's voucher mess, make time to call Abigail before bed, and figure out what on earth an influencer was.

Anyone who thought that running a theme park would be non-stop fun really had no idea.

Chapter Five

B eth winced at the sound of footsteps coming up the stairs. They weren't as enthusiastic as they had been the previous day. She knew why; she'd been stuck on her call and hadn't been able to call Abigail before bed.

Beth tried not to let the kids down, but sometimes her schedule just became so overwhelming that she couldn't help it. She put her pen down, stood up, and approached the door. In the hallway she spotted a pouting niece and offered her a sad smile.

"I'm so sorry I couldn't call last night," Beth said. She put her arms out. Abigail slowly walked towards her, and Beth wasn't unaware of the contrast from one day to the next. Yesterday she was a hero, today a disappointment.

Abigail gave her a tentative and short-lived hug. Guilt tore through Beth. She hated seeing her young niece like this. In her mind she rearranged her schedule—she'd just have to put some things on hold and get into the office a couple of hours earlier the next day.

"Would you like to spend the afternoon with me?" Beth asked. "We can have dinner at The Lunch Box."

Abigail's face showed the internal war. She wanted to be angry with her aunt who had ignored her and broken her heart, but she was also clearly very excited at the prospect of an afternoon with Beth.

"You'll go on the Runaway Express?" Abigail asked, the pouting lip still on full display.

"Three times," Beth promised.

A smile broke out across Abigail's face, and Beth breathed a silent sigh of relief that the younger generation were fairly easy to placate. That hadn't been her experience with adults.

Beth stood and held out her hand for Abigail to take. "Is Luke at football practice today?"

Abigail nodded. "Yes, Daddy picks him up at six."

"Excellent, then it will just be the two of us. Let's tell your father that we're having a girls' afternoon."

They walked along the corridor and into Cameron's office, where Beth told her brother that she'd be taking Abigail for the afternoon and for dinner. Cameron gave her a knowing smile and nodded his agreement, having not mentioned a word about the no doubt distraught state of his daughter the evening before. Beth was grateful for that. She knew she'd done wrong, and the extra guilt would have simply served to make her feel worse.

A few moments later they were in the park, and Abigail was practically bouncing with excitement.

"Where would you like to go first?"

"The Ferris wheel!" Abigail cried, having picked the first thing she spotted towering in the distance.

Beth happily nodded. It felt good to be able to say yes to anything Abigail wanted to do. The only rides that Beth hesitated about were the new roller coasters that they'd invested in over the last ten years. She'd been on every single ride in the park, but some she had only been on once and never intended to go on again. Her stomach had begun to rebel against a large number of inversions, especially ones taken at any speed.

Thankfully, Abigail was still too short to go on some of the more intense rides, much to the young girl's disappointment and Beth's relief.

Beth and Cameron had always instilled in the children that although they owned the park, it wasn't just theirs. They shared it with guests, and those guests had to come first. It was a lesson their own grandmother had instilled in them. Beth had always known that she was extremely blessed to be able to call Fraser Park her home and to spend as much time as she desired roaming the area and riding all the attractions.

It was important that the children understood that balance too, and Beth found herself beaming with pride at the way Abigail stood to one side and allowed another family to get into the queue before her.

Theme parks could sometimes be lawless places where people single-mindedly raced for whatever their heart desired. If they wanted popcorn, then they wanted popcorn then and there, and many would race to get into a queue before a slower guest. Parks were expensive and time was money.

In the queue for the Ferris wheel, Beth started to think about her meetings for the next day while Abigail rambled on about an incident involving some of her friends and a bedazzled phone case. Abigail, in a complete reversal of her father, hyperfocused on every single detail and passed them on when she told a story. Which she did endlessly.

The story continued throughout a trip on the Ferris wheel, two rides of the Runaway Express, a pass through Huffleton's Haunted Hall, and even into the queue for The Void. The Void was the most extreme roller coaster that Abigail was tall enough to ride. It took place mostly in the dark and had a backward portion of track, and so, to Abigail, it was the most incredible thing ever.

To Beth it was disorientating and gave her a neck ache. She didn't say anything because that information would be passed right back to her brother, and she'd be forever teased about it.

"Oh. My. God." Abigail's eyes widened, and she grabbed Beth's arm and pulled her to one side. "She's here, she's actually here!"

Beth pointlessly looked at the queue to see if she could figure out who Abigail was referring to. Not that she'd be able to recognise any celebrities of the day anyway.

"Who?" Beth asked, unable to see much in the dimly lit indoor queue.

"Do I look okay?" Abigail asked, which to Beth's mind was a ludicrous question for an eleven-year-old to be asking.

"Of course you do—you look perfect as always. Who are we impressing?" Beth looked again.

Abigail grabbed Beth's arm and dragged her into the queue. "Pretend we haven't noticed her."

"I haven't," Beth noted through a clenched whisper. She didn't have the strength to argue. Abigail was strong-willed, and Beth knew better than to try to reason with her.

They joined the queue, and Abigail did a typical eleven-year-old's impression of looking casual. Beth rolled her eyes and subtly looked around the queue line. And that was when she saw her, the influencer from the day before.

Beth casually made eye contact with Abigail and then cast a glance towards the young woman whose name had escaped her, to check if this was the person who had caused her niece to fly into a mess. Abigail nodded and made a big deal of looking at the themed computer console in the queue.

It suited Beth down to the ground. She didn't particularly want to engage with the supposed social media icon after her overreaction the day before. They were a few groups behind, and the woman didn't seem to be turning around, so they would hopefully be able to avoid her.

After a few minutes, they all moved forward in the winding queue, and that meant that the woman was out of sight.

There, that's sorted that out, Beth thought.

A few seconds passed before a ride operator called out, "Party of three?"

Everyone shook their heads.

"Party of two?"

Slowly the groups in front of them stood to one side one by one until the path cleared to Beth and Abigail.

Beth gestured for Abigail to go in front of her, and they weaved through the few groups of people to the front of the queue. They walked to the front of the ride where the operator was pointing.

"Hello, Abigail, hello, Miss Fraser," the operator greeted.

Beth smiled at the woman and started to board the vehicle. The smile abruptly fell from her face as she realised she was about to sit next to the influencer.

"Hello again," the young woman greeted brightly.

"Hello." Beth pulled the metal lap bar down and turned her attention to Abigail to be sure she was sitting correctly and the bar was securely fastened.

"Hi," Abigail called out. "I'm Abigail."

"I'm Jemma, nice to meet you, Abigail."

Jemma, that was it, Beth thought.

"I love your channel—I watch it every morning before school," Abigail said. "It's the best."

"Oh, wow, thank you so much. If it wasn't for people like you watching, I wouldn't be able to do it. So *you're* the best!"

Abigail giggled happily. Beth sat back in her seat and wished she could be anywhere else right then.

"Are you filming this ride?" Abigail asked.

"Not today, I'm just enjoying it," Jemma replied.

Beth rolled her eyes. She'd have to say something. "I misspoke the other day. I didn't realise you had been invited to tour. You can film on rides."

Anything Jemma was going to reply was eaten up by the sound of the ride starting. Flashing lights and loud music started, and an ominous voice spoke of the horrors that lay before them. Beth had heard it literally a hundred times before and tuned it out.

Fraser Park didn't technically have a rule regarding on-ride footage. Beth didn't approve, but Cameron didn't much care what guests did as long as they had fun. Beth had always thought that footage would detract from the experience and spoil a lot of the magic. Nothing had been set in stone.

Apparently, influencers and social media channels were now things that Beth needed to consider, and she wasn't sure she understood how all of that worked nor how it would impact on her no-filming rule.

They'd paid a handsome price for a professional to film all the on-ride POVs and uploaded them to the park's own YouTube channel, which had under a hundred subscribers. For some reason people weren't interested, and Beth couldn't really understand why. Why did they supposedly care about influencers but not the official park channels?

It seemed like only a few seconds had passed, but it must have been the two minutes and forty-two seconds that she knew was the actual duration of the ride, when they arrived in the unload station.

The ride safety measures clicked off, and the bars were released. The guest on the end of their row grabbed his bag from the pouch in front of him and exited the ride, followed by Jemma, Beth, and Abigail. Beth took Abigail's hand and hung back a little under the guise of checking something with the ride technician before they left. She hoped that would give Jemma enough time to disperse into the park somewhere.

"That was so cool," Abigail said.

"It was." Beth gestured for Abigail to walk in front of her down the long corridor towards the exit.

"We rode in the front with Jemma Johnson, so cool."

Beth rolled her eyes. Annoyingly, she felt a little jealous of Jemma. Abigail clearly idolised the young woman.

"You've never mentioned her before," Beth prodded.

"Haven't I?" Abigail asked.

Beth shook her head. Abigail talked. A lot. But she'd never mentioned an influencer or a YouTube channel that she liked.

"I suppose I just didn't think it was your kind of thing," Abigail mused.

But bedazzled phone cases are? Beth wondered.

Abigail opened the door and they exited into the park. Right in front of them, coming from the lockers, was Jemma. It seemed like Beth just wasn't going to be able to escape her.

"Hi again," Jemma greeted, hoisting a large camera bag onto her shoulder.

"Hey." Abigail was beaming, and Beth couldn't help but smile herself.

"What's next?" Jemma asked her. "The Galleon? The Depth?"

Abigail giggled and shook her head. "No, we're having dinner now."

"So am I, I'm eating at..." Jemma fished her phone out of her pocket and looked at the screen. "The Lunch Box?"

"That's where we're eating," Abigail cried happily. "Can we eat together?"

Jemma looked at Beth uncertainly, and Beth knew the ball was firmly in her court. She didn't particularly want to dine with Jemma. For one, she was still embarrassed at being caught off guard the day before. Not to mention that she had no idea what Jemma actually did, other than she allegedly attracted the attention of hundreds of thousands of people. But then Abigail seemed genuinely excited, and Beth could never deny her niece anything.

Dining with Jemma would give her the opportunity to smooth things over. And maybe figure out what a social media channel was and how being an influencer actually worked. Apparently, everyone knew except her.

"Sounds like a lovely idea—you're welcome to join us," Beth offered. "I'm Beth, by the way."

Jemma smiled. "That sounds great, Beth. Thank you."

❖

Jemma didn't know why she had accepted young Abigail's invitation. Probably something to do with the shiny big eyes and the pleading expression. How anyone could say no to her, she didn't know.

But that did mean she was now having dinner with the rude woman from the day before. Although, she had to admit, Beth seemed completely different today than she had in The Sleepy Glen the day before. She seemed a little more relaxed, playfully nudging Abigail with her elbow and causing her to giggle.

They were walking towards The Lunch Box where Jemma had four items that she needed to order, film, eat, and review. She wondered what kind of reaction that would get.

"So, what's your favourite thing to eat at The Lunch Box?" Jemma asked Abigail.

"She only ever eats chicken," Beth replied.

Abigail blushed. "I have the chicken fingers and chips," she acknowledged.

"When I was growing up, I only ever ate bread and chicken nuggets. Preferably shaped like dinosaurs," Jemma admitted.

"But as an adult, you know the importance of a balanced diet," Beth prompted and offered a meaningful look over the top of Abigail's head.

Jemma realised she'd put her foot in it and quickly backtracked. "Absolutely! I'm just saying that I did that for a few years until I started trying other foods and finding stuff I liked. In no time, I was eating vegetables every day."

Abigail looked distinctly unimpressed with that idea, but Beth gave her a grateful nod. Jemma realised then and there that Beth's approval was important to her. She'd always had a thing about authority figures and wanting to please them, and Beth very much seemed like an authority figure, judging by the way the staff nodded their greetings to her.

The restaurant was a quick service location with lots of themed seating and several counters where orders could be placed and food picked up.

"I bet you want to sit by the window," Abigail guessed.

Jemma chuckled. "Do I mention that a lot in my videos?"

"Yep, all the time, you say the light is better."

"That's true," Jemma managed to say before Abigail was rushing across the restaurant to a table in an alcove surrounded by three large windows.

Beth gestured for them to follow the girl. "Is that table suitable? We could find somewhere else."

Jemma recognised the olive branch and appreciated it. "It looks perfect."

They sat at the table, Jemma with her back to the central window for the best light, Abigail to her left, and, surprisingly, Beth to her right.

"We have mobile ordering now," Abigail said. "You order on your phone and then go and pick up. It's really easy."

Jemma caught the use of the word *we* and wondered again what Beth and Abigail's connection was to Fraser Park. It seemed rude to ask, so she decided to wait to see what information naturally came forth through the meal.

Of course, Jemma's research had already discovered the existence of the mobile ordering app. She'd spent a little time playing with it, so she'd understand how it worked and could easily record her phone screen later to insert it into a video.

She unlocked her phone, opened the app, and started to place her order. Abigail shuffled her seat a little closer.

"Are you having dessert?"

"Should I?" Jemma asked.

"Yeah, you should have the chocolate lava cake. It's really good."

Jemma angled her phone so Abigail could see her add the chocolate lava cake to her order. Abigail giggled, and Jemma finished up her order and paid. Beth had her phone out and appeared to be finishing up her own order.

"That was super easy," Jemma said. She'd experienced some mobile ordering before at theme parks, but often quick service restaurants just meant endless queues.

"What's your order number? I'll pick up both," Beth offered.

"Oh, thank you." Jemma held up her phone.

Beth read off the number and nodded. She stood up and looked at Abigail. "Stay right here," she instructed.

"I will," Abigail replied.

Once Beth was out of earshot, Jemma decided it was time to fish for some answers. "So, you come here a lot?"

Abigail nodded quickly. "I practically live here. I know everything there is to know. You can test me."

Jemma chuckled and leaned back, draping her arm along the windowsill. "Okay, what year did the Oasis waterfall open?"

Abigail scrunched her face up adorably as she thought. "1984."

"Wow, and what time does the park close tonight?"

"Midnight."

"Great. And where's the best popcorn?"

"By the main entrance, it's always the freshest because they top up the most because people buy more there than anywhere else."

Jemma looked impressed. "I see you do know everything. How does someone get lucky enough to practically live somewhere like this?"

"My daddy owns the park." Abigail's chest expanded with pride.

"Oh, I met him the other day, Cameron Fraser?"

"That's him."

"Wow, so you really must spend a lot of time here then." Jemma couldn't imagine owning a theme park. It must be a very interesting life.

"Yes. Me and my brother come here after school every single day. Everyone in the park knows us, and we can go anywhere we like. Except some backstage areas."

Jemma wondered what that must be like. Did they ever get bored with the park? Did they take it for granted? If Jemma had lived in a theme park when she was young, she wouldn't have felt the need to get out and explore when she grew up. Her life would have been completely different, stunted in many ways.

Remembering her day job, she reached down to her bag and unzipped it. "Sorry," she said to Abigail. "I need to film an intro if I'm going to eat all this food."

"Can I be in it?" Abigail asked eagerly.

Jemma shook her head. "Sorry, not without your parents' permission."

At that moment Beth was returning to the table with a tray of food and two members of staff carrying two extra trays with all of Jemma's food.

"Can I be in Jemma's video?" Abigail asked.

Beth looked confused. "I don't know if that's a good idea."

Abigail looked like she was about to argue, and Jemma desperately didn't want to upset the peace she'd built up with Beth.

She stood and took the trays from the staff members and thanked them for their help.

"You can help me with prep if you like," she offered.

"What kind of prep?" Abigail asked.

"Well, we need to do a lighting check," Jemma explained. "And then I need to know what I've ordered, what it's listed as on the menu, and what the price of each item is. And I always need extra napkins. Fancy being my assistant?"

Abigail beamed with excitement.

"Once you've eaten some of your own food," Jemma added, casting a glance to Beth and hoping to get a look of praise in return. The corner of Beth's mouth curled into a half grin, and Jemma felt that boost that she'd done the right thing.

Abigail sat down and started attacking her chicken strips.

Jemma glanced at the girl and then at Beth, her mother. They seemed a strange match, Beth and Cameron. They were like chalk and cheese. Disappointment lodged itself in Jemma's gut, a feeling that she tried to quickly sweep away. She couldn't be jealous at other people finding love and happiness, just because she was too busy with work to find anyone for herself.

She pushed the feelings away and focused on preparing for the video.

❖

Beth wasn't quite sure what she was witnessing. She'd taken a couple of mouthfuls of her salmon salad when Jemma whipped out a chunky camera with a lighting attachment and some kind of fluffy microphone accessory.

If she didn't know what an influencer did before, she was quite sure she had a ringside seat now. So far, she had ascertained it involved ordering an enormous amount of food. Beth had asked the team member to double-check the order when she saw the two trays stacked high.

There were four meals, three different sides, two desserts, and a bottle of water. It seemed ludicrous that the woman beside her was about to consume it all. Strangely, Abigail hadn't seemed at all puzzled by the arrival of enough food to feed a family. She'd simply helped Jemma line it all up.

"Right, let's get started," Jemma said. She turned to Abigail and asked, "Ready?"

Abigail nodded, sat back, and watched Jemma with a look that used to be reserved for the arrival of Father Christmas.

Jemma lifted the camera rig and turned to it face herself. She took a deep breath, smiled, and hit the record button.

"Here we are at The Lunch Box at Fraser Park, and as you've just seen it's super themed and fun in here. Loads of room, and the menu looks great. It's a quick service restaurant, and they have a mobile order function, so that makes things really super easy. I got a few of the favourites based on what my Instagram followers suggested, so let's dive in."

Jemma hit the button and turned to Abigail. "And that's the intro done."

Abigail frowned. "But you've not done the restaurant tour."

Jemma nodded knowingly. "I don't record the restaurant when I come in to eat. I do that another time when it's not lunch or dinner. Then I can guarantee that it will be a little quieter, and I won't be bothering people. I'll film that another day and edit it all together later."

Beth picked at her salad with her fork and listened intently. She really needed to figure out how to watch the content that Jemma created, so she could get an idea of the kind of things people were watching. She'd been under the impression that it was nothing more than a young blonde with an iPhone taking selfies of herself eating ice cream, but now she realised there was a lot more to it.

"Do you often film out of order?" Abigail asked.

"When I'm doing tours, yes. Like, I filmed a portion of my hotel tour early this morning, but I'll do the rest of it later and then stitch it together. It's easier when I'm filming forward, something in front of me—then I don't have to worry about the fact that I look like I'm changing clothes throughout one video."

Abigail's eyes widened at being brought in on a secret of the business. "That's really clever."

Jemma chuckled. "That's learning from experience. Trying to cram everything into one day is often *really* hard, especially if there are crowds by something when you want to film it, or if the weather isn't very good."

"How many takes do you do on average?" Abigail asked.

"How about you finish your food, allow Jemma to start hers, and then ask your questions?" Beth suggested kindly.

Abigail looked down at her food as if she'd forgotten all about it. She picked up another piece of chicken and started eating.

Jemma smiled at her, and Beth felt butterflies in her stomach. It had been a while since someone had looked at her like that. She was the boss, someone who people looked up to or disliked. Aside from her family, she was in a position of power over every single person she saw on a day-to-day basis. More casual interactions with peers were not something that happened anymore.

"Okay, I'm sorry, guys, but I'm going to be really rude and carry on working," Jemma said.

Beth waved her fork. "By all means, if you want to finish all that before the park closes, then you better get started."

Jemma smiled and set up her small tripod on the table. She lifted the viewfinder of her camera so she could see what she was recording, and then she hit the play button. Beth tried not to watch, but there was no way she could avoid what was happening right next to her.

Jemma was positively bouncing with energy. Her smile was so wide that Beth felt her cheeks hurt by proxy. She spoke of how excited she was to start eating and read each dish from the menu, including the ingredients and the price, before tucking in. She described the flavours and textures like a food critic would. While her style was upbeat and positive, she was also honest and not afraid to say what she thought. The chicken was a little dry, and the curried sauce was not spicy enough. The burger was standard theme park fare, but the mayonnaise relish was delicious.

Beth honestly couldn't imagine that people would actually

watch what she was seeing. She was sitting beside it and wanted it to stop. Although that was probably because a few tables nearby were looking over their shoulders. Beth didn't know if they were wondering who the bonkers woman narrating her meal was, or if they actually recognised Jemma. If she was as big a deal as Cameron suggested, then surely some of the park guests would know who Jemma was.

A few times Jemma misspoke or something happened that she wasn't happy with, and she covered the lens with her hand before starting over. The first time she did it, she explained to Abigail that it was her way of signalling there was a retake, so she'd see it later in the editing process.

The whole thing looked exhausting. There was something about always being on camera that Beth felt would suck the energy right out of her. Jemma seemed to be a fairly happy and bouncy sort anyway, but on camera that seemed to be dialled up even higher. Beth couldn't imagine smiling so much, nor narrating her thoughts on everything she ate, did, and saw.

After a while, Jemma stopped recording and blew out a little breath. "I'll leave it there for a while. Sorry to be interrupting your dinner—I'm a terrible dinner companion."

"Not at all, it's fascinating to see you...doing what you do," Beth said. She was going to say *work*, but she hadn't quite decided if it was work or not yet. She wondered how Jemma could support her lifestyle. Surely there was a pot of money behind her that allowed her to travel around the world, seemingly without a job. What a strange life to be living.

"It's so interesting!" Abigail enthused. Beth noticed that for once, she had almost finished a meal. Abigail'd been so entranced by Jemma and not wanting to interrupt that she had eaten without knowing it.

"I'm glad you think so," Jemma said with a smile. She picked up one of the meals she had sampled and started to eat a little more of it.

"I want to do what you do when I grow up," Abigail announced.

"We'll see," Beth interjected before Jemma gave her any

fanciful ideas that could never be met. She couldn't see Cameron financing that kind of lifestyle.

Jemma nodded in agreement. "Yeah, don't put all your eggs in the influencer basket. YouTube might not even exist when you grow up."

Abigail's eyes widened in shock as if someone had suggested that oxygen wouldn't be around in ten years. "Really?"

"Who knows?" Jemma shrugged. "The industry has changed so much since I started. I didn't use Instagram at first, and now it's my main channel for growth."

An alarm on Beth's phone pinged, reminding her that she needed to think about getting Abigail back to the office so her father could take her home.

"Do we need to go soon?" Abigail asked, knowing the sound of the endless alarms that Beth used to keep her day regimented.

"We do."

Abigail looked forlornly at Jemma. "Maybe I'll see you again before you go."

"I'm sure you will. I'll be here for the rest of the week, and you practically live here."

Beth smiled at the gentle way Jemma interacted with Abigail, mindful that she was a young and impressionable child and yet still speaking to her as though she was an adult. It was an art that Beth had learned through trial and error. As the children got older, they'd rolled their eyes and informed Beth of that very fact. She was often informed that she no longer needed to coddle them as they reached a certain age. Many an online search had taken place, so Beth had been fully prepared for how they would grow and when and how she should adapt to meet those challenges. She wondered if Jemma was naturally gifted when it came to speaking with people, including children. Some lucky people were.

"I'm sure you'll bump into Jemma soon," Beth told Abigail.

They stood, and Abigail gathered their empty food cartons onto a tray, ready to take it over to the recycling area.

"Can you come to the zoo with me and Daddy next week?" Abigail asked Beth, wide-eyed and innocent and no doubt asking while there was an audience in order to maximise the potential for a positive outcome.

Beth sadly shook her head. "I'm sorry, I have a lot of work to do at the moment." As much as she hated saying no to Abigail, she knew the pile of work wouldn't be going anywhere. She'd already taken more time off than she would have liked.

Abigail slumped in disappointment and slid the tray from the table. "Okay," she sighed as if she'd been told birthdays were no longer a thing. "Bye, Jemma."

Jemma gave her a sympathetic look. "Bye, I hope to see you around soon." She looked straight at Beth. "Both of you."

Beth's heart beat a little quicker at the unexpected attention.

"You should watch the fireworks tonight," Abigail added. "They are really pretty."

"I'll do that, and I'll report back to you when I see you," Jemma promised.

❖

Jemma watched the two leave and shook her head sadly. It was all too reminiscent of her own childhood. Begging her mother to go somewhere and do something but hearing that work had to come first. Of course, Jemma knew now as an adult that work *did* always come first. Food and shelter were the obvious priorities. But Jemma's parents had never lived a hand-to-mouth existence and could easily have taken an afternoon here or there to spend time with her. Beth appeared to be in a similar situation—a workforce of thousands, yet not even time to go to the zoo with her daughter.

She shrugged off the sadness that overcame her. It wasn't up to her to judge other people. There could be a whole lot going on that she didn't know about. She sucked in a deep and cleansing breath and set about putting on a brave face to finish off her food review. She definitely needed to do a couple more takes of things—having Beth watch her had been a bit of a distraction. A nice one, but Jemma had to push that thought to one side because she was obviously a married woman.

She hoped that Beth hadn't caught her glances—it wouldn't have been appropriate to have been watching her like that with her daughter at the table. But Jemma hadn't been able to help it. Beth was captivating in a way Jemma didn't quite understand. Beth was effortlessly attractive but aloof, and something about her just drew Jemma in.

She shook her head to try to get herself back on track.

Pushing those feelings down, she picked up her camera, took a couple of seconds to clear her expression and force a smile, and started to record. She did a few more takes of things that she knew would need a second go and filmed some more shots of the food. She checked the photos and video she had taken before to make sure everything was in order before looking at the list on her phone and ticking off the menu items that she had now bought and reviewed. It was a small dent in a large list, but it was a start, and she was on her way to having all the content she'd need to make an excellent series about Fraser Park.

She turned off her camera and took off the lens to pack her equipment away. A couple of people walked past her with raised eyebrows—she saw it all the time. They were probably wondering why one person needed so much food. People were hugely judgemental about things they didn't understand, and Jemma had learned to shrug it off for the most part.

Continuing to pack everything away, she felt someone approach.

"Eating us out of house and home, I see?"

She smiled at the familiar tone of Cameron Fraser. She turned. "Yes, that's what I'm here for, right?"

"Absolutely!" He grinned. "Can I get you dessert?"

"I had dessert, three in fact," she said.

He laughed. "My kind of dinner. Everything to your satisfaction?"

"Absolutely, even the company. I dined with your wife and daughter."

"That's unlikely," Cameron said without missing a beat. "My wife died seven years ago."

His expression never changed and Jemma wondered if it was some sick kind of joke.

"It was my sister, Beth," Cameron explained at Jemma's ongoing silence.

"Oh, I'm so sorry," Jemma said when she managed to find her tongue again. "I had no idea. They were together and…I just assumed. I'm so sorry for your loss."

Cameron smiled warmly. "Not a problem, it's an easy mistake to make. I miss my wife every single day, but she gave me my children, and for that I'll be forever grateful. I choose to celebrate the time we had together rather than mourn this time we have apart."

Jemma didn't think she had ever met someone who was so pragmatic about death. Especially the death of someone so close. She briefly wondered if it was all bluster and inside he was grieving deeply but couldn't show it for the sake of his children. But his eyes looked genuine, and in that moment she realised that he must have enormous personal strength and a personality to match. More than she suspected she had herself.

"That's an amazing way to see things," Jemma admitted.

He inclined his head slightly in acknowledgement of the compliment. "It wasn't easy," he confessed. He stood up tall, and the jovial expression return in a flash. "But you had a nice meal? Despite dining with my sister?"

She laughed at his joke. "She was very nice."

"She has her moments. We're twins—not that you'd know it to look at us."

Jemma's mouth dropped open in surprise. Siblings she could accept, but twins was a complete surprise; they were so very different. Cameron seemed to be constantly smiling, a positive ray of sunshine. While Beth was aloof and serious. She knew that siblings could often be different from one another, but these two were like night and day.

Cameron laughed and pointed to her expression. "Right?"

Jemma closed her mouth quickly. "Sorry, that was rude."

"Not at all, I know we don't seem like twins. We don't have that twin thing—like, I don't know what she's thinking. Ever." He chuckled before looking at his watch. "I better get going and find the two of them before I get in trouble."

The mention of her recent dining companions jolted something in Jemma's mind. "Is Abigail…?"

"Abigail's my daughter," Cameron confirmed. "Luke and Abigail are my children. Beth's a doting and wonderful aunt but doesn't have any of her own."

The realisation that Beth was likely single caused a smile to spread across Jemma's face. Now she didn't feel quite so bad for being so smitten with her.

"Anyway, I must dash. I hope you're having a good time. As I said before, if you need anything, let me know." Cameron was already walking away.

Jemma waved a farewell to him. "I will, thanks!"

She couldn't help but smile again at the thought that Beth was likely single. Probably straight, but at least she wasn't married with kids. Not that it particularly mattered as Jemma was unlikely to get the courage up to do anything about it. Such was the life of someone who never hung around in one place for very long.

"Jem? Oh my God, it is you? Can I have a selfie?"

Jemma turned and smiled brightly at the fan. "Absolutely!"

CHAPTER SIX

B eth stepped out of the offices and looked around the entrance plaza with a sigh. She'd expected Cameron to be in his office, as they had agreed upon, so she could drop Abigail off with him and get back to work, but for some reason he wasn't there. She'd attempted to call him, but as usual, his phone was switched off.

"Can I get some popcorn?" Abigail asked, pointing over to the popcorn handcart positioned near the exit.

Beth nodded. "Meet me back here."

Abigail happily skipped away.

"Hey, sis."

She turned to glare at her brother. "Where were you?"

Cameron balked a little at the greeting. "There was a problem down at the Mine Train. I checked everything was okay and spoke to guests while it was being fixed."

"Oh. Sorry, I just couldn't get hold of you. I was dropping Abigail off," Beth said, guilt at her harsh tone washing over her.

"I stopped by The Lunch Box as I thought you might be there, but seems I'd just missed you. I saw Jemma, though—you had dinner with her?" Cameron fished.

"Yes," she replied stiffly, not wishing to get into the conversation. "Abigail invited her."

"Good," he said. "Jemma seems to be having a nice time. Am I going to see you in any of her videos?"

Beth chuckled. "Certainly not. Although Abigail did ask, and Jemma, very wisely I might add, declined without parental permission. Which I recommend you don't give. You can't trust internet people."

Cameron blinked. "Who are internet people, and what nefarious thing are they actually going to do with a video of my daughter eating a chicken finger?"

"You never know." Beth didn't know either. "I still don't believe that people actually want to watch someone eat their dinner."

"Well, they do, in the thousands."

"Let's hope they also want to watch her looking at the spa," Beth commented. "We could do with getting some publicity there. Otherwise it's millions quite literally down a very expensive drain."

Cameron's eyes widened.

Beth looked at him, trying to ascertain what was wrong. And then it dawned on her. "You haven't told her about the spa?"

"Completely slipped my mind," he admitted.

"Our multi-million-pound spa that is haemorrhaging money and causing me sleepless nights slipped *your* mind?" Beth asked. She shook her head in despair. His carefree behaviour had been gradually increasing over the last few years, and she wasn't sure how much more she could take.

"One second, I can fix this." He got his phone out of his pocket and started tapping away at the screen.

"Honestly, Cam, this spa situation is something we need to get on top of. The market research says the clientele is out there—we just need to get the message out to them. Until we do, we have a very expensive series of pools and treatment rooms complete with qualified technicians sitting around and doing nothing." Beth could feel her headache returning with a vengeance. Every single piece of evidence they had gathered said the luxury spa would be a cash cow, but it had somehow turned into a money pit instead.

"I know, I know," he said, still typing on his phone.

"Seriously, Cam, we need to do something. The fact that you frequently forget it even exists doesn't fill me with hope that you're taking this issue seriously."

"I am, I promise."

Abigail returned with a cardboard box of hot popcorn, and

Beth's stomach turned at the smell. The stress was frequently making her lose her appetite, and occasionally even the smell of food made her feel sick. Not a problem Cameron had, judging by the way he reached down and picked up a couple of kernels and popped them in his mouth.

"Hey, Peanut, had a good afternoon?" he asked.

"The best, we had dinner with Jemma Johnson!"

"So I heard—you can tell me all about it when we get home," Cameron said. He looked confidently at Beth. "All fixed."

She folded her arms. "What do you mean all fixed?"

"I've just messaged Jemma and told her about the spa. She said she'd love to check it out. I told her you'd accompany her and show her around."

"You did what?" Beth exploded.

"Well, I can't show her around, can I? Her being a woman and me being...me." He picked up some more popcorn and shoved it in his mouth. "Besides, you've been looking a little frazzled lately. A day at the spa will do you good."

"Do you really think I have time to spend a day at the spa?" Beth demanded. "Why didn't you *ask* me?"

"I thought it would be a nice gesture. You know, getting Jemma to review it and giving you the day off."

She shook her head in dismay. He truly had no idea. "And who, precisely, deals with my workload while I'm at the spa? Honestly, you live in another world."

"I can show Jemma the spa," Abigail offered in a small voice, obviously detecting the rising tensions.

Beth looked Abigail in the eye, smiling brightly. "That would be wonderful, but unfortunately it will be during the day, and you'll be at school. But we'll definitely organise something for you to show to Jemma, maybe part of the nature reserve?"

Abigail beamed with pride at being given a job, and Beth looked up at Cameron with a glare that told him the argument wasn't over, merely suspended for the sake of his daughter. The look on his face suggested he received the message loud and clear.

"I'm sorry," he said. "I thought it would be a nice gesture. And it will help if one of us is there to show her around. Honestly, I think this will be great for the spa."

Beth stood and let out a sigh. "Let's hope you're right."

She didn't know whether or not it would be great for the spa, but she did know it wouldn't do much to reduce her mounting stress levels. Spas were not her natural habitat by any stretch of the imagination. Now she had to go to one with a young, perky, beautiful woman who she had only recently met.

❖

The daily alarm on Beth's computer signalled that it was time to stop working and head out for the nightly firework display. She always gave herself twenty minutes to close down what she was working on, tidy her desk, and make her way to her unique viewing platform.

When people asked why she watched the firework display every single evening, she always said that it was simply to make sure everything went well. Which wasn't at all necessary as several display technicians were hired to do just that. The truth was she adored the show.

The music, smoke effects, lasers, lighting, and fireworks were a magical display that helped Beth relax and forget all the stress that she felt submerged in throughout the day. She honestly believed that no one could help but be swept away by the enchanting story of hope and love that weaved its way through the nightly show.

The current show was called *Reflections* and had cost a pretty penny to be developed and programmed—not to mention shown every night—but Beth thought it was worth it and more. Nightly displays had been part of Fraser Park for the last sixty years, gradually growing in size to become the epic events they were now.

She switched off her computer and pulled on her coat and scarf. It had been a warm summer's day, but that wouldn't stop the chilly Scottish night from whipping up enough of a breeze to make a coat necessary.

A few moments later and she was out of the offices and into the park, marvelling as she always did at the streams of people heading home. They were literally fifteen minutes off seeing a fantastic and *free* show. But tired children, and adults, didn't want to wait. And Beth knew that some people didn't enjoy fireworks, loud music, or crowds anyway.

The numbers of people leaving was nothing in comparison to the thousands who were staying. Beth knew that the viewing areas around the central lake would be filling up. People would be finding benches, walls, as well as floor space to sit and wait for the show.

Thankfully, Beth had a better spot. She entered one of the gift shops in the land themed to mythical animals and nodded a greeting to the staff members at the tills. She walked behind a large fibreglass statue of a dragon and opened the hidden door in the wall with her key card. The magnet released the door, and she slipped out of sight and up the staircase.

Using her key card again, she accessed the roof of the gift shop. She closed the door behind her, plunging the rooftop into complete darkness. She sucked in a deep breath of fresh air and smiled to herself. It was the only place where she felt completely happy.

While it was well known that she viewed the display from the roof, no one ever interrupted her. She had the most perfect view of the display in the entire park, up high, front and centre, and right next to one of the speakers that pumped out the show music across the entire resort.

She approached the edge of the roof, reaching her hand out to grab the handrail that she knew was there but couldn't actually see because of the pitch-black darkness. Once she had a firm grip of it, she looked over the ledge of the roof to the crowds gathered below. They were illuminated by the street lighting that would be turned off once the show started. But for now, Beth could see all her guests waiting with excitement and anticipation. Many of them had snacks or drinks as they waited patiently. Some were wearing hoodies with the Fraser Park logo emblazoned on them, one of Cameron's few good ideas.

One person stood out to her, and she instantly recognised Jemma. The influencer was standing with a bulky looking camera attached to a heavy-duty tripod. She was on her phone, hunched over the screen and typing at a blistering rate.

Beth's mind drifted to the spa day and wondered just how she could get herself out of that situation. She didn't have time to take a full day off work. Nor did she want to spend a day with Jemma. What would they talk about? Beth didn't know the first thing about social media. Jemma would probably consider her old and thoroughly uncool, or whatever young people called people these days. She mused that there must be around fifteen years between them, a lifetime for many. Jemma seemed so young, perky, and perfect. Beth knew she was none of those things. Certainly not an ideal match for sharing a spa day.

And now her idiotic brother was planning to force them together. Beth knew she'd have to attempt to get herself out of that engagement, or face extreme embarrassment, but that was a problem for the next day.

The lights started to dim, and she knew the show was about to start.

She found herself watching Jemma as she put her phone in her back pocket and started to adjust the camera settings. She seemed fastidious about light and technical details, so Beth wasn't surprised to see her pressing all kinds of buttons.

Minutes went by, and Beth frowned. Jemma was still pressing buttons. If she didn't stop soon, then she would miss the start of the show.

She sucked in a deep breath to calm herself. It wasn't important, she reminded herself. She needed to take a few moments for herself and ignore whatever Jemma was doing below her.

Turning back to the lake, she saw more and more lights slowly dimming and could see the shadows of the speaker boxes rising out of their hidden positions around the park. No one wanted to see industrial speakers littered around the park for a twenty-minute show that only happened in the evening, and so they were all hidden away and only emerged for the display.

Curiosity got the better of her, and she glanced down to Jemma. Thankfully she had stopped fiddling with the camera but was now back on her phone typing. Beth let out a frustrated sigh. How could she be on her phone with less than thirty seconds to go before the show started?

Beth huffed and turned away, determined to enjoy the show even if Jemma wasn't. Even if it was at least the thousandth time she'd seen it.

The opening batch of fireworks shot into the sky and lit up the dark night. Beth smiled at the sound of the crowd reacting positively before the music burst into life. Beth considered the show the pinnacle of the park, the icing on the cake of a great day. A thank-you to the guests for coming and spending their time at Fraser Park and the best possible way to send them safely on their way with a smile on their faces.

One of the best things about the show was the sounds of the crowd. Hearing children's exclamations of awe or parents pointing something out to them. Beth had lost track of how many times she had seen someone get down on one knee to propose during the show.

It was pure magic.

She looked over the edge again to see Jemma was *still* on her phone.

Frustration filled her. How could the woman not take a few seconds from her damned device to see the magic happening in front of her. Was she so jaded by having seen so many amazing things that the show was just a throwaway experience for her? Beth felt sick at that thought—first for the prospect of their display being subpar to the competition, and second that someone couldn't see the beauty of the show.

She shook her head and took a few steps towards the middle of the roof space. She wasn't going to watch Jemma *not* watching the show. This was her time to relax and reflect, and Jemma Johnson wasn't going to ruin that.

Chapter Seven

Jemma woke up to birdsong and sighed with contentment. Fraser Park was turning out to be everything she'd ever dreamed as a child. There was something magical and captivating about the place. The park was beautiful and fun, the hotel cosy and welcoming. She already wanted to extend her stay and luxuriate in the location.

She picked up her phone and winced at the number of notifications she had. As expected, Instagram had exploded during the night after she live-streamed parts of the impressive firework display. She logged into YouTube and smiled at the huge number of hits the video she had scheduled for the night before had already received.

Immediately, she started replying to comments on both platforms, methodically working her way through each one and either adding a comment, an emoji, or just liking the comment if there was no reply she could give. Planning, recording, editing, and posting material were only part of her job. The other was replying to messages and showing that she was actively communicating with her fan base. And with the algorithmic clock always ticking, replying sooner was always better.

She knew she'd never get through all the comments before breakfast, but she could definitely get a way into the job before she got dressed and went downstairs to eat. Unfortunately, it was the morning that she wanted to film the breakfast buffet, which meant she needed to consider her hair, make-up, and outfit before she made her way downstairs.

She chuckled to herself as she realised she'd only been awake for a few short minutes, and she was *already* behind on her schedule.

Muscle memory allowed her to scroll and like and comment on each post with little thought, allowing her mind to wander. Cameron had messaged her to say that Beth wanted to show her the spa and would love to accompany her on a complimentary trip. The thought had sent butterflies swirling around Jemma's stomach, and she'd eagerly said yes. Clearly, she'd done something right over dinner if Beth was asking to spend more time with her. Of course, there was a possibility that Beth was just being polite or even that it was just a business thing and Beth happened to be the most well-versed in the spa. Jemma hoped not.

Beth Fraser had been front and centre in Jemma's thoughts ever since she found out that she was Cameron's sister and not his wife. Not that Jemma thought that someone as sophisticated and classy as Beth would even look twice at someone like her. And there was the small matter that she had no idea of Beth's sexuality. However, as Jemma didn't expect it to go anywhere and was happy just looking at Beth whenever she got the chance, it didn't really matter.

Jemma lowered her phone and let out a sigh. Not for the first time, she was reminded that being an influencer meant never being in one place for very long. She loved her job, adored seeing the world and all the tourist attractions it had to offer. But it took a toll on any thoughts of a love life. Flitting from place to place meant never being in one location long enough to strike up a decent conversation with someone, never mind anything more than that.

On top of that, there was the constant need to be perfect or at least portray perfection. That didn't always sit right with her. But it was the way it was. No influencer got anywhere by showing anything other than gloss and shine. And so Jemma kept up with the trends, even if it was utterly exhausting at times.

"Stop wallowing," she told herself.

She pushed back the bedding and forced herself to get out of bed. She'd need a good hour to get ready before she went down to breakfast, and her stomach was already complaining about being empty.

❖

Jemma arrived at the buffet an hour and ten minutes later and was grateful when the person who showed her to her seat didn't even blink after seeing she'd brought a top-of-the-range DSLR camera to the dining room.

She suspected that most of the staff in the hotel were aware of her visit. It was usually the case that word got out quickly that she was staying, and she found a few extra doors opened for her than might have if she had been an ordinary guest. Which was why Jemma liked to get all the hotel recording done in the first couple of days before word spread about her stay.

She ordered some green tea from the friendly waiter, then got up to visit the buffet. She'd already recorded her intro on the way down to breakfast and now needed to film all the food on offer, and then herself eating some of said food.

Filming yourself eat was a surreal experience, and Jemma had long ago become used to the strange looks she received. But there were still some locations where she received more strange looks than usual, one of them being hotels.

People filmed themselves doing all kinds of crazy things in theme parks, and guests had become used to it. Hotels were a different matter. Lots of different people stayed at hotels, even hotels attached to theme parks. And this hotel was attached to a nature reserve and a luxury spa, and it was in a picturesque part of Scotland that many people visited for holidays without visiting either of the resort's star attractions.

A quick glance around the dining room told Jemma that many of the theme park goers had already left to start their day. Remaining were a slightly older generation, people who looked like hikers, people wearing suits. She frowned. There were quite a few people wearing suits.

Is this a conference hotel?

Her stomach complained at the ongoing delay, and she got up and set up her camera. A few moments later, she sucked in a deep breath and started to film the breakfast buffet. She'd learned long ago that you couldn't be subtle when you were filming. For one, you had to narrate most of what you were doing and seeing. Any awkwardness that you felt, the viewer would feel, and no one wanted to feel awkward when watching a video about a holiday location or a tourist attraction. That was the quickest way to lose viewers.

Jemma alternated between filming herself speaking to camera and filming her surroundings and the food, being careful not to catch any unsuspecting hotel guests in her footage. While it was okay to capture people from a distance if you weren't focusing on them, she didn't want to get in the way of Agnes's morning haggis.

She managed to get around the whole buffet in just two takes. She stood to the side and reviewed her footage, checking that everything was in order, before actually getting some food to finally eat.

She heard a familiar voice in the distance and eagerly looked up to see Beth approaching one of the dining room team members. Jemma couldn't help the smile that spread across her face. She hadn't expected to see Beth, and the surprise appearance had made her morning.

Beth must have felt someone's laser vision burrowing into her and turned to look at Jemma. There was a brief hesitation before she smiled in greeting. She exchanged a few words with the person she was talking to before she came over.

"Good morning," Beth said.

"Morning," Jemma replied, hoping she didn't look too goofy with the smile on her face that she just couldn't get rid of.

"I hear my brother messaged you about the spa," Beth said. "I'm not sure I can spare a whole day, but I can set aside some time. What's your schedule like? I'm sure you're busy."

Jemma's heart sank. This didn't sound at all like someone who was *interested* in spending time with her. In fact, it sounded as if she'd entirely misread Cameron's message. She'd spent the last few hours on at least cloud five and a half, thinking that Beth had invited her to the spa, but now it seemed that wasn't quite what had happened.

"Um…" Jemma couldn't remember her schedule at all at that moment. It was pretty packed, but she could imagine that Beth's was far busier. "I can be flexible. When is good for you?"

Beth pulled her smartphone out of her jacket pocket and opened her calendar app. Jemma's eyes widened at the sheer number of appointments vying for attention. The multiple events were so closely packed together the text was unreadable.

"I have gaps, but it's hard to find an amount of time on the same day," Beth said. "Only this afternoon, which is too soon, I know."

"This afternoon is fine," Jemma blurted out. The chance of spending some quality one-on-one time with Beth seemed to be slipping away, and Jemma knew in that moment that she would happily throw out her entire schedule for a few hours with this woman.

"Oh." Beth sounded unsure, possibly unhappy with that answer. Or was Jemma projecting her own doubts and insecurities?

"If that's okay?" Jemma asked. She sucked in a quick breath. "I mean, I'm sure it would be best if you showed me around, so I can capture everything you need. I'll be honest—I didn't know there was a spa here, and I'm sure I'm not the only one."

Jemma felt a tiny bit guilty at pressuring Beth like that. She had known there was a spa, but it was very poorly advertised, and it was only because Jemma was ruthless in her planning that she had noticed it. When Cameron hadn't initially extended an invitation to the spa, she thought that he had wished her to focus on the theme park side of things.

Her little white lie and gently applied pressure seemed to work. Beth sharply nodded her head. "Of course, of course. We're pleased to have you here, and I'd love to show you around. Shall we say two o'clock?"

Jemma grinned. "Absolutely. Do we need to book treatments in?"

Beth seemed to hesitate. "I hadn't considered that—sorry, this has all been a bit last-minute." She looked at her calendar again, and Jemma could feel the panicked stress radiating from her.

"I can do it, if you'd like?" Jemma offered. "It will make a good video intro. I can look at the options and book some things in for us. Just a couple of little things, to get an idea of the services." Beth remained hesitant, and Jemma flashed what she knew was a winning smile. "I'd love to—it will be great material for my channel."

"If you're sure?" Beth asked.

"Absolutely. And I'll meet you by the spa at two. Bring your bathing suit. Or bikini. Or…whatever. Anyway, I better get to eating breakfast before they close." Jemma could feel the heat of the blush on her cheeks and needed to get away from Beth before her growing crush made itself too well known.

"Yes, of course. I'll, um, see you at two." Beth hurried away, and Jemma wondered if she had detected Jemma's interest and was running away in fear.

Dammit, she thought.

❖

Beth escaped the dining room and made her way towards the conference facilities. She'd hoped that suggesting a time so soon would clash with Jemma's schedule, and they'd have to cancel. At no point had she thought that Jemma would happily dump her entire afternoon and spend the day with her.

"Don't influencers have schedules?" she mumbled to herself.

On top of everything else, Beth now had to have treatments in the spa that afternoon. And look like she was enjoying it. Which was utterly impossible because Beth didn't do spas. The only times Beth had set foot in a spa was when she was researching and had attended a luxury spa in London for a half-hour whistle-stop tour. And then the day the Fraser Park Resort Spa opened its doors.

Beth just didn't have time to lie on a table and listen to whale song, or to sit in warm water and consider the healing powers of nature. There was a very real chance that if she relaxed for too long, her brother would seriously consider selling the resort for a magic bean.

She winced at the unkind thought. That wasn't true at all.

Cameron did his best. He might appear to be off the rails at times, but that was only because of his poorly hidden grief. Beth knew that despite his reassurances that he was fine, her brother had changed since losing the love of his life. She did her best to absorb the results of his new unruly behaviours, but her ability to do so was wearing thin. As was her patience sometimes.

She was simply tired and struggling to keep up with the pace at work at the moment. Whispers that the board were not happy just at the time they were in the middle of building a very expensive water park were not what she needed to hear.

She hoped the meeting they were about to have with the board members would put a lot of her doubts to rest. Speaking face to face with them would allow her to put her case forward, show the figures, the projections, and the costs. Once she had done that, they would surely be appeased and would go back to doing whatever it was they did every day that wasn't breathing down her neck. And after all that, she had to carve out a few hours in the afternoon to have treatments in the spa. She hoped they wouldn't be too involved or time-consuming.

"Hey, sis," Cameron greeted as she walked into the boardroom.

He sat at the head of the conference table with his feet up on the edge.

"Put your feet down," she told him.

He sighed but did as she asked. "And how are you this fine morning?"

She approached the head of the table, where the paperwork she had been working on sat, and stared pointedly at him. He stood and took one of the chairs to the side of the head.

"Oh, I'm peachy," she said. "I have this meeting which I really don't have time for, to calm the tempers of grouchy old men who know nothing about running a theme park. Then I have all my usual work to cram into a few short hours before I spend the afternoon at the spa with an influencer, whatever one of them *actually* is."

"I told you, she has a channel—"

"Yes, yes." She sat down and batted away his explanation.

"But what does it all mean? How does she get paid? Is she really an influencer, or is this some kind of scam? I need to research it, but I just haven't had the time."

"Ask her."

Beth chuckled. "Very funny."

"I'm serious. The whole sector is new—I'm sure she explains it to people all the time. She can answer all your techie financial questions. She's really nice."

Beth had to admit that Jemma did seem to be a very nice person. A little too bubbly and excitable, but certainly a nice spirit. She supposed that was essential in her line of work.

"By the way," he continued, "I promised I'd tell you about things before I did them, and so consider this advance notice of me suggesting we run some digital advertising. I spoke to a pal from uni who does this kind of thing, and he says we're missing a trick. He thinks we need about a ten grand a month budget—"

She held up her hand. "Absolutely not. Now is not the time to be trialling expensive new advertising. Especially not with the board watching every penny we spend. We need to halt extra spending until we've got the water park funding all secured and we're nearer to completion."

"Beth, we have to stay competitive," he argued. "We're stuck in the dark ages—unless we start shaking things up, we're going to sink."

Beth glanced at the door, checking that no one was lurking outside and eavesdropping on a conversation she'd really rather not have just before a very important meeting.

"Keep your voice down," she berated him. "We're not sinking. Everything is fine. And we can trial new advertising once things have settled down. I don't need to remind you that we no longer have full control of the company."

"They are supposed to be silent partners," he pointed out.

"Well, they found a voice." She pinched the bridge of her nose. "Bottom line, we need their money, and they will cut us off if they think we don't know what we're doing. It's in the lending contract, Cam. You read it."

He slumped in his chair.

"You *did* read it, didn't you?" she demanded.

He shrugged. "I can't remember. You're better with the details and, you know, the numbers and stuff. I can't remember it all right now."

"Please tell me you read it. Please tell me you didn't just sign it without reading it. You can't put this on my shoulders." Beth didn't really think that he would do such a thing, but her grief-stricken brother had been unpredictable for a while now. She tried to soften the blows of his supposedly carefree nature, but sometimes she really needed his support. Sometimes she couldn't cover for him.

"I'm not."

"You are. If you're not reading contracts, then it automatically becomes my fault when something goes wrong."

Cameron smiled and shook his head. "Nothing is going to go wrong, Beth. Really, you need to not worry so much."

Beth counted to five in her head to prevent herself from launching across the conference table and throttling him as they frequently had done to each other when they were kids. They were adults now, and they knew better. Or at least she did.

"Will you at least run through these figures with me before they all arrive?" Beth asked, tapping one of the folders in front of her with her finger.

"Sure." He grabbed the folder and started to read.

Beth wondered if he was really taking any of it in or if his mind was away with the fairies as it so often was. There was little she could do about it now. She knew she couldn't rely on him for things like this. As usual, it rested heavily on her and her alone.

Her heart started racing again, and she sucked in a breath and locked it in her lungs to try to centre the spinning room. A few seconds later, the haze cleared, and she felt her heart rate normalise again.

It will be fine, she thought. *Just relax.*

❖

The meeting had gone to hell. Beth knew it. Every member of the board there knew it. Even the secretary taking minutes knew it. Cameron was the only person who seemed to think nothing untoward had happened.

After the meeting, he slapped his sister on the back, gave her a broad smile, and told her that she was worried about nothing before heading back to the park.

Beth shook her head as she watched his retreating form, wondering if it was some kind of defence mechanism or if he really was that unaware of what was happening around him.

Not that she had much time to think about her brother's mental state—she needed to get home, grab some lunch, and prepare for the spa. Even if the details of the meeting did niggle at her. In the car on the short drive to her cottage she replayed the meeting over and over again. It had been an ambush. The sudden request to have an in-person meeting was unusual to say the least. Beth wondered if there was more to it than she was currently aware, or if her over-active and negative imagination was drawing conclusions out of thin air. Ever since she had brought more board members into the business, she had felt as though an invisible knife was pressed against her throat. At first, she had assumed it was paranoia because as long as the existing board, as well as herself and Cameron, all voted together, then they would always have the deciding vote.

And then Robert McLaughlin had passed away, and a new board member, loyal to the new investors, had been voted in. The balance of power shifted, and it made Beth feel very nervous.

Her hands gripped at the steering wheel.

"One problem at a time," she reminded herself. The next task was getting the spa profitable, and if spending a few hours with Jemma would help with that, then that's exactly what she'd do.

She frowned as she tried to recall all the features the spa had. She'd need to know if Jemma started asking any questions.

"Six treatment rooms," she reminded herself. "Indoor swimming pool, with two spa baths. Outdoor—*heated* outdoor swimming pool with hot tub. Sauna and steam rooms. Relaxation room. Full gym and two fitness studios."

She pulled into her driveway and parked up. She cocked her head to the side to see if she had remembered everything.

"Treatment rooms, indoor pool, outdoor pool, sauna, steam, gym, studios, relaxation room," she repeated.

She caught her reflection in the rear-view mirror and sighed. She looked tired, her eyes were drawn, her hair was limp, and she was sure she had a few more wrinkles around the eyes than she did that morning.

Ironically, she absolutely needed a relaxing spa day and some treatments. Unfortunately, she didn't have the time to properly unwind, nor would it be very easy to relax with a stranger next to her, presumably filming everything they did.

A nervous tingle ran up her spine as she wondered what Jemma would film. Would she film her?

The thought caused Beth to hurry from the car. She only had a couple of hours before she got back to the resort, and she needed to prepare herself. Starting with figuring out where on earth her black one-piece swimming costume was.

CHAPTER EIGHT

Jemma waited in the corridor next to the entrance to the spa. She was early as she'd wanted to film an introduction and had spoken to staff and gotten their sign-off to film in the facilities as well.

During her morning in the park she had mainly focused on shopping and Fraser Park merchandise, which had allowed her some time to look at all the treatments on offer at the spa.

In honesty, she could do with the eighty-five minute Drift Away massage package but didn't think that was appropriate, considering she'd have company. She'd book a couple of short things, not wanting to overload Beth's already hectic schedule.

"Am I late?"

She turned and smiled as Beth approached her, a look of concern on her face.

"No, I'm early." Jemma held up her camera. "Had to film my intro."

"Will you be filming in the spa?" Beth asked, a hint of worry in her tone.

"Yes, I've spoken with your spa manager, and she's given me the okay to film the facilities once we're done, as long as there is no one in there. I won't be filming us."

Beth visibly relaxed. But only slightly. Beth Fraser seemed to naturally be tense, Jemma had noticed.

"You have a really good treatment package on offer," Jemma said, trying to put Beth at ease. "I booked us in for the twenty-minute media massage—it focuses on neck, shoulders, and back. And then the twenty-minute express power facial."

"Power facial?" Beth chuckled. "Is that where they pressure wash your face?"

Jemma hadn't expected the joke and burst out laughing. "No, sadly it's not. It's a facial consisting of oats, honey, and fruit juices. Then a cleanse, a mask, and a mini massage."

"Have you memorised the treatment list?" Beth asked suspiciously.

"A little," Jemma admitted. "I had to do a few takes of my introduction because I kept getting it wrong or someone interrupted."

"You must get that a lot—people interrupting, I mean."

"All the time. But it's fine. I'm the weird person filming myself all day long, after all. It's a great package of treatments, though. And I love that it mentions same-sex couples on the couples' treatments. That's rare, but it's a nice inclusive touch."

Beth looked like she wanted to say something else but before long the moment seemed to pass, and she gestured towards the doors. "Shall we?"

They entered the spa and checked in before being led to the ladies' changing area and instructed to change into their bathing suits before donning a complimentary fluffy white robe and matching slippers.

Jemma had planned ahead and wore her red and white striped bikini under her clothes, and so she was ready and out of her changing cubicle and into the spa area in under five minutes. She placed her bag and her equipment bag on one of the wooden benches and explored the area.

She'd been in other spas before, from small hotel additions to full spa facilities that encompassed multiple levels. Fraser Resort Spa was a nice in-between. It was big enough that it had many facilities but small enough that it didn't feel like you were being swamped by too many options.

"Your first treatment starts in thirty-five-minutes," the technician explained. "In the meantime, feel free to explore the spa and go in the pools or the hot tubs. We'll come and get you when it's time, so no need to watch the clock. And if you need anything, just let us know."

"Thank you so much," Jemma said. She sucked in a deep and relaxing breath and slowly let it out again. It would be good to have some time in the spa and just chill out. Her schedule had been pretty packed lately, and the thought of just resting on a sunbed and listening to the sound of water trickling into the pool from the faux rockwork sounded like heaven.

Beth appeared from the changing area, and Jemma felt her eyebrows rise without her permission. Thankfully, Beth hadn't seen her leering, and so Jemma had the chance to pretend she hadn't seen her and continued looking at the indoor pool.

Don't stare, don't stare, don't stare, she chanted to herself.

Had it really been that long since she'd seen an attractive woman? Jemma didn't know why she was reacting so strongly to Beth Fraser, but for some reason, she was no longer in control. Her heart thudded against her ribcage, her eyes widened of their own accord, and her breath caught in her throat.

Any thought of calming her growing crush was all but lost. If Jemma hadn't already been aware that she was most definitely developing a thing for Beth, she was now.

Beth stood beside her in a simple but elegant black one-piece and started to put on the robe she had been holding when she arrived poolside. Jemma thanked her lucky stars that the robe was going on as that would hopefully prevent her malfunctioning body from spending too much time ogling Beth.

"The spa was completed just under a year ago," Beth explained in a formal tone. "There are six treatment rooms, an indoor pool which houses two spas, an outdoor pool that is heated—"

"—and has its own hot tub," Jemma finished. "I read the brochure."

Beth's cheeks lightly flushed, and Jemma felt a little guilty for shutting her down like that. It had been a knee-jerk reaction, in response to wanting to believe that Beth wanted to spend time with her that afternoon rather than acting as some kind of put-upon tour guide.

"It's a great place," Jemma said brightly, trying to soothe her harsh words. It wasn't Beth's fault that Jemma had been hoping to connect with the busy woman who clearly had no personal interest in her. "I like the design, a mix of Middle Eastern and African."

"Thank you, I spoke at length with some designers about it. We wanted to honour but not appropriate culture. It's a fine balance." Beth looked around the large space with a wistful look.

"So you were directly involved in designing the spa?" Jemma asked.

"I was directly involved with everything," Beth said in a soft voice, still looking around the space as if she hadn't seen it for a while and was only now realising how beautiful it was. "We have a small team here at Fraser Park. Everyone has to muck in."

"I get the feeling you muck in more than most," Jemma said. "Shall we try out the outdoor pool? I adore a heated outdoor pool."

Again, Beth seemed to hesitate for a moment but soon nodded her agreement. Jemma tried to think what it was that was throwing Beth off her stride. Every other time she saw her, she had been poised and in control. Here, in a place of supposed tranquillity and relaxation, she seemed on edge and a little lost.

"Do you come to the spa often?" Jemma asked, opening the door for Beth and gesturing for her to exit the glassed spa area first.

Beth laughed. "No, I'm not really a spa person."

That explains it, Jemma thought.

They approached the large outdoor pool, and Jemma admired the wisps of condensation rising from the warm water where it met the chill in the air.

"Yet you built a spa?" Jemma asked.

"The resort needed one. I researched it, brought in experts, and oversaw the build. But…" She paused a moment before continuing, "To be honest, I'm just not that good at relaxing."

Jemma felt as though she had broken through some wall. Beth was opening up. She smiled brightly at Beth and shucked out of her robe and tossed it on a nearby sunbed. "Let's see what we can do about that."

She took a running leap into the water.

❖

Beth laughed at the enthusiastic dive-bomb Jemma took into the water. A few moments passed before Jemma resurfaced, hair stuck to her face and a wide grin across it.

"The water's lovely," she called. "Come on in."

Beth pointed over to the shallow end and the built-in steps. "Excuse me if I take the old-fashioned route."

Jemma simply nodded before taking in a big breath and diving under the water. Beth watched her gliding through the water like a child who had recently discovered they could swim. She wished the water park was more than just a series of piles of dirt and construction equipment. Jemma would truly enjoy that experience.

Her heart started to thud at the thought of the build, the debt, the board, and everything else she associated with the water park.

"Are you okay?"

Beth turned to see a concerned looking face peeking over the edge of the pool in her direction. Beth didn't really have an answer. No, she wasn't okay. But this wasn't the right person to tell. While Beth knew that her family loved her and cared deeply for her, she couldn't remember the last time they had genuinely asked if she was okay. And Beth could tell that Jemma was genuine—it was clear in her worried eyes. It was nice, not to mention surprising, to know that Jemma cared. She felt an unfamiliar warmth flow through her body.

She nodded. "Yes, I'm fine. Just lost in thought about work for a moment."

"That's precisely what you're supposed to *not* do in a spa," Jemma informed her.

Beth chuckled. "Sorry, I'm a spa novice."

"I can tell. You're still not enjoying the water."

Beth rolled her eyes playfully and walked around the pool towards the steps. Once she was sure Jemma was swimming and not looking, she peeled off her robe and quickly climbed down the steps and into the water.

The last time she was in a swimming costume with another woman was when she was a child with her grandmother. It struck her that may well have been the last time she'd holidayed.

"So, what do you do outside of work?" Jemma asked, swimming over.

"I garden," Beth said, "and spend time with my niece and nephew."

It was technically true, but the idea of having time outside of work almost caused Beth to laugh. She did enjoy gardening but never got a chance to, especially since the storm of seven years ago which had effectively destroyed her grandmother's beloved garden.

The truth was, she didn't do anything outside of work. She worked both weekdays and weekends, she rarely took holiday, and if she did she was always on call.

"What about you?" Beth asked, eager to move the conversation away from her.

"Can you really call what I do work?" Jemma asked.

"I'm afraid I don't really know what it is you do," Beth admitted. She swam over to one of the submerged seating areas, and Jemma followed.

"I create travel content," Jemma explained. "I travel, film everything I see and do, edit it, upload it, and repeat with a different location."

They sat side by side but with a sizeable gap between them. For the first time ever, Beth was pleased that the spa was underutilised, and they were the only ones there.

"How do you pay for all that travel?" Beth asked the question she had been wondering from the start.

"Advertising pays for everything," Jemma explained.

Beth must have looked blank as Jemma took one look at her face and chuckled.

"So, when I upload content to YouTube, I can choose to monetise my videos. Which basically means putting ads onto them. I get paid a tiny amount when those ads are seen and a little bit more when those ads are clicked on."

Beth blinked. "And that pays...well?" She couldn't imagine

that a few pennies here and there could be enough to cover a person's travel expenses.

"Yeah, it pays very well," Jemma said. "I make between three and five US dollars per one thousand views."

Beth tried to do the math to figure out what Jemma's videos might pay her. Cameron had mentioned a quarter of a million views, or was that subscribers? She couldn't recall.

"I have nearly a million subscribers. They don't all watch all my videos, but I have a pretty good retention rate. I have about three and a half thousand videos, and I average around a hundred thousand to two hundred thousand views per video. Some go up to a million—some have even hit four million when they get trending," Jemma continued. She sat on the submerged seat, her feet sticking out in front of her, and gently slapping the water with her toes.

Beth still couldn't quite fathom all what Jemma was saying. It just seemed like a load of numbers that she couldn't make head nor tail of.

"In an average month, I make around thirty thousand pounds," Jemma added.

"A month?" Beth snapped her head around to look at the young woman, shyly batting her feet in the water.

"Yeah, there's…tax and stuff. And it goes up and down every month. And it wasn't always like that—it's because I have a big back catalogue of videos. Travel videos are always popular. People are always searching for them. I have some great fans and subscribers who help me by commenting and sharing. And I work really hard on the algorithms and stuff."

Beth reached her hand out and placed it on Jemma's shoulder. "You don't have to explain. You've clearly built up a spectacular business, well done. You should be proud. Hell, I'm proud of you." She retracted her hand, realising she was touching the bare skin of a woman she hardly knew. "You clearly saw the opportunity and worked hard. Well done, I'm stunned that filming yourself eating a cheeseburger can make that kind of money, but that doesn't take away anything from your obvious success."

Jemma looked bashfully at her. "Thank you."

"So, do you post content every day? How does it work?"

Beth was fascinated. She'd thought the very idea of filming yourself eat, watch fireworks, shop, and have a spa trip was simple narcissism. It appeared she was grossly underestimating the influencer business, to the tune of at least three hundred and sixty thousand pounds per year. Jemma paid more in *tax* than the entire management team at Fraser Park *earned*. She also suspected that Jemma was underestimating the amount, judging from the blush on the tips of her ears and her clear embarrassment when she stated such a large figure.

Wanting to save Jemma from her blushes, Beth decided to move away from the money side of the business and onto the practicalities. She was still wildly curious about what an influencer did and how.

"I try to post every day. I used to post more than once a day, maybe two or three smaller videos. But the algorithm doesn't really respond to that, and people are more likely to sit down and watch one well-edited, longer video from me than small bits and pieces here and there."

"How long is a longer video?" Beth questioned.

"About twenty-five to thirty-five minutes. Sometimes I drift up to an hour but not often and never over that. People have limited attention spans."

Beth laughed. "That they do. How long does it take to edit a video?"

Jemma blew out a breath and stared up at the sky as she thought about it. "No less than triple the length of the original video. You have to watch it all through once at the start and once at the end, at least. I don't do a lot of editing, mainly cuts, or I could literally spend days on each video."

Beth considered that for a moment and quickly totalled up the timeline. "So if you were to create a finished, uploadable, video of half an hour, that would require more footage. Maybe an hour?"

Jemma nodded.

"And then you have to edit that, which will take, what, another three hours?"

Jemma nodded again.

"That's four hours for thirty minutes of video, and then you have to upload it?"

"Yes, and then I have to engage with it for the algorithm," Jemma added.

"What is this algorithm you keep mentioning?" Beth asked.

Jemma smiled. "The algorithm is like my boss. It's the coding behind each social media platform, and it decides if the platform will help you get your content seen. If I posted on Instagram and never engaged with my replies, Instagram wouldn't show my posts as often. If I reply to comments, the algorithm will see I'm engaged with my followers and will help to show my post to more people who might like my content. Which increases my followers, which is the aim of the game."

Beth felt exhausted just thinking about it. Suddenly Jemma wasn't a person who filmed herself with a colourful cocktail in a glamourous location and got paid through the nose for the privilege. She worked hard, and Beth was only aware of the very tip of the influencer iceberg.

"Well, I have more information to provide you with an answer now," Beth said.

"An answer to what?" Jemma frowned.

"You asked if you can call what you do work. It's clear that it is. You presumably spend hours planning content, filming, and then editing it. Beyond that you must spend a lot of time engaging with your followers, especially if you're closing in on a million of them. The real question is…do you find time to sleep?"

Jemma beamed. Beth wondered if people often stopped to think of the intricacies of her job and understood the sheer volume of work that must go into maintaining her online presence. Beth was impressed, and she hardly knew a thing about it. All she did know was that Jemma clearly worked extremely hard. Perhaps they did have something in common after all.

"You see why I need a spa day now?" Jemma asked, pushing away from the seat and floating in the water in front of Beth.

"Absolutely. If anyone deserves to have their face power washed, then it's you," Beth joked.

Beth decided then and there that the first opportunity she had, she'd look at Jemma's channel and see exactly what it was she did. Admittedly, she'd belittled the very notion of an influencer at first. But there had to be something to it. Hundreds of thousands of people watched Jemma's content, and she made extremely good money doing it.

She supposed it was like a television production company. The company would research content, produce, edit, and distribute that content, and potentially millions of people would watch it.

The difference was that Jemma seemed to manage it all on her own. She'd harnessed the power of new and accessible technologies and had built up her own production company. Not only that, she seemed to have done it alone.

Beth couldn't help but feel impressed.

While Jemma couldn't actually see Beth, she could sense that she had finally relaxed a little. Stress had radiated off Beth during the side by side media massage they had both experienced. Jemma had loved the feeling of the masseuse's hands running over her neck, shoulders, and back and easing out all the tension caused by too many hours hunched over her laptop or her phone.

Unfortunately, Beth hadn't seemed to be a fan. Jemma didn't mention it, not wanting to embarrass her. Or draw attention to the fact that she was highly attuned to Beth's presence.

But once the face masks had been applied and the technicians had left them alone in the dimly lit room, Beth finally seemed to let some of the stress ease away. Jemma wondered if it was the presence of the technicians, technically her staff, that had put Beth on edge or if she was simply so wound up that she needed time to let go of whatever was bothering her.

Jemma decided that some casual conversation might help to make Beth a little more relaxed.

"Abigail's cute as a button," she mused.

"She is," Beth replied, warmth in her tone.

"She clearly adores you," Jemma said.

"And you. Apparently she's a big fan—she was quite star-struck when she first saw you. Not that she'd thank me for telling you that."

"I'll keep it between us," Jemma promised. "Actually, when I first saw you, I thought you were her mother."

Beth laughed as if the very thought was preposterous.

"What? You two are very close," Jemma pointed out.

"We are, but I'm not mother material."

"You seemed to be," Jemma pressed. "Don't sell yourself short."

"I could never replace Diane," Beth said.

Jemma wished she could see her, but the dim light in the room meant she could only just make out a shadow of the woman next to her. She didn't want to overstep but wanted Beth to understand that she meant it as a compliment, but somehow the conversation was unravelling.

"I didn't mean that," Jemma said softly.

There was a pause before Beth ejected a small sigh. "I know, I'm sorry. It's a difficult subject. We lost Diane seven years ago, and it's just as raw today as it was back then."

"May I ask what happened?"

"A heart attack," Beth explained, her voice weak. "No one knew she had a problem with her heart, and one morning she just didn't wake up."

Jemma felt her own heart clench at the very thought of something like that happening. "I'm so sorry."

"Thank you. Cameron has been incredibly strong throughout. He has the biggest heart and wears it more publicly than anyone I know. He mourns, obviously, but he made the decision to celebrate Diane's life rather than mourn her death. Easier said than done some of the time." Beth let out a breath. "But we're a resilient family."

"Is it just you, Cameron, and the children?"

"It is. Our mother left when we were children, and our father died when we were teenagers. Our grandmother brought us up, even before Daddy died."

Jemma couldn't imagine such loss. Her parents had been a bit of a thorn in her side sometimes, but she couldn't imagine them not being there. Jemma could hardly remember her own grandmother, but she hadn't been a kindly sort. She'd been cold and miserable, hardened by years of perceived injustice and formed into a selfish and unlikeable person. She hoped that Beth hadn't endured that on top of everything else.

"There's no special someone in your life?" Jemma asked, hoping to goodness she wasn't about to uncover yet another layer of horror.

Beth snorted a laugh. "No. There's not many people in this part of Scotland who'd be suitable."

Jemma couldn't think what Beth could possibly be alluding to. "Suitable?"

"The mention of same-sex couples on the spa treatment list isn't an afterthought," Beth explained. "There aren't many women of my persuasion around here."

Jemma's heart soared. Beth was a lesbian, or bisexual, or something. She was certainly interested in women. And she was single. Excitement at the prospect that she might just be in with a chance of something with Beth clogged up her thought process, and she struggled to know what to say. Beth hadn't laid a path for a simple *me too*.

The door opened and light from the corridor rudely interrupted the moment.

"Miss Fraser, I'm so sorry to interrupt, but there's a call for you," the technician said, holding out a cordless handset. "They said it was urgent."

"Thank you." Beth held out her hand and took the phone.

Jemma attempted to look like she wasn't listening, which was hard once they were both plunged back into darkness and sitting less than a metre apart. Beth spoke in clipped tones. Whatever had happened clearly wasn't good.

"I'll be there as soon as I can." Beth pressed a button and hung up the call. "I'm sorry, I'm going to have to cut this short."

"I'm sorry you'll miss the power washing part," Jemma joked, trying to lighten the situation. She got up and opened the door again, calling out to the technician. "Hello? Miss Fraser has to go. Can you help her get ready?"

A few moments later two technicians arrived and quickly set about helping Beth remove the face mask. They insisted on applying a light moisturiser, and within minutes Beth was ready to leave.

She stood in front of Jemma looking apologetic. "Really, I am very sorry about this."

"It's fine—I get a chance to dive-bomb the pool again and film everything," Jemma reassured her. "I had a great time."

Beth smiled and looked like she was going to reciprocate the comment. She hesitated and finally said, "Good, if you need anything else, then you have my brother's details."

It stung. Jemma had hoped that they'd bonded in some way in the hour or so they'd spent together, but it seemed Beth was eager to put the wedge between them again.

"I do, thank you for your time," Jemma said, trying her best to not look as devastated as she felt.

CHAPTER NINE

With the late afternoon suddenly available to her again, Jemma naturally found herself back in Fraser Park. She had managed to see everything at least once in the time she had already spent there, but the level of detail had her wanting to explore areas multiple times.

Jemma hadn't understood the difference between a theme park and an amusement park when she had started vlogging. It wasn't something that had really been on her radar, until one day she went to a *real* theme park.

It sounded obvious now, but at the time it had eluded her until she had seen it with her own eyes. An amusement park delivered thrills and entertainment; a theme park transported people to another world.

It hadn't seemed important in her youth, but when you filmed a theme park and had to verbalise what you were seeing, it suddenly became very clear the level of work and detail that went into everything.

Jemma found herself in the medieval land of Fraser Park, admiring the family crests that adorned the castle-like brick wall of a gift shop. The thing Jemma liked most about theme parks was they went above and beyond, often in a way that was probably unnecessary. She knew of a merry-go-round in the Netherlands that was decorated with real gold. Hardly anyone would notice or care, but for the few who did, it was like a little bit of secret magic sprinkled in.

"Jemma!"

She was used to hearing her name called when she was out and about—one of the problems with being famous was that people thought they knew you. And disconcertingly sometimes that you should know them. Being on someone's television set, for those who cast from a mobile device to the big screen, meant people developed a very real connection.

She turned and was relieved and pleased to see Abigail weaving her way through a crowd of people to get to Jemma. She smiled. "Hey! Great to see you again."

Abigail came to an excited skidding halt. Her cheeks were red from the exertion. A boy jogged to catch up to her—he was older and definitely related.

"This is my brother, Luke," Abigail introduced.

"Hi, Luke, great to meet you," Jemma said.

He smiled but looked a little shy. "Is that the G5?" he asked, nodding to her camera.

"It is. I usually use the G7, but this does low light so much better," she replied. He looked no older than early teens, but Jemma had learned long ago that when children got to a certain age, it was far better to treat them like adults.

"Are you filming the fireworks?" Luke quizzed, eyeing her equipment bag that was slung over her shoulder.

"Yep, I filmed it last night from a fixed point, and today I'll film it actively, and then I'll chop the two together," she explained.

Luke nodded knowingly but Abigail frowned. "What do you mean film actively?"

"I'll focus on certain bits—like, I might zoom in, or out, depending on what the show is doing. The fixed-point filming is like a backing track I can rely on whenever I need to, but the active footage is the important bit." She leaned in close, as if divulging a secret. "I don't watch the show much the first time, and then I focus on certain aspects the next time, and if I'm lucky enough to see it a *third* time, which I will do here, then I don't film it at all, and I just enjoy it."

"Dad says we can't watch it all the time like Aunty Beth does." Abigail sighed.

"Does she watch it every night?" Jemma asked, intrigued.

"Yes, she has a secret place where she can watch it alone—" Abigail stopped when Luke gave her a sharp look that seemed to imply that was sensitive information.

Jemma decided it was time to switch gears and talk about the kids rather than fish for information on their attractive aunt. "So, do you two just get to hang out here whenever you like?" she asked.

"Sure." Luke shrugged nonchalantly. "We come here after school—we have for ages."

"I don't think my parents would have been chilled enough to let me hang out in a theme park every evening," Jemma admitted.

"Everyone knows us," Luke said. He turned and smiled and waved at a member of staff who happened to be walking by.

"Hey, Luke," she replied with a wide smile. "Hi, Abigail."

Jemma considered that the kids probably had a few hundred people to watch over them when they spent time in Fraser Park.

"Will you come on No Way with us?" Abigail asked.

Jemma regarded the girl for a moment. "Are you tall enough for No Way?"

"Just," Luke said. "She finally grew this year."

Abigail poked her tongue out at him.

Jemma considered the request. The two were fans of her channel, and their father was the co-owner of the park. They seemed like nice kids, and she'd like to spend time with them, but she couldn't shake the feeling that it wasn't really appropriate to do so.

"I'd love to, but I have so much filming to do." It wasn't a lie—she did a have a lot that she needed to get through for her upcoming park tour video.

"Can we join you?" Abigail asked. "We won't get in the way."

Jemma couldn't exactly say no. Not that she wanted to, and it seemed to be a good compromise.

"Sure, you can tell me all the little details and Easter eggs that no one else knows about," Jemma suggested.

Luke's eyes widened with interest. "We know a lot of secrets about the park—like, our great-grandmother planted lilac bushes by the entrance because they were her favourite. They are still there today, and that means they're over eighty years old."

"Wow, that's amazing. Yes, anything like that would be great for the channel," she confessed. Little insider bits of information were always eaten up by theme park enthusiasts.

"We should start by the Chinese dragon," Luke said. "Did you know that it was made by real Chinese woodcarvers?"

"And it was sent in a box all the way from China, and it took six months to get here," Abigail added.

Jemma was already aware of both facts as she had extensively studied the park, but she didn't want to dampen their enthusiasm and cause them to clam up.

"Really? That's so cool. Tell me more…"

"Have you seen the children?" Beth asked Jon, one of the attendants at the haunted house attraction that the kids loved so much.

Cameron sent her an email explaining that he would be stuck on a telephone conference call and asked if she could find the kids and perhaps feed them dinner. Beth happily put aside the financial forecast that had been causing a deep indent in her forehead.

Any relaxing she'd managed to do at the spa was shattered after three members of staff didn't turn up for their shifts, which meant Beth had to switch up the roster and call on off-duty staff to fill the gaps. Then there was the temporary power outage which had caused the internet connectivity to disappear, which meant card payments had to be suspended for fifteen minutes while the routers rebooted.

After all that, she'd sat down to look at the forecasts which she'd been struggling with for days. The idea of going to get the kids and spending an hour or two with them before getting back to work seemed like a nice plan.

Unfortunately, finding the children wasn't always easy. Luke had a mobile phone, but it was frequently off, on silent, or out of range. The problem with the vast park was that the mobile signal was patchy at best.

Beth had considered asking Luke to carry one of the staff walkie-talkies, but she knew he'd lose it in minutes.

"Haven't seen them," Jon said.

Beth raised an eyebrow. It was unusual that neither of them had been by the haunted house as it was by far their favourite walk-through attraction. Especially as Jon was well-known for handing out candy to them.

Jon gestured to his walkie-talkie. "Want me to put out a call to see if anyone has seen them?"

Beth had hoped to avoid that, but she'd been walking around for twenty minutes with no luck at all. She nodded. "Please, it's not urgent, though."

"Anyone seen Abigail or Luke? Not urgent, just looking for a location," Jon spoke into the device.

Beth felt a little anxious. Cameron insisted that the kids could roam the park and enjoy any of the attractions they desired without company. She knew the park was a relatively safe environment but had never been able to fully relax into the idea.

"They are by the carousel with a woman. They've been there for about half an hour with her," a voice crackled through the walkie-talkie.

Beth thanked Jon and hurried away. The kids had both declared the carousel to be boring many years ago, so the fact they were there was a surprise. And who on earth were they hanging out with for half an hour?

Panic raced through her, and she found herself jogging through the various lands on her way to their location. She'd never forgive Cameron's lax behaviour if something had happened to them. Why was he always so chilled about everything? Did he have no idea of the world around him?

She knew the answer: not lately. Cameron lived in a bubble where everything was possible, and everyone was kind. It seemed to be the only way he could deal with his grief, to counteract the negative feelings with as much positivity as possible. Sometimes, unrealistic positivity. Beth wished she could live in that world, but she was firmly rooted in reality.

Taking a shortcut through a restaurant that connected to a gift shop, she burst through the door and into the large plaza. Her gaze darted around before resting on Abigail. She sighed in relief at seeing the happy, smiling girl. Despite the worst-case scenario running though her mind, everything seemed fine.

She approached and was surprised to see Jemma with them. She was speaking to a camera that Luke was holding.

Abigail saw Beth and ran over. "Luke's helping Jemma—isn't that cool! He's a cameraman."

"Very cool," Beth murmured, eyes fixed on Jemma.

The woman was casually speaking about the carousel behind her, explaining its history, the craftmanship, pointing out details, and generally enthusing about the park's oldest ride.

For the first time, Beth could see the appeal of watching this kind of content. Jemma was full of positive energy, talking to the camera as if she was addressing a best friend. Her smile was infectious, and people who passed by couldn't help but smile as they saw her. Beth wondered if they knew who she was. Surely some of them must if her fan base was so large.

"And so, I'll leave you with some footage onboard this fantastic carousel. Remember to subscribe to the channel if you haven't already, and please, please, give this video a thumbs-up if you enjoyed it. Have a perfect day!"

Luke pressed a button, and Jemma approached him, the two of them huddled over the viewfinder and discussing something.

"Have a perfect day," Beth mumbled under her breath.

"That's Jemma's sign-off. She ends every video with that," Abigail explained.

"Seems like a stretch," Beth muttered. She couldn't remember a perfect day. In fact, it had been so long since she'd had a *good* day that she couldn't even possibly imagine what a perfect one would look like.

"Hi, Beth, great to see you again," Jemma said. "Did you get your work thing sorted?"

"I did, thank you. Sorry again for abandoning you like that."

"Not a problem, I'm glad we had the time we could together." Jemma's eyes sparkled, and Beth found herself swallowing and having to look away. Did the woman have any idea how attractive she was?

She looked at Luke and Abigail. "Your father is going to be delayed. He's asked me to make sure you eat dinner at a reasonable hour—"

"Crêpes!" Abigail demanded. "By the lake!"

"Yes, crêpes." Luke nodded hard. "Can Jemma come?"

Beth felt cornered. She'd hoped to scoop the kids up and take them away, preferably to a nice sit-down restaurant. Now she was, yet again, being asked to dine with Jemma.

"Jemma might be busy," Beth told Luke softly.

"I'm not."

Beth's gaze met Jemma's. She was smiling and packing her camera equipment into her bag. Beth couldn't fathom why Jemma would want to spend her time with the three of them. Surely she was busy?

"Have you tried the crêpes yet?" Abigail asked.

"Nope, but they are on my list of things to try. If you don't mind me filming?"

"Can I hold the camera again?" Luke asked.

"Only once you've eaten. Can't have a hungry cameraman. They get really shaky." Jemma took hold of Luke's shoulders and playfully shook him. "And then the footage looks like this."

Luke giggled in a way Beth hadn't heard in years. She smiled at the knowledge that the little boy she once knew was still in there somewhere, buried behind all the effort involved in becoming a man.

Jemma stopped shaking him and held him steady while peering over his head at Beth. "What do you say? Can I join the fun?"

Beth couldn't help but smile and nod. Crêpes by the lake it was.

❖

The crêpe stand was designed to look like a traditional forest green pavilion for renting boats for the lake. It served sweet and savoury crêpes, and the only reason Jemma didn't order a large sweet dessert with lashings of ice cream was because she assumed Beth would want her to set a better tone for the children.

When her chicken, spinach, feta, and mushroom feast of a crêpe arrived, she was very happy indeed. A lot of theme park fare was burgers and chicken nuggets, which Jemma loved but could also become bored with.

Some resorts were now upping their game and serving food from around the world, as well as hosting other restaurants inside their gates. Jemma was pleased that Fraser Park was on the right track and not in danger of falling behind the competition. There was something about the resort that Jemma just adored, and she already knew she'd be coming back often.

Watching Beth hand the children napkins and direct them towards an available picnic table, she wondered how much the attractive executive had to do with her decision to make a return visit to the resort.

Jemma waited with Beth while her crepe was cooked and prepared.

"Thank you for entertaining them this afternoon," Beth said, her head tilting towards the kids.

"Not a problem, they were super helpful actually. They know a lot about the resort."

Beth grimaced. "Comes from spending every second of their spare time here, I suppose."

Jemma hesitated a moment, wondering if she should share the sensitive information the children had confessed to her.

"What is it?" Beth asked, immediately detecting the change in atmosphere.

"I probably shouldn't say anything," Jemma said.

"Well, now that you've said that, you'll have to."

Jemma checked the children were still eating their crêpes and well out of listening range. "We were chatting—I wasn't prying or anything. The kids kind of mentioned that you and their father were always busy. They said that the business always comes first. And they didn't seem so happy about it."

"They said that?" Beth asked, clearly surprised.

Jemma felt a little guilty, both for sharing the kids' secret and for dumping it onto Beth's shoulders. However, she couldn't help but think she would have had a better childhood herself if someone had said something similar to her own parents.

Beth paled and looked a little unsteady on her feet. Jemma held her elbow to steady her.

"Whoa, are you okay?"

Beth blinked a few times before swallowing and slowly nodding. "Yes, yes, I'm fine. I'm sorry. I…I had no idea they felt that way."

"Maybe I shouldn't have said anything," Jemma wondered aloud, removing her hand reluctantly.

"No, you're right to tell me. I'll speak with Cam. They've been through enough. It's disheartening to think that they think they can't speak with us. But that just makes it more important to fix."

"They are great kids," Jemma said. She noticed Beth's glassy eyes and pale skin and wondered if she was going to be sick. "I'm sure you can all figure it out," she reassured.

"I hope so," Beth said wistfully, staring over to the picnic bench.

"Miss Fraser?" A crêpe, wrapped in a branded cardboard holder, was held out through the window of the pavilion.

"Thank you," Beth said, taking the crêpe.

They slowly walked over to the picnic bench, and Jemma took the opportunity to look out at the lake where pedalos and cute wooden boats glided through the water. On the banks were a vast array of ducks stomping around the various diners and hoping for a bite to eat. It was idyllic. But Beth seemed completely unaware of it, lost in her own thoughts.

Jemma wondered if this was what happened when you spent too much time at a resort, that you became blind to it. Had Beth become so consumed by the management of the resort that she no longer stopped to smell the roses? If that was the case, then it was a terrible thing to have happened.

"I've finished if you want me to film," Luke said, eagerly wiping his fingers on a napkin.

Jemma looked down at her crêpe and realised, for the first time in a very long time, that she had entirely forgotten that she was supposed to be filming her meal. Thankfully, she hadn't taken a bite of it. Not that it would have been the end of the world, but it would have annoyed her that she'd forgotten.

"That would be great." Jemma gently lowered her equipment bag to the table.

"Same settings?" Luke asked.

"We'll test, but I think we'll need a higher ISO because of the lighting here."

"Right."

He was already opening the bag and setting up the lens and camera as she had shown him earlier. It was actually nice to have two little assistants. Abigail was a perfect gopher and excelled at running around getting anything that Jemma might need, from her lip gloss from her make-up bag to a bottle of water. Luke was a little older and clearly knew his way around a camera. Between the three of them, they made an excellent team.

Beth sat on the picnic bench and placed a soft kiss into Abigail's hair. Jemma felt a pang of jealousy. She'd never had a close relationship with any of her family. They were good people and they loved each other, but they just didn't really know how to show it. But for the small stab of jealousy there was a tidal wave of affection behind it.

The Fraser family were adorable, and Jemma only hoped they knew how lucky they all were.

Chapter Ten

B eth stepped into the hallway of her cottage and let out a long
sigh. It had been a long, strange day. From board meetings in
the morning, to the spa in the afternoon, to a cluster of disasters,
dinner with Jemima, and then back to work.

Even the evening display had done little to soothe her mood.
Especially when there had been an overcrowding issue when one of
the old gates at the west entrance had refused to open.

She shrugged out of her coat and hung it on the rack before
moving into the living room and turning on all the lights. The
problem with living alone was that the solitude was always so
apparent when you got home. The silence and darkness served as a
reminder that the property was empty, and no one had come or gone
since you'd left that morning.

Pausing by the patio doors, Beth nervously licked her lips and
looked at the darkness outside. She knew she shouldn't torment
herself even further, but she just couldn't help herself. She held her
breath for a moment before switching the garden lights on.

She didn't know why she tortured herself by looking out into
the ruined garden, but she frequently did. Maybe she hoped that
some magic from the park would one day follow her home and her
grandmother's garden would suddenly be restored to its former
glory.

Clearly, today wasn't the day that particular fairy tale was
going to come true.

The large fallen trees still lay at awkward angles across the former flower beds, the battered greenhouse, and the rockery. Mud littered everything in sight, having been dragged in by the torrential downpour from the storm seven years ago.

Beth had watched from the upstairs window that fateful evening, knowing that the nearby river would burst its banks and that a torrent of water was on its way. Little had she known then that the force of the water would uproot several trees and effectively wreck the entire garden. A garden her grandmother had lovingly tended all her life. Beth had maintained the cottage and the garden after she moved in when her grandmother had passed, but that night changed everything.

She'd tried to fix it, but she wasn't enough for Mother Nature's forces and couldn't find anyone willing to help. She'd long ago been labelled as an impossible to please perfectionist by the local tradespeople. After the storm, she'd called everyone she could think of only to find they were either too busy or simply never returned her calls. The cottage was in the middle of nowhere, and with the locals ignoring her, and people further afield unwilling to make the long journey, she was stuck. Now it was just a given that her garden was gone forever.

Beth switched off the light and shook her head. It was a problem for another day. Like so many of them were.

She felt the worst kind of tired, the one where exhaustion grasped at your eyelids to tug them down while your brain hurled a thousand and one thoughts into your consciousness like a toddler searching through a toy box.

Tea was most definitely in order. She filled the kettle and flipped the switch and wondered how to spend her evening. She had reports to read, forecasts to create, research to conduct. And yet, her focus kept drifting towards the same thing. Jemma.

They'd spent a lovely evening by the lake with the kids. After crêpes were eaten and filmed, they'd taken a four-person pedalo out onto the water. Beth couldn't remember the last time she'd been on the lake. It had been a spur-of-the-moment decision that Jemma had suggested. The children jumped at the idea, and Beth found it impossible to say no.

After that they walked around the lake, Abigail excitedly pointing out all the animals she saw. Beth had lost track of time, and Cameron had come to find them with a grin on his face at the knowledge that his sister wasn't always perfect at timekeeping.

Then Beth knew she had to get back to the office, and Jemma had said she hoped to see her again soon. For some reason those words had lingered in Beth's mind all evening.

Tea made, she set up her iPad at the kitchen island and searched Google for *Jemma travel channel*—she couldn't remember what the channel was called, and she wasn't about to ask Cameron for the exact details. She was sure she could locate it herself.

Sure enough, Jemma's beaming face appeared at the top of the search results. It seemed she had a YouTube channel called *Life with Jem*. She also had a Facebook page, a Twitter account, and an Instagram account.

Beth had never really been one for social media, but she had learned how to add oil to her car from YouTube before so knew it had its uses. She clicked on the YouTube channel.

She blinked. Jemma had over nine hundred and seventy thousand followers. Beth couldn't even process how many people that actually was. She scrolled through the video thumbnails and noticed that Jemma's videos were getting hundreds of thousands of views.

A video caught her eye about packing only hand luggage for a transatlantic trip.

"Impossible," Beth murmured.

She clicked the video and sipped her tea as Jemma explained how she was going to spend five days in California with only one piece of hand luggage and a small handbag. Jemma showed everything she was packing—clothing, toiletries, shoes, accessories, and electronics. She then showed the bag she was using and provided pricing and information on other packing essentials.

A cleverly edited montage showed her packing her bag at great speed, and before long she was standing with the bag in her hand, ready to go.

Beth had to admit she was impressed. She definitely didn't

think Jemma would be able to get everything she needed for such a trip into just hand luggage. She hit the little thumbs-up icon and saw another video that caught her interest about hitting five London tourist hotspots in one day without breaking the bank.

Before long, Beth had spent over an hour watching various videos. Some she watched from start to end, frustrated when the adverts interrupted, and some she skimmed through. She was beginning to understand the draw of Jemma's channel. She spoke to the camera as if she was a friend, and you were following her on her adventures. In many ways Jemma seemed to pull the viewer into the adventure. Beth had noticed that Jemma used *we* a lot in her videos, speaking to the viewers as if they were there with her, and they were all making a choice at the same time. When she looked at the menu of a restaurant, she'd wonder what *we* should have. It was a small thing but incredible powerful, making Beth feel as if she was there. And as if she was a personal friend of Jemma's.

A video finished, and Beth smothered a yawn. She was eager to watch more, but she was tired. It was only now that she could understand Abigail's and Luke's excitement at watching the channel. Jemma was like a fun friend coming to visit and telling you all the exciting things they did when they were somewhere interesting that you wanted to go.

The editing was slick, with background music and clean cuts. Beth could tell that a fair amount of effort went into production. However, she did wonder if it was quite fair to show something that wasn't entirely accurate. She'd seen Jemma filming food a couple of times now. She plumped it up, put it in the right light, and filmed it at its very best. She wasn't being deceitful as such, but it wasn't *quite* true to life.

Beth supposed that was all part of the channel. No one wanted to see a half-melted ice cream and a sad looking burger. They wanted it to look delicious.

With a little understanding of the behind the scenes work, Beth had to wonder about the other videos she'd watched. How much effort had gone into making them look…perfect?

It was even Jemma's sign-off on her videos—*Have a perfect day!*

But could something really be described as perfect if it was being manipulated and edited?

Beth sighed and ran a hand through her hair. She was putting far too much thought into it. It wasn't her channel, or any of her business. Clearly almost a million people frequently watched *Life with Jem*, and they loved it. Jemma had cultivated a channel that worked.

"How does anyone get a million people to do anything?" Beth wondered. She tapped into the comments section and started to read some of the comments to the videos and Jemma's replies. She was surprised by how many Jemma replied to.

A small part of Beth had wondered if Jemma's fame was because she was young and attractive. Everyone knew those two things got you very far in this world. Now and then a comment appeared that stated how gorgeous Jemma was, but there were not many of them. The vast majority were simply people saying how much they liked the video, telling Jemma where she should eat while at that location or where she should travel to next, or even asking for advice. It appeared that Jemma had created a community of like-minded travellers.

She clicked on the channel again and looked at the variety of thumbnail images, all featuring Jemma in various poses.

She's very attractive, Beth thought to herself. *Not to mention kind, energetic, friendly, and intelligent.*

She laughed out loud at her ridiculousness. Jemma could be all those things and more, but it was completely irrelevant. She was straight, and she was far too young and far too attractive to be interested in someone like Beth. The fact that Jemma's gaze lingered a little longer than was usual was probably just her way of being friendly.

People who had perfect days were not interested in people who couldn't even describe a perfect day. With a tired sigh Beth turned the iPad off and went to prepare for bed.

❖

Jemma sat crossed-legged on the bed and hunched over her laptop. She'd downloaded all the day's footage from her memory card, and now she was organising and clipping it.

She still hadn't entirely decided how to frame the content she had recorded. It always fell into one of two options—a mega vlog that showed her day in the park as it happened, or many small clips focusing on certain elements.

One of the biggest advantages of the smaller uploads was that they took a lot less work, and she'd be able to get a video up that evening.

Before she got that far, she needed to organise all the clips into folders, so she knew what she had and could get a handle on what she could do with it. She picked up her pen and crossed off a few items on her to-do list. She'd not gotten through enough of the park's signature snacks as she would have liked by this point in the trip. Which meant an ice cream heavy day the next day.

Her stomach lurched at the thought.

While ice cream was nice, she had her limits, especially as a standard vanilla cone was hardly available in theme parks anymore—it was always multiple flavours, mountains of whipped cream, masses of sauce, and more. To eat one delicious ice cream was great, but to have to get through several in one day and attempt to look happy while doing so was tough going.

Have to get back on that pedalo. A smile crossed her face at the thought. Being on the lake with Beth and the kids had been so much fun, and much needed after Jemma polished off her savoury crêpe with a sweet one.

At one point she and the kids stopped pedaling to see if Beth would notice. The boat lurched to a far slower speed, and Beth had looked over the side, wondering if they'd gotten caught up in something. Beth promised her vengeance on their joke and spent the rest of the trip with her legs raised up off the pedals and simply enjoying the scenery.

Jemma had been glad to take the extra strain, especially as Beth seemed so tired. She hid it well from the kids, but Beth looked like a woman who needed a month on a beach somewhere. Her exhaustion didn't change the fact that she looked gorgeous, and Jemma took every opportunity to steal glances, wondering if Beth could ever look twice at someone like her. She doubted it. They were from different worlds. The busy executive and the influencer.

Glancing at the video that was processing, she caught a glimpse of Luke, who was the very spitting image of his father. Jemma still couldn't quite comprehend that Cameron and Beth were twins. To say they were polar opposites wouldn't cover it.

There were physical similarities, but their personalities couldn't be more different. Cameron seemed fun but disorganised. He was very personable but almost a little bumbling in his cluelessness. Not at all like his sister, who was probably the most capable person Jemma had ever met. Beth just had an air of confidence and professionalism about her that Jemma found incredibly attractive.

Jemma shook her head and refocused her attention on the footage and her problem of how to curate her content. She knew one thing—she wanted to leave the firework display for another separate video. It was too impressive to shove onto the end of a normal day vlog. It was clear that a lot of thought and heart had gone into the production. She jotted a note down to ask Cameron about it when she saw him for the interview that still wasn't quite in the schedule yet. She hammered out a quick message on Instagram to Cameron to remind him. She suspected he needed reminding.

She dragged her laptop a little closer and started picking through the footage. She needed to double-check what Luke had filmed for her, just to make sure that it was up to scratch. He looked like he had been focusing, but she thought it was a little much to ask of a fourteen-year-old to always be on point.

Sadly, the only way to check it fully was to watch it. Putting her AirPods in, she started one of the videos. The first two minutes were full of Luke and Jemma chatting about lighting and getting the right angles before Jemma started talking to camera. It all seemed fine; Luke held the camera steady like a pro.

It was a video of the lake from that evening, and Jemma saw Abigail and Beth in the background. Her attention drifted from checking the footage to watching the two women in the background feeding the ducks. It was a few minutes before she realised that she'd not listened to a word of what she'd been saying on film.

She paused the video and sucked in a deep breath. Even when she wasn't there in person, Beth Fraser had the ability to distract her.

"Focus," she reminded herself.

CHAPTER ELEVEN

The next morning, Jemma was up and out of the hotel in good time to get to the park just after opening. Some theme park guests were what was referred to as rope droppers—people who arrived for rope drop, the unofficial term for park opening. Parks were no longer opened by a rope being dropped, but the terminology stuck.

People who rope dropped often arrived up to an hour before the park opened, mainly because many parks would open around half an hour before the listed opening time. It was a nice little Easter egg that those in the know got to enjoy.

The problem was that these people caused queues, and Jemma wasn't one for queues. Firstly, she was impatient, secondly, she couldn't film in them, and thirdly, she often got stuck with someone who recognised her from her channel. She loved her fans, but some of them were a little much, and being stuck in a queue with them with nowhere to escape was zero fun.

So Jemma now timed her morning arrival for just after the rope drop crowd had dissipated but before the next wave of crowds arrived. It was a science. Everything about travel and theme parks was. She should know—she made a living off telling people about it.

She strolled through the hotel gardens towards the park, enjoying the little extra theming that wasn't necessary but was definitely appreciated. The path meandered around trees and over small channels of water, all to keep the guest caught up in the bubble of theming. In essence, it was a very clever method of crowd control.

There could be a large concrete plaza that led from Fraser Hall to Fraser Park, a straight line with nothing to engage the senses. But a themed garden made the Hall feel secluded and special and allowed the park to be revealed after a short journey through a tranquil garden.

The calm scene was shattered by a blur of activity out of the corner of her eye. Jemma only just managed to recognise Beth speeding her way from the hotel along one of the other paths. Jemma hurried her pace, knowing that the paths converged a little further up.

"Beth?" she called out.

Beth was ahead of her and stopped dead, turning around with a confused expression on her face. It softened when she saw Jemma.

"Hey, good morning," Jemma said as she approached.

Beth tried to smile, but it was obvious she wasn't feeling it. "Good morning."

"I'm detecting that maybe it isn't a good morning?" Jemma asked. She saw the warring emotions on Beth's face, a struggle between honesty and the desire to maintain a professional appearance. "Do I need to karate chop someone?" Jemma asked playfully, holding her arm out straight and swooshing it through the air.

It worked, and Beth chuckled. "Yes, I have a list of people. You'll need to take extensive notes."

"It's early in the day, and you already have a list?"

Beth nodded. "Yes, we have a lot of…meetings at the moment. And my brother will insist on not taking anything seriously. So I'm left looking like the negative one when I point out all the flaws in his plans."

"I can imagine your brother not taking much seriously," Jemma admitted. "I'm sorry, that sounds like a hard situation to be in. No one likes the party pooper."

"Exactly." Beth's eyes shone bright. "I'm the party pooper. He makes me the party pooper. I don't want to be the—"

Jemma held her hand up. "I'm going to have to stop you saying party pooper. Join me for coffee? We can talk about it—I promise to keep it just between us, and I guarantee you'll feel better afterwards."

Beth hesitated, and Jemma prepared herself for another rejection.

"You know what? That sounds wonderful," Beth said, surprising Jemma.

"Really?" Jemma hated how desperate and shocked she sounded, but she couldn't help it. She'd never been cool and reserved when it came to a crush.

"Not in the park, though," Beth said. "How about in the nature reserve? Have you been yet?"

Jemma shook her head. She'd planned to go the next day but would happily follow Beth there now and tear up her schedule. Jemma was usually so meticulous about her planning, but Beth didn't have to do much to convince her to change her plans. Jemma felt as if her time at Fraser Resort was ticking away, and she needed to grab on to every possible moment with Beth.

"I'll show you one of my favourite places, as long as you promise not to film it and share my secret with the world." Beth's tone was good-humoured and her smile casual. It was obvious that the thought of getting away from work for a while was exactly what she needed.

"I swear to keep your secrets," Jemma said, performing a mock salute. "Lead the way."

Beth offered a lopsided grin, and they walked along the path, this time in a different direction.

"I shouldn't really be taking time off like this," Beth confessed. "I have so much to do."

"Do you ever take time off?" Jemma asked.

Beth laughed heartily. "No, when you're the boss, time off is a luxury you can't afford."

"Then what's the point in being the boss? Unless you really enjoy your work?"

"I do, I love Fraser Resort," Beth said quickly.

"I know you love the resort, but do you love your work?" Jemma asked.

Beth remained silent, her pensive expression suggesting she was tossing and turning the question over in her mind. Jemma waited patiently for an answer.

Jemma had spent a lot of time on YouTube over the years, and it was easy to get lost down various rabbit holes. Once you showed an interest in something, YouTube showed you more of that thing. And so, in between the travel channels and the theme park news, Jemma followed a number of lifestyle channels that spoke of work-life balance and finding joy in life. Some of it was nonsense—one woman thought you should throw away anything you didn't use in a three-month period. Which would mean Jemma throwing away her entire winter wardrobe, something she knew she would very much regret.

However, many of the channels offered helpful advice, especially in a time when people weren't always following the age-old practice of getting married and having children, living a predetermined script that had been planned out for them by tradition alone.

One of the things that Jemma had learned and desperately wanted to impart to Beth was the importance of happiness. It sounded ridiculous, but it was an important part of life and living that so many people overlooked for one reason or another. It was something that Jemma herself had snubbed. Her parents had never been very in touch with their feelings, and that was something they had passed down to Jemma when she was a child. It was only as an adult that she had started to realise that life was about more than just going to work and making money.

Though, if she was honest with herself, lately she had been asking herself whether or not she truly loved her job as much as she used to. She knew she was blessed to have the success that she did, but some of the negative aspects of her job had started to niggle at her lately. Social media was becoming a harsher world to live in as it grew in popularity. She knew she wasn't as happy as she had once been, and that was something she needed to work on.

"Without my work, there would be no Fraser Resort," Beth eventually said. "So, by default, I must enjoy it."

It didn't sound like a thundering approval, but Jemma didn't want to press too hard.

"It must be a lot of work to keep everything running, especially as your brother seems..."

"Useless," Beth provided.

"Easily distracted," Jemma suggested.

"That too." Beth grinned.

They arrived at the entrance to the nature reserve, and Beth led them to the staff entrance, greeting the staff member on duty as she walked through the open gate. Like the theme park next door, Fraser Nature Reserve had a large themed entry square that allowed guests to pick their own adventure by way of a number of paths to different lands.

Beth gestured towards the first path that indicated they were heading towards the African-inspired area. As they walked down the path, the trees, foliage, and even background music changed to indicate they were in a different themed land. Jemma risked a little glimpse at Beth and was pleased to see a small smile now adorned her otherwise tense face.

The path became a solid bridge with a beautiful waterway flowing beneath them, a waterfall in the distance. The amount of work and detail that had gone into the area had Jemma staring with an open mouth. She'd thought the nature reserve would be little more than fields and paddocks with animals visible in the distance. In reality, it was as themed as the park next door. Fraser Resort seriously needed to do something about their marketing. She supposed by issuing an invitation to her, that was exactly what they were doing.

Beth led the way down a path towards a rest area designed to give the feeling of the downtown area of an African city. Only the familiar branding of a local Scottish coffee producer on the side of one of the walls spoiled the illusion, but Jemma didn't mind.

They'd passed a few other guests on the way and now stood in a small queue of people. Jemma mused that better advertising of the resort would surely mean that it would be packed with guests. People travelled to other *countries* for this level of theming and experience, and she doubted many knew just how much work and effort had gone into making Fraser Resort, especially the reserve which was very much left in the shadow of the theme park next door. She had certainly been unaware, and she was a travel vlogger. None of her research had uncovered this, and she suspected the other influencers and vloggers who had been through the doors were the ones solely interested in intense rides, or food.

She'd definitely be back to Fraser Resort, hosted or not. They clearly needed a lot of help with their marketing, and Jemma knew she could help. It didn't hurt her channel that she would be one of the few influencers in the country able to uncover such a hidden gem in the UK tourism industry. Not that she'd mention that fact right now to Beth and antagonise the executive further. Right now, they were two almost-friends sharing a calming drink and some quiet time together.

The queue moved quickly, and soon they both ordered coconut lattes that were highly recommended according to the overhead menu that was written on a chalkboard. A few minutes later they had takeaway coffee mugs, and Beth quietly led the way around the seating area and down a short flight of stairs. With a quick check that no one was behind them, Beth opened a staff-only gate and held it open for Jemma.

Jemma walked around the corner and gasped at the little oasis that Beth had brought her to. Technically it was nothing more than a pathway, a handrail made of thick branches and rope and protected from the splashing waterfall in front of them by a rock overhang, but it was an idyllic getaway. It was quiet, except for the waterfall, peaceful, and well out of the way of guests.

"This is gorgeous," Jemma said, staring up at the rock and wondering if the green algae was real or theming.

"No filming," Beth teased.

"Definitely not, some things need to remain secret," Jemma agreed.

They both leaned on the handrail, coffees in hand, and looked at the waterfall in front of them.

"So, come here often?" Jemma asked.

Beth chuckled. "Not as often as I'd like."

Jemma bit her lip and wondered how far she should push. She wasn't friends with Beth. In fact, she was the influencer who Beth might view as a sneaky journalist looking for a scoop. If there was a chance that she could get Beth to confide in her, she'd try it. Beth's beautiful face had gradually become more troubled each time Jemma saw her lately. If she could help in any way, she would.

"So, this list of people I need to karate chop?" Jemma asked playfully.

Beth smiled. "I shouldn't have said that—I'm sorry."

"Don't be sorry. You looked like someone had taken away your birthday. I'm sorry that you're having a bad morning." Jemma took a sip of her coffee, silently hoping that Beth would take the bait and start to open up about whatever weight rested on her shoulders.

"It's just…business things," Beth admitted softly.

"I thought it was because you're a renowned party pooper?" Jemma joked.

Beth smiled at her. "Well, some would definitely tell you that."

"Party poopers don't share the best view in a nature reserve with someone else," Jemma said, gesturing to the secluded path they were on.

"I doubt they'd want to share this view with me," Beth mused.

"Their loss." Jemma didn't say if she meant the company or the view, but in her heart she knew they could be standing in front of the rhino enclosure complete with that interesting smell and a keeper shovelling excrement, and she'd still have a light feeling in her heart if she had Beth beside her.

"We have a hostile board," Beth confessed.

Jemma sort of knew that wasn't good news but also had no idea what it actually meant. "I thought you and Cameron owned the resort."

"In name only." Beth sipped her latte and turned to face Jemma. "The resort was falling behind the competition, we wanted to make it bigger and better, and for that we needed a lot of investment. At first, we found local investors who knew us, knew the resort. But then we needed more investment for the water park that's being constructed."

Jemma had seen signs for the water park but had no idea how far along it was. None of the messaging had a completion date. "And some of those investors are...hostile?"

Beth nodded. "Possibly. We lost one of our older board members a while ago, which meant a shift in power. Cameron and I still have the numbers, but they only need to turn one of the original investors, and they can vote against us. Or call for a vote of no confidence in one of us, those making our vote void. They seem to be targeting me to try to turn the votes."

Jemma felt outraged on Beth's behalf. "That's not fair."

Beth smiled softly. "That's business."

"Why would they do that? The resort is great—what does it achieve to backstab you?"

"Money," Beth stated simply. "They can choose to change the way the park is run, and they can make it more profitable. I'm a thorn in their side. I like things to be done right. And when things are done right, they generally cost more."

Jemma suddenly had a very strong suspicion that Beth was the reason behind the exceptional level of detail at Fraser Resort. The theming that wasn't absolutely necessary but meant everything to the fans and was the heart and soul of a resort was created by the woman in front of her. No wonder Jemma had been attracted to her; they both had a passion for the magic of a tourist attraction done well.

"What can I do to help?" Jemma asked, eager to move mountains if she had to.

Beth kindly smiled but shook her head. "There's little that can be done. I need to keep fighting them. If the resort is doing well, they have little to complain about. It's just a little exhausting at the moment because I'm running everything on top of securing plans and funding for the water park."

"What's your brother doing during all this?" Jemma asked, not even attempting to hide her frustrated tone. It was clear that Beth was taking on too much and with little or possibly no support at all. No wonder she'd had trouble relaxing in the spa the previous day.

"He does his best, but Cameron is more a people person," Beth explained. "He can relate to people better than I can. If there's ever a problem in the park with guests or staff, he can always smooth it over better than I can. I think he has a special magical twinkle in his eye or something."

"I'm sure you have that too," Jemma said. She forced herself to look out towards the waterfall and not into Beth's eyes where she knew she would get lost. "What's your favourite snack in the park?"

"My favourite snack?" Beth asked in confusion.

"It's something I ask everyone," Jemma explained. "And I'm meant to be making you feel better about your hostile board situation, not making you dwell on it."

"Ah. I'm not sure. I suppose if I had to choose one, then it would be popcorn."

Jemma slowly turned her head and glared at Beth. "Popcorn? That's it? Just plain popcorn?"

Beth laughed. "Sorry, yes, just plain popcorn. But it's not just plain popcorn, not when you really think about it. It's the smell that first greets you when you come into the park in the morning—it wafts around most of the resort. It's fresh, warm, buttery, and perfectly seasoned. Never burnt, never under- or overcooked. It comes in a box that's thick enough to keep its shape but thin enough to warm your fingers on a chilly morning. It's shareable and you always want more. It's *never* plain. It might not be a fashionable freakshake or ice cream mega concoction, but it's never plain."

And with that one sentence, Jemma's crush on Beth developed beyond merely thinking she was a confident and attractive-looking woman. Now she was poetic and wise and really understood the emotions of a theme park. Jemma smiled wistfully. "You know, I hadn't thought of it like that. You're right—popcorn can be the only real answer. Unfortunately, because of the Instagramability of your amazing snacks, I have a day of eating myself sick on ice cream ahead of me."

"Is that a word?" Beth asked with a lopsided grin.

"Absolutely."

"Well, I would apologise for the Instagramawhatsit of said snacks, but if they get more guests to the park, then I'm afraid I can't. You'll simply have to eat them all. And enjoy them, of course."

Jemma laughed. "I'll do my best."

"Do have some real food in between all the ice cream, though, to give your stomach a fighting chance."

"I will. I've learned to pace myself."

"Have you really? I believe I saw you eat your way around a theme park in Tokyo just four months ago."

Jemma's eyes widened and her heart soared. Beth had watched her channel. She desperately wanted Beth's opinion on what she had found there, what videos she liked, what styles she enjoyed, but was almost too afraid to ask.

"You saw that?" Jemma whispered.

"Oh yes. I honestly thought you were going to throw up."

"I did." Jemma shuddered at the memory. It had been a stupid clickbait experiment designed to attract new viewers. It was only when she was halfway through her challenge and feeling sick that she wondered why on earth she'd taken it on. By then she had already teased the concept on Instagram and was forced to follow it through. And now Beth had seen it and probably thought she was a complete idiot.

"Ah, you edited that out?"

"Yeah, it wasn't pleasant." Jemma bit her lip. "I'm not like that...It was just a silly idea."

"Cameron once bet me I couldn't drink all the new milkshake flavours at The Diner," Beth mused. "I got a third into the third one, and...well, that evening I regretted my decisions."

Jemma laughed. It seemed there was another side to the normally strait-laced Beth. She wondered if this was a recent event or something that had happened when they were younger. She didn't ask in case Beth admitted she was a child at the time and made Jemma feel even less mature than she currently felt.

"I was very impressed with your travelling to California with hand luggage only," Beth said.

Jemma felt a blush touch her cheeks. "Thank you. I'd seen a couple of other videos of people doing it and wanted to see if I could manage it. Could have done with another sweater for a chilly evening or two, but on the whole, it worked out."

"Thank you for making me take some time out," Beth suddenly said. "I hadn't realised how much I needed it." She glanced at her watch and sighed. "But I really must think about getting back."

"Ten more minutes," Jemma pleaded. "Please, what's ten minutes? I'm not sure I've fully delivered on my guarantee that you'll feel better. I'd hate to get a negative review of my cheering-up abilities."

Beth chuckled. "Very well, ten more minutes. Tell me, what's your favourite snack?"

Jemma considered the question. She'd eaten a lot of delicious food in a lot of different places. It often depended on her mood, which was the problem with being a food vlogger. You couldn't eat just what you fancied—you had to eat the entire menu while you were there. But right then, all she could think about was sharing a box of warm, fresh popcorn with Beth.

"Mochi in Japan," Jemma lied.

"I've never been to Japan. What's it like?" Beth asked.

Jemma smiled and bit her lip. "Wow, how do you explain Japan?" she started.

❖

Later that morning, Jemma stood by the entrance to Fraser Park, waiting for Cameron to come and meet her for their interview. He had finally sent her a message to organise the chat, basically explaining that he could do whenever she was free. Jemma strongly suspected that wasn't a kindness afforded to her because she was an influencer, but more an indication of his woefully empty schedule.

The fact that she now knew that Beth was rushed off her feet while Cameron had little to do frustrated her. She'd only been in the resort a few days, and she could already see the immense stress that Beth was under. Why couldn't Cameron? He didn't seem the sort to be cruel, so had he just not realised?

She noticed him walking across the entrance plaza, a bright smile on his face as he waved hello to staff members. Beth had said that they'd both been in the same board meeting that morning, the one that had left Beth with a twitching vein her forehead that looked like it might explode any moment. Cameron was either doing an exceptionally good job of pretending he hadn't been in a disastrous meeting, or he didn't care.

"Good afternoon," he greeted. "I'm ready to be grilled."

Jemma smiled. "I don't grill—I lightly flambé."

He laughed and looked up at the cloudy sky. "I thought we might film outside somewhere, but I have a feeling the Scottish rain is on its way. Maybe we should do this in my office?"

The thought of a glimpse behind the scenes had Jemma quickly nodding in agreement. There was also the fact that Cameron's office was surely near to Beth's. Cameron led the way towards a cluster of farmhouse cottages just off the entrance plaza that Jemma had strongly suspected were either office space or just fake frontages.

Theme parks were littered with large painted facades that looked like buildings but were simply wooden frames with nothing behind them. Some were so well constructed that the optical illusion was faultless, until you saw it from the side.

"Are these cottages original?" she asked as Cameron opened the door and gestured for her to step inside.

"Yep. They used to be for the farmers who owned the fields on the other side of the nature reserve, but after a few years of really bad harvests they decided to sell up." Cameron gestured for her to go up the stairs. "Now the farms are the overflow car park and the animal hospital for the reserve, and these cottages are the main offices for the resort."

The individual cottages had all been knocked through to create a series of narrow hallways to connect them. The upstairs resembled more a rabbit warren than an office space. Jemma eagerly looked around for any sign of Beth but was disappointed when Cameron indicated his office was the first one along a corridor.

They stepped inside and he closed the door. "I haven't prepared anything," he confessed. "I didn't know what you'd be asking me."

"Nothing you won't know the answer to, I'm sure," Jemma said. She lowered her equipment bag to the floor and looked around the space. "Can we move that chair closer to the window?"

Cameron grabbed the wingback chair and slid it closer to the window. "Here?"

"Perfect." Jemma opened her bag, got her tripod and camera, and started to set up.

"So, how was the spa?" he asked, flopping into the chair and picking lint off his trousers.

"It was great. I ended up with a lot more content than I expected. I had no idea it was so big. You really need to advertise that place more."

Cameron sighed and nodded. "I know. Please, tell my sister that."

Jemma bit her lip. She didn't want to get involved in whatever argument the siblings had previously had on the matter. "Well, I think Beth has enough on her plate, from what I've seen," she mumbled. She focused her attention on attaching the camera to the tripod, but she knew Cameron was looking at her.

"That's true," he admitted. "Did she say anything?"

"No." Jemma stood up and met his gaze. "No, we're not that close. But I know when I see a woman who has a lot on her shoulders. I don't know her that well, and I don't think she'd ever actually *admit* she's overworked, but I think she is."

A tiny imperceptible smile crept onto his face and vanished again as soon as it arrived. "That's true. Beth doesn't really open up."

Jemma wondered if she'd shown her hand and quickly looked away. She walked around the room, turning some lamps on and some lights off until she found a good balance.

"I'm sorry I didn't mention the spa before when we were arranging your visit," he said. "It completely slipped my mind. I don't know what your schedule is like, but if you'd like to stay longer, I can definitely extend your time at the hotel and add days to your resort pass. I wouldn't want you to have to hurry or not get the content you need because of my lapse."

She'd already made the decision that she would stay longer. Even though she knew she had more than enough footage and time to make a set of videos on Fraser Resort, she wanted to stay and see and do more. She couldn't ignore the fact that one of the reasons for that desire was a wish to see more of Beth. Even though she knew it was highly unlikely that anything could happen between them. She could always admire from afar.

"That actually sounds like a great idea," Jemma said as casually as she could manage.

"Excellent. I'll add another week on. You might not want all that time, but it secures the room for you." He got his phone out of his jacket pocket and started tapping away on the screen.

An extra week seemed like a long time. She'd spent far less time at far bigger resorts. But she couldn't bring herself to argue. She wanted an extra week. She'd have to figure out how to frame her content to stretch that amount of time. She didn't want her audience to become bored with Fraser Resort, but she also didn't want to not post anything on some days. Most of her audience enjoyed everything she did, but a dedicated few liked to complain any time she did something they didn't agree with. While she knew she shouldn't spend too much time attempting to appease a minority, they still often factored into her decisions.

"Thank you, I really appreciate that," she said.

"I appreciate what you're doing for us," he replied. "I've seen that mentions of Fraser Resort have gone up on social media channels since you've been here and posted a couple of videos.

And your live stream on Instagram got us a lot of traction, and new followers. And it's nice to see you and Beth getting on."

Jemma felt her cheeks heat up, and she quickly ducked behind the camera under the guise of checking the setup. "Oh, I hardly see her."

"You've been here, what, three days? You've had dinner together twice, you've been to the spa together, and I saw you both disappear into the nature reserve this morning." Cameron wore a knowing grin.

Jemma looked at him, attempting to appear as innocent as she could muster. "I suppose so. We just seem to bump into each other a lot."

"You're blushing," he pointed out.

"It's warm in here."

"These windows are a hundred and fifty years old. It's never warm in here," he pointed out. He leaned back in the armchair and regarded her with a knowing smile. "Jemma Johnson, are you interested in my sister?"

Jemma's heart pounded so hard she was certain he'd be able to hear it smashing against the inside of her ribcage.

"No!" She winced. The overly dramatic denial had probably sealed her fate.

His grin widened. "You are. Oh, this is perfect."

Jemma held up her hand. "No, please. Look, I may have a tiny little crush, but it's nothing. Really nothing. Beth has no idea, and I'd really like to keep it that way. Please?"

Cameron stopped smiling, clearly detecting her distress. He nodded seriously. "Okay, sure. I won't say a word."

Jemma breathed a big sigh of relief. "Thank you."

"May I ask why? I would have thought you two might be a good fit."

Jemma couldn't help the bitter laugh that burst from her. "No, we're not. I mean, Beth's great. But I'm just not right for her."

He cocked his head to the side and regarded her. "I'm lost. Why not?"

Jemma didn't want to spill all her faults right there and then to a man she hardly knew, no matter how kind and genuine he seemed. She smiled sadly. "Could we just"—she gestured to the camera— "do the interview? I'm sorry, I just don't really want to talk about this. And you must be busy."

He looked at his watch and winced. "I do have an off-site meeting for lunch. Sorry, I won't pry. And I definitely won't say a word to Beth. I'm sorry if I overstepped."

"You didn't. It's just embarrassing. And I don't want to make Beth feel awkward." Jemma stood behind the camera, loosely holding the tripod in front of her like a shield.

"Say no more—we'll pretend it never happened. Now, about that flambé?"

Just like that, the tension was defused. Cameron smiled easily and sat casually in front of the camera, ready for whatever Jemma would throw at him. Any playful teasing about her crush on his sister had evaporated into thin air. Jemma couldn't help but be relieved but made a mental note to herself to make sure she kept her crush in check in the future. If Cameron had seen it so easily, then others might too. Especially now that she was staying another week.

CHAPTER TWELVE

A nd that's it for another wonderful day at Fraser Park." Jemma spoke to the camera as she walked towards the exit. "We got to eat at The Glass House, went on a ton of great rides, ate probably the best candy apple in Britain, and got to see a brilliant fountain show over at the main lake. It's been a great day, and I hope you'll join me again tomorrow for more fun, snacks, rides, and top tips to make your visit to Fraser Park the very best." Jemma stopped and smiled warmly. "Have a perfect day!"

It was her second outro, one filmed while walking away from the lake, and this one filmed on the main path towards the exit. She'd have a look at them both that evening and decide which one was best. Despite it only being early afternoon, she was feeling tired and hoped that she'd managed to keep her energy levels up during filming.

Now she was planning to head back to the room to have a long bath and then maybe a cheeky nap before heading out for dinner at a top-rated and highly recommended restaurant in the nature reserve.

She put her camera away in her equipment bag and continued her walk towards the exit. As she got closer, she realised it was becoming a little more crowded than she was used to. Or, more accurately, people were hanging around.

There were quite a few more staff members than usual around the main entrance plaza, and many of them were talking to guests. Jemma could tell that something had happened, but she wasn't entirely sure what.

She spotted Beth, a walkie-talkie in one hand, the other gesturing for a member of staff to go and do something. She looked serious, concerned, but definitely in control. Jemma couldn't help but walk over to see what was happening.

Beth offered her a tight grin when she saw her.

"Hey, everything okay?" Jemma asked.

Beth looked around to check no one was close enough to eavesdrop. "A woman has been injured at one of the children's playgrounds. We're just waiting for an ambulance to arrive." Beth gestured to some gates that were usually closed but were now wide open. "We like to keep things like this a little quiet, but unfortunately this will be the easiest and quickest route for the paramedics to drive to her location."

Jemma winced at the thought of a brightly coloured emergency vehicle, presumably with blue lights flashing, crawling through the main gate of the park. It wasn't a great look.

Beth held the walkie-talkie to her mouth. "Can we ensure the parade is altered to the secondary route. It looks like this might take a little longer than we'd like."

"I don't suppose there's anything I can do?" Jemma offered, knowing it was pointless.

Beth shook her head. "No. Maybe don't film this?" There was a lightness to her tone, and Jemma chuckled.

"Yeah, no worries, I try to encourage people to travel. Not put them off. How badly is this woman injured, anyway?"

Beth winced. "It didn't look good from what I heard. She climbed some children's equipment and fell from the top. Onto her face, I believe."

"Yikes. How old is she?"

"Old enough to know better," Beth murmured. She reached into her pocket and pulled out her mobile phone. She looked at the screen and answered the call with a stressed, "Hello?"

Jemma could see the ambulance arriving in the distance, slowly making its way through the pedestrianised area that led from the car park to the main gates.

"Is she okay?" Beth asked.

Jemma couldn't help but catch the panicked tone and looked at Beth, who was rapidly losing her calm composure.

"Right, well, I'll...I'll try to find him, and I'll get him to call you. Or I'll come. I'll figure something out. Yes, yes, thank you for letting me know." Beth hung up the call and again lifted the walkie-talkie. "Has anyone seen or heard from my brother?"

"He went out for lunch off-site a couple of hours ago," Jemma explained. "After our interview, he grabbed his car keys and said he was running late."

Beth was already making a call on her mobile phone. "I'll kill him."

"What's going on?" Jemma asked.

Beth held the phone to her ear while looking from the ambulance to the growing crowd of people who were standing in the way and gawking.

"Abigail's been sick, and so the school wants to send her home. They couldn't reach Cameron, so they called me. Ordinarily, I'd go and get her, but I can't leave now." Beth groaned. She hung up and shook her head. "Voicemail. I'll have to call them and ask them to keep her a while longer." She looked at her watch and let out a frustrated sigh.

"I can pick her up," Jemma offered without a second thought. She felt sorry for Abigail being stuck at school while not feeling well, not to mention that Beth looked so stressed she'd need the ambulance herself in a moment.

Beth looked at her in surprise. "Um, I don't..."

"Who knows where your brother is? And you can't leave in the middle of all this. I can pick her up and take her back to the hotel. Please, let me help," Jemma asked. "I don't mind."

"Beth, the husband is kicking off and talking about calling the police. Can you come over to the playground?" a voice requested through the walkie-talkie.

"Which school is she at?" Jemma asked, eager to help. "You can trust me—I'm good with kids."

"I don't doubt that," Beth acknowledged quickly. "I just…this isn't something you should need to get involved in. We should be able to cope."

"I can get an Uber," Jemma said, her phone in her hand already. "Do you even have Uber around here? I can get a cab if you don't. It's fine."

"Beth, do you copy?"

"One moment," Beth replied into the walkie-talkie. She held Jemma's gaze for a few seconds. Finally, she nodded gratefully. "Thank you so much. I really can't repay you enough for this."

"Not a problem. Which school is it?"

Beth reached into her pocket and pulled out a set of keys. "Take my car. It's parked in bay four in the first row of the car park. If you access the satnav, the school is saved there. It's St. Philomena's. Could you take her to my place? Again, it's saved in the satnav under *home*."

Jemma took the car keys. "St. Philomena's and back to home. Got it." She turned to leave.

"Jemma?"

She stopped and turned back to Beth with a questioning eyebrow raised.

"Thank you. Really, I can't thank you enough for this." Relief flooded Beth's expression, and Jemma felt a little lighter at being able to aid Beth in some small way.

"It's not a problem, really. Just call the school and let them know to expect me, so I don't get arrested."

Beth's eyes widened as if she had only just considered that. "I'll do that right away."

❖

Jemma pressed the key fob, and the lights to the car flashed. For some reason she was surprised that Beth drove a 4x4 soft-roader. She'd expected something practical and businesslike, sleek like a Mercedes. But the Toyota in bay four was well-used and caked with mud, completely the opposite of what Jemma thought she'd find.

She got into the car and adjusted the seat and mirrors. Happy to help the Fraser family out, she also knew this was a chance to maybe impress Beth. Although she wouldn't do that if she crashed the car.

Once she was sure that everything was right, she started up the engine and accessed the satnav. In a sad indication of a life not lived, the address book had three entries: school, home, and Cameron. Jemma didn't think that it was an oversight or a lack of time to input more addresses. Why would she save addresses of places that she no doubt knew by heart? It indicated some kind of desire to use a feature of her car, perhaps when she'd first purchased it. But after those three entries, the well had run dry.

Selecting the school option, she waited a few seconds while the on-board computer calculated a route. She drummed her fingers on the steering wheel and looked around the cabin. The back seat had a child's booster seat, another indication of Beth's involvement in her niece's and nephew's lives.

In the door pocket was a packet of mints, a pack of tissues, and some wet wipes. Jemma didn't know what she expected to find, or why she was even snooping around Beth's car. It felt a little naughty, and so she returned her attention to the satnav, which had finished its job and declared it was just fourteen minutes to the destination. Jemma carefully reversed out of the space and was soon on her way.

The radio was tuned to a classical music channel that Jemma presumed was supposed to be calming, an effect that was lost by the fact that the signal vanished every now and then.

Jemma found she had to concentrate hard on the narrow roads that were most definitely not reminiscent of where she learned to drive in London. She couldn't remember the last time she drove a car; she'd sold her own BMW some time ago when she realised it was going to waste in the garage of a house she hardly ever saw. When she travelled, she frequently took public transport or taxis so she could continue to film while on her way to wherever she was going. Thankfully, it came back to her pretty quickly, and before long she was navigating the narrow Scottish lanes like a pro. A nervous pro, but a pro.

By the time she arrived at the school, she realised she had been holding her breath for most of the journey and let out a huge sigh. Thankfully, the school had a small car park with a drop off area that was empty.

She was barely out of the car when the door opened, and Abigail and a kindly looking elderly lady appeared.

"Hello there, dear. Beth called to let me know you'd be coming for Abigail."

Abigail looked a little green and feverish, and Jemma briefly wondered if maybe she didn't want to be locked in a car with her for the journey to Beth's home. She pushed that feeling aside quickly. If she got sick, then she got sick. It was a price she'd be willing to pay to get Abigail home.

"How are you doing, Abigail?" Jemma asked.

Abigail leaned against her teacher a little and shrugged lightly. It was clear she was very poorly, nothing like the effervescent girl she knew.

"She's been a wee bit sick, but it's nothing a little lie-down and some rest won't cure," the teacher said, gently patting Abigail's shoulder.

Jemma thanked the teacher for her help and got Abigail settled in the car. She programmed the satnav for Beth's house and slowly pulled away from the school, careful not to shake Abigail about too much and ruin the interior of the car.

"Sorry you're not feeling well," Jemma said, glancing in the rear-view mirror to see Abigail.

"S'okay. Thanks for coming to get me. Where's Daddy?"

"We couldn't get hold of him, probably somewhere with a bad signal," Jemma said, hoping that was true. If he'd deliberately ignored the call, she'd kill him. Not that she could imagine Cameron doing such a thing. He was undoubtedly useless some of the time, but he seemed to be a dedicated father.

"Where are we going?" Abigail asked.

"Beth asked me to take you to hers."

Abigail simply nodded at that, her heavy eyelids struggling to stay up. Jemma decided to let her rest if she could and remained silent for the rest of the journey. The narrow country lanes didn't change, but thankfully she didn't meet any other traffic on the way. The lanes got narrower and narrower, and she was about to confirm with Abigail they were going the right way, when the car told her she would arrive at the property in a moment. The hedgerow gave way to a small driveway, and Jemma took a gamble and did as she was told.

Beyond the hedge was a beautiful, large cottage that had clearly been around for a very long time. The immaculate gravel drive at the front and the hanging baskets filled with bright flowers and trailing plants indicated a level of pride in the appearance of the property.

She likes gardening, Jemma reminded herself.

She pulled up, and Abigail was already unclipping her belt and getting out of the car, which Jemma took as confirmation that they were definitely at the right place.

She got out of the car and looked at the stone-built cottage in awe. "This is gorgeous."

"It was my great-great-grandmother's," Abigail explained. "And then my great-grandmother's, and now Aunty Beth's."

"Maybe one day it will be yours," Jemma suggested. She held up the keys. "Do you know which one?"

Abigail nodded, took the set of keys, plucked the correct one, and put it in the lock, turning it and pressing heavily on the old wooden door. Jemma followed her into the house, locking the car behind them even though that seemed redundant considering they were in the middle of nowhere. She closed the front door and followed Abigail into the house.

"Do you want anything to eat or drink?" she asked, having no idea if there was anything to be offered.

"Can I have some juice?"

"Let's see if we can find any." Jemma gestured for Abigail to lead the way.

The interior of the cottage was large, spacious, and modern. It had clearly had a lot of work done and now retained original features alongside modern design. Jemma itched to look around and see what she could find out about Beth. There was a big bookshelf that was stuffed with books and CDs, and she couldn't help but glance at it.

Jemma was a terrible snoop. It wasn't a habit she was particularly proud of, but it was one whose origins she could pinpoint with accuracy—her mother. Alison Johnson was a class one curtain twitcher and knew everything that was happening in her neighbourhood. Growing up with someone who was constantly in other people's business had definitely rubbed off on Jemma.

The truth was that it was a great way to get to know someone. A few seconds' glance at a bookshelf could tell more about a person than an hour's worth of conversation. Music, reading, and media choices could express so much about someone's personality and preferences. And if that bookshelf was in a public part of the house, then it was almost *expected* to be looked at.

Look after Abigail before you go snooping, she told herself.

She turned to go into the kitchen but stopped dead and stared through the patio doors to the back garden. "What on earth happened?" she asked, her jaw falling open as she took in the sight before her.

"A storm came and wrecked the garden. I was little," Abigail explained. "It makes Aunty Beth very sad, but she can't get it fixed. She says she will, one day."

Jemma approached the glass and looked at the ruined garden. The first thing she noticed was mud, piles and piles of mud. Sludge surrounded fallen trees that lay haphazardly across the garden. The middle of a hedgerow was all but missing. It looked like someone had taken a giant gardening fork and turned over the entire garden multiple times before dousing it in gallons of water.

She tore her gaze away from the garden and reminded herself to focus on looking after Abigail. In the kitchen she unsurprisingly found juice and treats for the children. Jemma gave Abigail a very small snack plate to settle her stomach.

"Do you want to lie on the sofa and watch TV?" Jemma offered, a while after Abigail had finished eating.

"No, I think I want to go to sleep if that's okay. You won't be bored, will you?"

Jemma's heart melted at the thoughtfulness. "Absolutely not, don't worry about me," Jemma said.

"Will you tuck me in?" Abigail asked, suddenly looking very small and shy.

"Of course." Jemma felt pride swell in her chest that Abigail had plucked up the courage to ask. It clearly meant that she was in favour.

She was surprised when Abigail led them through the kitchen and living room and into the hallway. When they got to the staircase and Jemma realised she was heading upstairs, she couldn't help but wonder where they were going.

On the top landing, Abigail opened a door and entered a bedroom that very clearly was a child's room. Jemma wondered just how often Abigail had sleepovers with her aunt. She wished she'd had similar when she was a child, but both of her parents were only children, and there were no kindly aunts or uncles to go and stay with.

The girl picked up a very old and worn cuddly toy in the shape of a dog and hugged it to her chest before kicking off her school shoes.

"You should probably take your school cardigan off in case you get too warm," Jemma suggested, noting that Abigail still looked a little flushed.

Abigail agreed and quickly shrugged out of the cardigan and tossed it to the end of the bed. A few moments later, Abigail was under the covers, cuddling her toy, and looking very small.

"If you need anything, you give me a call—I'll be downstairs," Jemma promised.

Abigail slowly nodded. "Thank you for coming to get me, Jemma." Her eyelids were already starting to close.

"Not a problem," Jemma whispered.

❖

Beth worried her hands in her lap. She was trying to look calm and collected, but inside she was nearly bubbling over with anxiety. The taxi was taking its sweet time in taking her home. She had been so overwhelmed by all the stress the day had brought that she only realised that she would need a taxi to get home when she arrived at her empty parking spot.

The medical emergency, the probably pointless lawsuit, and the crowd management had taken far longer than she would have liked. At the back of her mind was the niggling knowledge that she had sent a practical stranger off, in her car, to pick up her niece.

Part of her trusted Jemma implicitly, but there was a loud part of her that worried about child trafficking and pictured Jemma taking Abigail to the airport at that very moment. She knew it was nonsense, but her brain often enjoyed sabotaging her calm with worst-case scenarios straight out of horror movies.

She'd left three voicemails for Cameron. That was another cause for concern. On one hand, it was almost certain that he was somewhere with no mobile signal, but on the other hand there was a small possibility that he was dead in a ditch.

She sucked in a deep breath and blew it out again. She needed to calm down and stop overreacting. Jemma, Abigail, and Cameron were all just fine.

"It's just here on the right," she told the driver, knowing that most people sailed right past the concealed driveway to the cottage.

He slowed down and crawled along the road at such a slow pace that Beth seriously considered getting out and walking to hurry the matter up. Eventually, after an absolute age, they pulled into the driveway, and he came to a stop. She paid him and quickly approached the door and knocked. It was a strange sensation to be knocking on her own front door, and she again wondered what possessed her to give her keys, car, home, and niece to a total stranger.

Jemma opened the door and smiled warmly at her, a mug of hot liquid in her hand, her hair tied up in a messy bun, and a sweater casually wrapped around her shoulders. She looked at home.

That was what possessed you, Beth thought. It was Jemma's relaxed and utterly trustworthy personality. The fact that despite spending only a small handful of hours with the woman, she already felt she knew her well. Beth was jealous at how effortlessly Jemma could interact with people and put them at ease. It was something she struggled with frequently.

Jemma stood back and gestured for Beth to come in. "Abigail's asleep upstairs. I gave her a little something to eat and drink to try to settle her stomach. She's not been sick again since she's been back. I checked on her a couple of times and she's sound asleep."

Beth entered the hallway and felt embarrassed that she had been so concerned about accepting Jemma's help. Of course nothing untoward happened—the thought was ridiculous and she'd been watching too many crime shows.

"I helped myself to some tea, I hope you don't mind," Jemma asked.

"Absolutely not, I'm so grateful you could step in and get Abigail for me." Beth looked at the stairwell. She was eager to go up and check in on her.

Jemma seemed to read her mind. "I'll put the kettle on. You go and say hi to Abigail, and I'll see you down here when you're done."

Jemma left for the living room, and Beth dropped her bag and hurried up the stairs. Guilt weighed heavily that she hadn't been there for Abigail, to pick her up in her moment of need.

She crept into the guest room and could see Abigail sleeping soundly and hugging Muttley, the cuddly toy from Beth's own youth. She sat on the edge of the bed and wiped some stray hairs away from Abigail's face.

"Aunty Beth?" Abigail mumbled.

"Hello, sweetheart, how are you feeling?" Beth couldn't be sad that she'd awoken the girl. While she wanted her to sleep, she also wanted to check that she was doing better.

"Jemma Johnson picked me up from school. Alex and Marie are going to be so jealous," Abigail said, a small smile forming on her face.

"Do you still feel sick?" Beth asked, shifting the conversation to slightly more pressing matters.

"No, just tired. Where's Daddy?"

"He's in a meeting, and we can't get hold of him," Beth lied smoothly. "If he knew you were unwell, he'd be here in a flash."

Abigail sighed sleepily and nodded. "I know."

Beth placed a kiss on her forehead. "Go back to sleep, and I'll wake you when it's time for dinner."

Abigail was already falling asleep again as Beth stood up. She wished she still had that ability as an adult, to just drift off to sleep whenever and wherever. Nowadays it took hours of tossing and turning.

Assured that Abigail was well, she headed back downstairs to profusely thank Jemma for picking up the slack. It had been a random series of badly timed events, but Beth felt so utterly crushed at not being able to cope with everything at once. That was part of her role in life, to manage crises and bring order to chaos. But that afternoon had created one too many problems for her to be able to cope with, and the reality of that made her feel sick.

In the kitchen, Jemma stood by a freshly boiled kettle and gestured to a mug that proudly stated *Beth's Mug* in big letters. A Christmas gift from her brother many years before.

"I took a wild guess that was yours," Jemma joked.

"Very perceptive," Beth replied. "And thank you, again."

"Not a problem." Jemma picked up her own tea mug and gave Beth space to make her drink.

Beth looked at her vast array of supposedly calming teas and picked the one that she always picked, camomile. It did little to calm her, but the taste and scent were nice enough. It was also nice to come home to someone, even if it was a strange circumstance. Something as simple as a mug being ready for her and the lights being on felt such a stark contrast to the evening before.

"Did everything work out okay at the park?" Jemma asked.

"It did." Beth wasn't entirely sure it had. There was still a potential lawsuit, not that she had much to worry about regarding that. Signage around the playground made it very clear that the equipment was for children, was supposed to be used in a certain way, and that guests took their own risks upon entering the site. It was just an irritation, another thorn in her side that made running the park needlessly more difficult than it should be.

"You have a lovely home," Jemma said.

"Thank you, it was my great-grandmother's."

"Abigail said as much. Must be nice to have a house with so much history."

"It has its ups and downs," Beth confessed.

"Is the garden one of those downs?" Jemma asked knowingly.

Beth looked out of the window and sighed. She didn't often see the chaos that was the back garden in the daylight. It looked so much worse when you could see it all in one go rather than in a small spotlight cast by the security light of an evening.

"Abigail said it was a storm?" Jemma pressed.

"Yes." Beth folded her arms and leaned against the kitchen counter. "A big storm, seven years ago. The river burst its banks and brought the top layer of three fields down the hill and into the garden. Uprooting trees along the way."

"Were you here when it happened?"

"Yes, upstairs, looking out of the window in horror. Nothing could be done, just nature taking its course."

"I'm sorry about the garden, but I'm glad you're okay. It sounds pretty scary."

Beth looked up and saw real concern in Jemma's eyes. She rarely stopped to think about how lucky she was to have been uninjured that night, too swept up in the damage to the garden and the downstairs of the cottage to think of what might have been.

"My grandmother kept all kind of things in the attic space. I can almost guarantee there's a canoe up there," Beth joked.

Jemma smiled and looked at the garden. "May I ask why you haven't had it fixed? Seven years is a long time."

Beth felt a stabbing pain in her chest at the exhausting memories of all the times she'd attempted to put the garden right. She took a sip of tea. "Well...to be honest, people have been very busy and unable to help. It's not a small job, and there were lots of other people needing help after the storms. The tradespeople were so very busy."

Jemma looked at her with kindness in her eyes. "Busy for seven years?"

"Well, yes."

"Everyone?"

"It's a very small town," Beth explained. "There aren't many contractors as it is."

"How about the next town over?"

Beth chuckled. "That's some distance. I'm stuck with the locals."

"And every single one of them has been busy...for seven years?"

Beth nervously licked her lips at her subterfuge being so easily uncovered. She put her mug down and prepared herself to be honest with Jemma.

"I'm...not well-liked around here," she confessed. "I have a bit of a reputation for being a perfectionist. So no one is willing to come and help, and I can't do it alone." She walked into the living room and over to the bookshelf, lifting out one of the old photo albums. Jemma followed and sat next to her on the sofa to look at the book.

"My great-grandmother and my grandmother were both very keen gardeners. They tended this garden for many years." Beth flipped through the pages to find the photos of the garden. Her heart clenched when she saw them, blooming in all its glory as it had done for much of her life.

"The house got passed down to me when my grandmother died. Cameron had already moved out and was house-sharing with friends from university. I took on the cottage and the garden, as I think it had always been planned that I should do." Beth turned the page and a photo of her as a child with a tiny spade came into view.

Jemma's hand pounced on the page before Beth could turn it again. "Is that you? It is—I can see the eyes. You're adorable!"

Beth chuckled and wrestled the photo album away from her. "Yes, it's me. I'm supposed to be showing you the garden."

"Right, yes, the garden. Carry on. I must compliment you on that adorable little shovel, though." Jemma removed her hand and allowed Beth to turn the page again.

She found another picture of the garden in full bloom and ignored Jemma's comment as she said, "As you can see, it was incredible. I don't think I can ever get it back to its former glory."

Jemma grabbed Beth's hand in hers and held it firmly. "You will. I haven't known you for long, but I know that you are a go-getter, and I honestly believe you can do whatever you put your mind to."

"But the local tradespeople won't come. Honestly, I'm not exaggerating. We have to get people from outside the area to come and build and maintain things at the park. I was quite forceful in my younger days, headstrong and not right for management. I made a few enemies with the local workers."

Beth couldn't help but notice her hand remained in Jemma's. She could easily pull it away, but she didn't want to. Jemma's hand was soft and warm, and the heat from her body beside her felt almost like an embrace. It had been a very long time since she'd sat and spilled her emotions to someone. The moment held a warmth that she realised she'd been missing.

"You should talk to them. I'm sure you can make them understand," Jemma suggested.

"I'm not good with people," Beth admitted. "That's Cameron's department, not mine."

"I think you're perfectly good with people," Jemma said seriously.

Beth's eyes flickered up to meet Jemma's, which were boring into her. Any possibility that Beth had been reading too much into Jemma's casual glances was blown out of the water by the look of sheer want in Jemma's eyes.

Every reason why it was a bad idea to think of Jemma that way came flooding through her mind. Jemma would be leaving soon. She was an influencer and could easily spread negative comments about Fraser Resort. The age difference. The fact that Beth had no idea what someone like Jemma could possibly see in someone like her.

Negative thoughts bounced around her brain like a trapped fly.

But then she looked into Jemma's eyes and saw nothing but honesty and hope. Beth couldn't understand it but could recognise it. She drifted closer, acknowledging that she was also interested but encouraging Jemma to close the gap herself. Beth couldn't remember the last time she had been kissed. She clutched the photo album with her free hand in the hope it would give her some much needed strength. She didn't want Jemma to know she was shaking.

"Sis?" Cameron's voice boomed as he opened the front door.

Jemma leaned back quickly. Beth jumped to her feet, only just catching the album and putting it safely on the sofa.

"In here," she said, her voice sounding shrill to her own ears.

Cameron stepped into the room, the look of a panicked parent in his eyes. "I'm so sorry—my phone was off. I thought I'd restarted it, but I obviously didn't switch it back on properly. I got your message but couldn't get hold of you."

Beth closed her eyes and attempted to get her breathing back to normal. She'd left her phone in her bag in the hallway, out of range for her to be able to hear the ringtone.

"Abigail's fine. She's upstairs asleep," Jemma said, smoothly stepping in and filling the silence.

Cameron looked from Beth to Jemma with confusion.

"I picked her up. Beth was dealing with a few things at the park and couldn't get away," Jemma added.

"You?" Cameron blinked and looked speechless. "I…I'm so sorry. I honestly had no idea my phone was off. Gosh, Jemma, thank you so much for helping out. I'm sorry Beth, I really am."

Beth just nodded, unable to say anything. She'd very nearly kissed Jemma, and she wasn't entirely sure how she felt about that. Nearly being caught by her brother of all people made matters so much worse. What was she doing with someone as young and perfect as Jemma? And what on earth could Jemma want in her? The thought crossed her mind that Jemma wanted a simple fling. Maybe this was a frequent thing for her, a way to pass the time while travelling the world. A modern-day equivalent to a girl in every port. That was the only reason Beth could possibly compute why Jemma would have any interest in her.

"Is she upstairs?" Cameron asked.

"Yes," Beth replied, suddenly able to find her voice. "Yes, you should say hello. She asked after you. I said you were in a meeting, and we couldn't get hold of you."

Cameron nodded gratefully. "I'll make it up to you, I promise." He looked lost and dazed by the sudden turn of events.

"Maybe you should let her stay here tonight," Beth suggested, suddenly not wanting to be alone. The thought of everyone leaving left a pit in her stomach.

Cameron considered the idea and then nodded. "Yes, she'd probably like that. I have to go and get Luke from sports club anyway. If you're sure that's okay?"

Beth nodded. "Of course, I left everything with Pete when I came back. They aren't expecting me back today."

Cameron looked ashamed. "I made a right mess of things for everyone, didn't I?" He shook his head, clearly angry with himself. He looked at Jemma. "I'm sorry for putting you out. This really shouldn't have fallen to you. I'm so sorry, Jemma. Let me give you a lift back to the hotel."

Jemma looked panicked. "Um…"

"What a lovely idea, good plan," Beth said. Fear at what might have happened and what might still happen pricked at her. It was better for all of them if Jemma went back to the hotel, as soon as possible. "I'm just going to make some phone calls, check that everything is in order at the park."

She turned to Jemma and addressed her without making real eye contact. "Thank you again for helping with Abigail. It was so, so appreciated. Cameron will give you a lift back, and I'm sure I'll see you around the resort."

She hurried off to her home office, feeling embarrassed and lost.

❖

Jemma did her very best not to slump into the front passenger seat of Cameron's car. The last thing she needed was the brother of her crush questioning exactly what he had walked in to.

The previous five minutes had passed in a depressing flash. From Cameron's arrival to them both being hurried out of the cottage and sent on their way. Beth had hid in her office, phone stuck to her ear in a very obvious attempt to look busy so Jemma wouldn't speak to her.

Yet again, Jemma found herself hurting because Beth had effectively thrown her away. Everything had been so perfect one moment and then completely the opposite the next. Jemma didn't know what had happened, but Beth had gone from very clearly wanting to kiss her to not being able to remove her from the house quickly enough.

The only logical conclusion was that she was embarrassed of Jemma. She swallowed hard. It was a bitter pill to swallow but was as she suspected. She just wasn't good enough for someone like Beth Fraser.

Cameron got into the car and clicked his seat belt into place. "Again, Jemma, I'm so sorry about all this."

He'd been bumbling around issuing multiple apologies to Beth, Abigail, and Jemma since he'd arrived. It was very clear to see that he was devastated by his mistake. Jemma couldn't be angry at him. The whole sequence of events might have led to her heart being broken, but before then she'd been only too happy to help.

"It's fine—everything worked out," Jemma said.

"I'll get you back to the hotel," he said, pulling out of the driveway and onto the narrow country lane.

The silence inside the car was claustrophobic, and Jemma could easily sense that Cameron was trying to figure out how to say what was on his mind. She remained quiet, not wanting to speak about what he was no doubt about to bring up.

"I sense," he began, "that I might have interrupted something back there."

"Good thing you did. She clearly regretted it," Jemma said, unable to hold back the bitterness in her tone. "Nothing happened."

"Looks like I messed that up as well," he muttered to himself.

"You didn't. I just…I thought something was there, but I was obviously very wrong."

"Beth's not good with people," he attempted to explain.

"Yeah, she kind of said as much. Contractors won't come and help her fix the garden, she explained."

"No, that's not what I mean. I mean she pushes people away." He let out a long sigh. "Beth thinks that people always leave. Because they kinda have. Our mother left when we were young, our father died, our grandmother died, my wife died. Beth finds it hard—we both do. But Beth suffers with it more than I do. I have lots of friends, and I live my life. Beth pushes people away and focuses on work."

Jemma reluctantly put herself in Beth's position and couldn't imagine the tremendous feelings of loss. To lose both parents and then a beloved guardian was bad enough. To then watch your twin lose their partner must have been too much to bear.

"I think she was going to kiss me," Jemma said. "But she changed her mind when she saw you. It's like I said to you this afternoon—I'm not right for her. She realised that. She was embarrassed for you to see her with me."

Cameron stopped the car in the middle of the lane.

Jemma sat up straight and looked around. "You're blocking the road."

"Only Beth and I ever use it. We're in the middle of nowhere." He turned to face her. "I may be her twin, but I don't pretend to know every thought that runs through my sister's head. However, I can tell you with absolute certainty that she would never be embarrassed to be seen with you."

Jemma felt herself blush and looked away.

"I don't want to sound like I'm hitting on you," Cameron hastily added. "I'm absolutely not, but no one could fail to see what a beautiful, intelligent, kind woman you are. Anyone would be lucky to be seen with you. I know my sister would feel the same. I don't know why she changed her mind and pushed you away, but I'd bet money that it has more to do with her fear of losing people and the fact she knows you're leaving soon than anything else."

Jemma remained silent and stared out of the passenger window at the hedgerow. It made sense, but the pain of the rejection still stung. Not to mention the probability that there was little she'd be able to do to change Beth's mind. She couldn't promise she wasn't going anywhere when she was a travel vlogger and always on the move. She'd already booked her flight to Germany from Edinburgh airport for two weeks' time to attend a festival she'd been invited to.

Cameron continued driving. Jemma knew she just had to put her crush on Beth to one side. She couldn't follow it and allow herself to be hurt again, and she certainly didn't want to hurt Beth. If Beth already understandably suffered from abandonment issues, then the last thing Jemma wanted to do was make it even worse when she'd inevitably have to leave.

No matter how hard she tried, she couldn't shake the feeling that part of the rejection stemmed from Beth thinking that Jemma was just too immature for her. Beth ran a resort where thousands of people relied on her, she was clever and capable, and Jemma was just someone who ate doughnuts on camera for clicks.

Beth was a powerhouse; Jemma most certainly wasn't. She thought again of how obvious Beth's overwork was to her and turned to face Cameron. "Your sister needs more support," she said. "She's at breaking point. I know you don't see it, but I do."

Cameron looked surprised. "Breaking point?"

"She's stressed, like, beyond belief stressed. She couldn't calm down in the spa, and she's constantly on edge. I can see it in her eyes and the way she acts—she needs help. I don't think you fully understand the amount of stress she is under. You need to help her."

Cameron nodded. "I—I'll do better. Thank you for letting me know. I'll keep an eye on her."

Even after having her heart broken, Jemma couldn't resist trying to help Beth. She turned her attention to her phone. There were always new comments to deal with, and that would take up the rest of the journey back to the hotel. She could feel a depressive cloud settling in over her. Falling for Beth was one thing. Being so obviously rejected was quite another.

❖

It was early evening, and Jemma had already cast off her clothes in favour of comfortable pyjamas. She'd ordered room service and had decided to not go back to the park that evening.

In her mind she had framed it as a great opportunity to get some video production and marketing done, but the truth was she didn't feel like having fun. She knew in her heart that any footage she filmed that evening would be unusable because her facial expression and her voice would be dead giveaways that she was unhappy.

Beth's dismissal had dredged up old wounds. While Jemma attempted to keep the thoughts at bay, it was impossible to deny her past, which often seeped into her present.

Jemma had always been endlessly positive. At least, that was how she portrayed herself. No matter what was happening on the inside, she projected a positive demeanour. At school, that had resulted in a lot of bullying being directed her way. While other kids were up and down with mood swings, Jemma had happily metaphorically skipped around the classroom, trying to show what a perfect life she had.

It was all a lie, of course. But Jemma had learned early on that you could appear happy even when you weren't. Most people became cheered by your good mood, and the cycle continued. Sadly, there was always a cluster of people who didn't enjoy other people's happiness.

Jemma's childhood wasn't terrible—she knew many people who had it far worse. And so, in many ways, she didn't feel that she had the right to complain. She lived a comfortable life, never had to worry about shelter, food, or money. It was just that her parents weren't exactly the loving sort. They'd left emotional wounds that Jemma felt embarrassed admitting to as they were so trivial compared to what she knew others went through.

Being happy became a defence mechanism. Finding the positive in everything she saw allowed her to feel happy, even if it was an act. It wasn't until she was older that she realised other unhappy people didn't deal with things the way she had. Instead, they wanted to make everyone else feel as miserable as they did. So it was inevitable that Jemma's positivity would become a magnet for the bullies.

She picked up her laptop and opened a folder that she only ever opened when she was wallowing. It contained screenshots of social media comments from people she had known when growing up. She knew it was petty, but whenever someone from her childhood left a positive comment on her channel, she took a screenshot and saved it.

Jemma would never be so mean as to reply to their comments with anything other than positivity and appreciation, but alone on her hotel room bed in her scruffy pyjamas she could look at the comments and feel that while she had lost the battles as a child she had won the war.

Their bullying had very nearly ended her social media career before it began. Her first few videos were quickly found by her haters and deluged with negative comments. But the next morning she discovered that their noticing her channel had somehow achieved the opposite of their goals—it had given her a small audience. And her new audience was appreciative of her attitude, and they'd given her the validation she needed to carry on.

She read through the saved comments. She'd read them so often that she knew them by heart. There was Samantha who wanted to show off that she was friends with Jemma way back when, then Ella, who had four children and a husband she hated and commented often that she wished she was wherever Jemma was posting from.

Jemma chuckled to herself. If her wider audience knew that she had crippling self-doubt, they'd be stunned. Most wouldn't even believe it. She'd been masking so well and for so long that it would probably seem absolutely ridiculous.

The other not so small factor was that she had no right at all to be miserable. She was rich, successful, and famous. Her life was a dream—she travelled the world and saw whatever she liked, whenever she liked.

She rubbed her face with the palms of her hands and blew out a long sigh. She closed down the folder and opened up the video editing software. She didn't have time to wallow in self-pity. She had work to do and a schedule to replan. It was time to throw herself into work and try to forget about the whole day.

CHAPTER THIRTEEN

Jemma felt much better the next day. She'd pushed all negative thoughts to one side and put on her biggest smile and set to work. By midday she had filmed several ride and merchandise pieces as well as a number of reviews of ice cream snacks.

After her fourth ice cream meal, she sat down not far from the central lake and the carousel, to give herself a chance to digest, and had a fantastic view of people passing by. She set up her camera on a tripod beside the bench to take some generic crowd shots—she often used them when she did voice-overs for information bursts.

She looked at the crowd and spotted a familiar face. She sighed. Obviously, she wasn't going to be able to avoid Beth forever, but she had hoped for a little more than half a day.

Beth was talking to an older man in a suit. No, not talking to, talking *at*. Beth was all smiles and nervous energy and was clearly trying to impress him. But it was painfully obvious he wasn't having any of it. It was awkward to watch, like a student trying to suck up to a professor who had zero interest.

Who was he?

Beth was almost tripping over her own feet trying to speak to the strict looking man. Whatever she was saying, it wasn't hitting the mark at all. Jemma felt sorry for her, despite everything.

Jemma pretended she was fully engrossed in answering comments on her phone, but one eye was always on Beth and the painfully awkward scene unfolding in the distance.

It doesn't matter, it's nothing to do with you, Jemma thought.

After a few more agonising minutes of Beth attempting to tell a joke that apparently fell flat, the man patted Beth on the shoulder and took his leave. Beth seemed to slump in defeat and watched him walk away. When she turned around, she noticed Jemma.

Jemma quickly lowered her eyes and focused on what she was doing, hoping that Beth would use the opportunity to make her escape. Sadly, that wasn't to be, and Beth soon approached.

"May I sit with you?" Beth asked, a touch of hesitation to her tone.

Jemma nodded without looking up. "Of course, you own the park after all."

Beth sat down. "I wanted to apologise about last night. I put you in a difficult situation, and I shouldn't have done that. I'd like it if we could go back to how we were."

"Strangers?" Jemma asked, finally looking up.

Beth looked hurt. "I thought we were friends, or at least on our way to being friends."

Jemma winced at her own harsh words. It wasn't Beth's fault that she'd developed a crush, and she was nice enough to come over and apologise. Jemma was acting immature, the exact reason Beth was probably uninterested in her in the first place.

She sat up a little straighter. "We were. Are. Sorry. Yes, let's go back to the way we were. How are you, and who was that very bored looking man?"

Beth chuckled. "He is a representative of the chair of the board, who decided to come for a visit without telling anyone. We've never met face to face, and I was trying, and apparently failing, to connect with him."

"Is it usual for the chair to send a representative without telling anyone?"

"No." Beth leaned back on the bench and sighed. Jemma could tell she was tired and itched to be able to do something to soothe the troubled expression. "Anyway, enough about me. What are you up to?"

Jemma gestured to the camera beside her. "I'm just getting some generic crowd shots."

"Oh, you're filming?" Beth looked concerned. "Should I go?"

"No, no, it's just background stuff for any voice-overs."

Beth looked confused and Jemma explained. "Like, if I want to say the park opening hours and the times of the parades and stuff like that, that could be a couple of minutes of talking, and what would be on the screen during that time? I might flash up some text, but there needs to be something beneath that. So I always take tons of crowd shots for that."

"Ah, I see. And how is the crowd performing? Are they going to make the cut?" Beth joked.

"Actually, probably not," Jemma confessed. "There's been a few crying children, a man jumped in front of a pigeon to scare it off, and a woman was wearing a top with a questionable slogan on it."

Beth blinked. "I was joking."

"I know," she acknowledged. "But seriously, I need good background material. A lot of it gets cut away. Like everything else, I record a lot and only use a little."

Beth looked away, and Jemma just knew she was holding something back.

"What is it?" Jemma encouraged.

Beth casually waved away the question. "Nothing, I'm not the expert here."

"No, go on, I'd like to know what you think."

Beth took a breath and then looked at Jemma again. "I'm just wondering if it's not all…a bit of a fib."

Jemma smiled. "Well, in some ways, I suppose it *could* be considered a lie, yes. But that's what people want to see. They don't want to see a bad day when everything went wrong—they want to see the good day."

"But you're a travel channel, showing people all these places around the world, yes?" Beth asked. At Jemma's nod, she continued, "And yet the content you produce is so highly polished it's questionable that you are even showing them the reality of these places. Yes, Fraser Park has a man that stamps his feet when he sees a pigeon. But you're cutting that out, so your viewers don't see. Is that a realistic view of a visit here?"

Jemma mulled that over for a second. "Well, it's more about being an influencer, and all influencers do this. Things are a little more glossy than real life, and sometimes things are edited. People know that."

"People know it's not real?" Beth asked.

"Yes," Jemma said.

"Do they, though?"

Jemma swallowed. The truth was, she wasn't sure. The thought had niggled at her in the past. When she'd first started doing retakes and editing content, she told herself she was producing a show, and it had to be perfect. But was she producing a show or an accurate view of travel? The lines had become blurred. Now it was just natural to edit everything—anything that wasn't *perfect* was gone. It was just the way it was.

"Take Abigail," Beth continued. "When she sees shiny footage of a day trip to London, not a missed bus, not a drunk shouting in the street, not a homeless person at the station, not a downpour of rain, is she getting a realistic view of what London is like? Does she know what you've shown her isn't based in reality?"

Jemma couldn't answer. That was an ethical question that she had pushed to one side when building her channel. It was a question that some of the social media naysayers continued to ask. Jemma had swept it to one side, but thinking about it on a personal level made it different. Abigail, or any children her age, wouldn't know that she was editing out anything she didn't think was perfect. Or if they did know she was editing, they wouldn't know *what* she was adding or subtracting.

"I'm sorry," Beth said. "As I say, it's nothing to do with me. You're the expert."

"No, no, I'm glad you mentioned it," Jemma replied. "Food for thought."

"Ladies, good to see you both."

Jemma turned to see Cameron approaching them, a knowing grin on his face. If he said one word to Beth about what they'd privately discussed the previous evening, she would have to run away, never to be seen again.

"Sis, I spoke to Steve about that thing, and he is going to sort it tomorrow." Cameron shoved his hands into his pockets and rocked on his feet like a small child wanting praise from Mummy for doing something right.

"Good, thank you," Beth said, providing him with the approval he so clearly sought.

"Have you booked in your interview with Beth yet?" Cameron asked Jemma before addressing his sister again. "She interviewed me yesterday, but she'll have to talk to you too to get all the bits I no doubt missed."

Beth opened and closed her mouth a couple of times. "An interview? Me? I...I'm not good at that kind of thing. Especially not on film."

Jemma didn't know whether to press ahead and try to get an interview for the sake of equality, or to let Beth wriggle out of it. Clearly, she didn't want to, but it seemed to be more about not feeling capable rather than not wanting to spend time alone with Jemma.

"Well, she can't interview me and not you," Cameron continued. "It will look awfully sexist of us."

Jemma resisted the urge to glare at him and bit the bullet. "I'd love to interview you if I can. Cameron's interview was *okay*, but he waffled a lot and didn't really get to the point at all. If I can cut in pieces of a real interview with you, I think it would be much better."

"Oh. Well, yes, that makes sense. Let me see when I'm free," Beth said.

Beth looked at her schedule on her phone, and Jemma looked at Cameron and offered a sarcastic smile. He held his hand over his heart as if he had been wounded but was smiling from ear to ear as he did.

Jemma rolled her eyes and smiled back. He didn't know about the awkwardness and discomfort between her and Beth. All he knew was that Jemma was interested, and they'd almost kissed. He was trying to play matchmaker and set them up, which seemed to be so typically Cameron. A ham-fisted attempt at fixing things. Jemma couldn't be angry at him even if she did want to give him that kick to the shins.

❖

Beth flew through the door to Cameron's office and glared at him. He'd vanished soon after an interview time had been set. Beth had hung around with Jemma for a few moments, so it didn't look like she was running away. As soon as it seemed an appropriate time to remember a call she needed to make, she made a dash for the offices.

"What was all that about?" she demanded.

Her brother sat at his desk, peeling an orange and smiling pleasantly at her as if she hadn't just stormed into his office and commanded an explanation for his behaviour.

"What was all what about?" he asked casually.

"Setting up that interview with Jemma." Beth seethed. He'd put them both on the spot and hadn't left until they'd agreed, and then he'd sauntered on his way as if he hadn't just wedged a large spanner in Beth's plans.

She didn't have time to do an interview—she wasn't the right kind of person to be interviewed. And, most of all, she didn't want to have to spend alone time with Jemma. She wasn't entirely sure what Jemma's expectations of her were, but it was clear that Beth had hurt her. Which was the last thing she had wanted to do.

There was a strong possibility that she had overreacted the night before, and if that was the case, then she would make it right. But that would only work if Beth kept a respectable distance and limited the amount of time they would see each other. She didn't know if she was strong enough to push Jemma away a second time.

"You're as much Fraser Park as I am," he said. "I do all the interviews—it's not fair on you."

"I *like* you doing the interviews," she explained. "Because I'm bad at them. It's the thing you do."

She wanted to add that it was one of the few things he did *well*, but she was cooling off from her anger and didn't want to be outright mean to him. After all, he had no idea of the hornets' nest he had bumbled his way into.

"I think you're fine at them, and you certainly would be if you did more of them," Cameron said. "It can't always be me, sis. You've got to admit that there's a perception that I run this place. The local newspaper doesn't know you exist."

Beth had to admit that was true. And it did annoy her when people asked to speak to the owner, meaning her brother and not her.

She paced the room for a moment, wondering how to explain to him that she wanted to be treated like an equal, but being interviewed by Jemma would just complicate an already delicate matter. In the end, no words came to her. Just exhaustion. She slumped on the sofa and sighed.

"Are you okay?" Cameron asked, concern etched on his face.

The ringing in her ears and the pounding of her heart told her quite clearly that no, she wasn't okay. But she had to be okay. Falling apart wasn't an option, not now. Not because of the financial problems, not because of overwork, not because of the board. And most certainly not because of Jemma.

"I'm fine, just didn't sleep very well last night," she lied.

He regarded her for a couple of moments before seemingly accepting the lie. "I wanted to talk to you about extending our winter hours."

Beth shook her head. "We spoke about this and agreed not to do it."

"I'd like to talk about it again, maybe run a survey amongst guests."

"We've learned from past experience that guests aren't necessarily that honest in surveys. If you ask them if they want something, they say yes. But whether they'll actually attend something is another matter." Beth rubbed at her aching temples.

"Remember when we asked if people would like a big bonfire for November fifth, and the resounding response was yes? And then we did it and couldn't even sell half the tickets?"

"I just think that opening longer and offering more during the quieter months might draw people in." He ate a segment of orange, chewing loudly.

"It costs a lot to keep the park open, especially when it's a cold winter night and most people won't want to stay. It will be a loss."

Cameron sat up, frustration clear. "See? This is what the board doesn't like."

Beth raised an eyebrow. "Oh, please, do enlighten me."

"You're negative. I'm suggesting something, and without even really thinking about it, you're shooting it down."

Beth opened her mouth in shock. "I don't need to think about it. It's obvious."

"But it's negative. You swoop in and say no to everything, usually before someone has even finished speaking."

She jumped to her feet. "It's not my fault that I'm the only practical person around here."

Cameron leaned back in his chair and rolled his eyes. "See? You get defensive. Negative and then defensive. It's hard to talk to you sometimes, Beth."

"What you're suggesting is something that I know will cost a lot of money with no chance of making it back," she argued.

"Maybe, but there are other ways to say that," he said. "You get...uppity."

"Uppity?"

"Yes, like that. Anyway, I thought I'd point it out. I get you don't see it, but I am trying to help you, sis. If you want people to like you, you have to temper that desire to tell people no, or that they're wrong. Even if they are wrong. No one likes negative people."

Beth opened and closed her mouth in anger for a few seconds before storming away.

❖

Jemma sucked in a deep breath to steady her nerves. The last thing she wanted to do that afternoon was interview Beth, but she didn't want Beth to feel that she was avoiding her. Especially after Beth had made a sort of effort to clear the air.

Friends she had called them. Jemma didn't know how she felt about that. Since the first moment she saw Beth, she could imagine being so much more than just friends. Could she maintain a friendship with the beautiful woman, or would she always be wanting more?

The knowledge that Beth had attempted to initiate a kiss didn't make the matter any easier. How was Jemma supposed to maintain a respectable distance if she always wondered if there was a chance that Beth would want more?

She shook her head to get rid of the thoughts and entered the main office building. She approached the receptionist and smiled. "Hey, I'm Jemma Johnson. Here to see Beth Fraser."

The receptionist returned the smile. "Of course, she's expecting you. If you just go up those stairs, turn right along the landing, and it's the second door on the left."

Jemma thanked the woman and headed up the stairs. She'd hardly prepped for the interview, wanting to book it in for as soon as possible and get it over and done with. A gap in Beth's diary meant only an hour and a half had elapsed from Cameron badgering them both into doing it and the actual interview taking place.

Luckily, Jemma had conducted a lot of interviews in her time and could probably perform one in her sleep. Although she doubted the same could be said of Beth if the panicked look in her eyes was anything to go by.

The office door was open. Jemma peeked around the corner, hoping she wasn't intruding on Beth's busy schedule. Beth's office was similar to Cameron's—a dark wooden floor with a red tartan rug that matched the cushions on the leather sofa. Original windows with strips of wrought iron making a neat set of crosses looked out over the entrance courtyard. A mix of paint and wallpaper that showed the room was once a house and retained some of those charms. A large desk, rows of filing cabinets and bookshelves, and a desktop photocopier were all reminders that this was now an office, even if the room seemed at odds with it.

Beth was hurrying around the room, moving stacks of paper and seemingly cleaning up.

"Hey," Jemma greeted when she realised Beth had no idea she was standing in the doorway.

Beth jumped. "Oh...I didn't know the time." Beth looked at her watch as she dumped a stack of files and papers on top of a filing cabinet. "Come in, I'm sorry about the mess."

Jemma wouldn't say it was messy in the room, just there were signs of a lot of work that had been done and even more that needed to be done. She entered the room and lowered her equipment bag to the floor beside the sofa.

Beth closed the office door and peered into a mirror fitted to the back of the door, fluffing her hair. "Do you think I'm negative?"

Jemma blinked at the sudden question. "Well, I don't know you that well..."

"You must have some idea," Beth pressed.

Jemma shrugged. "Okay, yes, you do seem a little on the negative side."

Beth spun around and planted her hands on her hips. "No, I'm not."

Jemma chuckled. "You can't ask my opinion and then disagree. You have to admit, you're not super positive about things."

Beth hesitated a moment. "Cameron called me negative."

Jemma crouched down to open her bag and begin to set up. "I'm not getting in the middle of that."

"He said that's why the board and others are often against me."

Jemma smiled to herself, realising that this wasn't a conversation that was going to go away anytime soon. "We all catch more flies with honey." She pulled out the tripod and started to set it up.

"I can't help being honest and practical," Beth argued.

"No, but you can choose how to phrase something. Like just now, you asked me if I thought you were negative, and when I said yes, you immediately denied it. If you'd said, say, that you didn't realise people saw you that way, it would be a softer way to say the same kind of thing." Jemma looked around the room. "Do you want to sit at your desk, or on the sofa for this interview?"

"My desk," Beth said.

Jemma looked at her and made a face.

"What?" Beth asked.

"You'll look more casual sitting on the sofa."

"I'm not casual."

"No, but it might be nice to pretend for a while." Jemma flashed her a cheeky smile and was relieved when Beth chuckled.

"I'm not good at this kind of thing," Beth said. "Cameras make me very nervous."

Jemma thought Beth looked cute when she was uneasy. But she also knew that Beth wouldn't want to be caught on camera looking nervous, and so she needed to relax her somehow.

"Come and sit down," Jemma suggested, gesturing to the sofa.

Beth did as she was told, sitting so close against the arm of the sofa that she looked like she was trying to hide. Jemma carried on setting up her camera and portable lighting rig to try to set up the best light, while not having all the equipment right in Beth's face.

"Do I need to soften my approach?" Beth asked, apparently still hung up on the previous conversation.

"I don't know," Jemma said honestly. "Does it bother you that people might find you negative?"

"Of course, no one wants to be thought of as negative. Do they?"

Jemma shrugged. "We're all different."

"I suppose we are. Maybe it's irrelevant anyway—I am what I am. I can't just go from being me to being someone else."

Jemma looked through the viewfinder to set up her shot and saw Beth staring off into the distance, seemingly deep in thought and obviously not particularly happy about her brother's comments on her persona.

"I don't think it's about completely changing your personality," Jemma said. "It's about taking a step back and softening what you say. Or if you really have nothing nice to say about something, then avoiding that subject and not saying anything at all."

Jemma picked up the lighting rig and moved it to the side of the sofa. "Take the way you talk to the kids. You're kind, calm, patient. You listen to Abigail drone on and on about whatever issues she's having with the girls at school, about bedroom wall colours or whether or not they can get their ears pierced. Just because it's a grown man in a suit doesn't mean you need to treat them any differently."

Beth smirked. "Are you seriously telling me I should talk to a board member the way I speak to a child?"

"Why not?"

"Because...because they are men in their fifties and sixties who care about business, and not ear piercings."

"But the principle is the same," Jemma pointed out. "Take my job, for example. The media calls me an influencer. And that's fair, because I influence people's opinions on things. I edit and present an image of either myself or a location that I want people to see. Sometimes I'm having a bad day, but I still smile and put on an act that I'm just as happy as I was the day before. I show a version of myself that's appropriate to the audience. When I'm filming, I show my channel face. When I'm talking to my mum, I'm a different person. When I'm talking to my financial adviser, I'm different again. You told me that you're bad with people—I think you're fine with people. You might just need to stop and think about who you're talking to."

Jemma continued to fiddle with the lighting rig, increasing and decreasing the brightness. She realised Beth hadn't replied and slowly turned around, fearful she had gone too far. Beth was smiling at her.

"What?" Jemma asked.

"Thank you," Beth said. "That was...helpful to hear."

Jemma beamed. "You're welcome. You ready to start?"

"No." Beth chuckled.

"Let's try. It will be easy, just a conversation between you and me. I'll keep the camera rolling, and I'm sure you'll ease into it."

Jemma pulled up a chair out of shot, turned the camera on, and sat down. She sighed when she saw Beth looked so tense that she could snap in half.

"Don't worry—when all this is over, I'll buy you some fresh, warm popcorn," Jemma said.

Beth smiled. "I'm trying to cut back on the popcorn. It's no longer a treat when you have it every other day."

"You have to celebrate the wins," Jemma said.

"Is this a win?" Beth asked.

"It will be when we have it done. You'll have done something you didn't think you could do, and then you should absolutely go and celebrate. I do it all the time. Anytime I meet a goal or do something the scares me, I have a celebratory drink or a snack, or I do something just for me."

Beth didn't look too convinced and looked away from the camera, fluffing up the cushion beside her.

Jemma fidgeted nervously in her seat. "I'm sorry. I know that's really immature."

Beth's head snapped up. "It's not immature."

"It is. We should be able to get on with life without giving ourselves little treats and pats on the back. It's silly." Jemma gazed down at the floor, wishing she'd kept her mouth shut. Her habit of bribing herself with treats to do things she didn't want, and rewarding herself for having done things she didn't want to do in the same way, was the peak of childishness. She knew that. And now she'd said it to Beth, who already no doubt thought that Jemma was a bit of a child.

"It's not at all immature," Beth repeated. "It's a good idea. The reason I looked the way I did is…Well, it's because I don't believe I will feel any better after this interview. I think it's going to be a mess, and nothing worth celebrating." Beth laughed to herself. "And I think I have my answer on that whole am-I-negative question."

An idea hit Jemma. She stood and went to the camera, hitting some buttons to turn off the recording light. "Okay, I'm going to turn this off for a while, and we can just chat to get comfortable. Just do a sort of run-through, how's that?"

"Sounds like a good idea," Beth agreed. She visibly relaxed.

Jemma felt a little bad for lying to her, but Beth's problem seemed to be some kind of performance anxiety. If Beth thought the camera was off, then she was much more likely to be herself. Of course, she'd give Beth final approval of any footage she wanted to use.

"How long have you worked at Fraser Resort?" Jemma asked, taking her seat again.

Beth laughed. "I was in a television advertisement for the park when I was three. Does that count?"

"Is there footage of this ad?" Jemma asked. She'd seen a young Beth in a photo the day before and would love to see more.

"Probably somewhere," Beth replied, a smile on her face. "I was on the spinning teacups with my grandmother, Lillian Fraser. She took over from her mother, Agnes, who was the founder."

"So it's always been a female-run business?"

"Yes, I run the resort with my brother Cameron, but it was founded and has been run by women since it was opened in 1911. And I don't have to tell you that it was quite the feat for a woman to be a businesswoman back then."

"Do you think women make better leaders and managers?" Jemma asked.

Beth considered the question for a moment. "I don't think it's that cut and dried. I think women bring a different skill set to anything we do. But not all women are the same—broadly speaking, we are similar in some respects, but it would be unfair to paint an entire gender with the same brush." She crossed her legs and smoothed out the creases in her skirt. "I do think that my brother and I have differences, but we complement one another. I think that's helped to make Fraser Resort what it is today."

"Is there something that's changed about the resort in the last, say, twenty years that you're most proud of?"

Beth laughed. "So much has changed in the last twenty years—I couldn't possibly pick one thing."

"Go on, try," Jemma pressed with a big smile on her face. It was nice to see Beth relax and almost settle into the idea of an interview.

"Gosh." Beth sighed and looked up to the ceiling. "I'd like to say the spa, but then there's the evening show, and then there's the number of new rides and attractions we've added in that time. Actually, you know, I do know the proudest moment. It was when we brought my brother's firstborn here. He was just a baby, and I held him as we brought him into the park one evening, and we realised that we had an heir. That, if he chooses, he would one day be the next Fraser to call this amazing place home. He could be the one making the decisions in fifty years about what should come next. That was a very special moment for all of us."

Jemma felt the familiar rush of warmth that washed over her whenever she thought about the Fraser family. They were a small group, and they had their differences, but the love they had for one another and for the concept of family shone through.

❖

Beth couldn't help but laugh. In fact, she was nearly crying with laughter. She couldn't remember the last time she'd had so much fun. Her interview prep with Jemma had started off well with lots of pertinent questions about the resort and its features but had now descended into a sort of rapid-fire Twenty Questions of whatever random topic entered Jemma's mind.

"My favourite member of Little Mix?" Beth gently wiped at the corner of her eye with a tissue. "I couldn't name any of them to save my life."

Jemma shook her head. "Unbelievable, we'll have to educate you."

"Abigail has been threatening to do so, but luckily, I'm busy running a business." Beth smirked and gestured around her office.

"Lasagne or cannoli?" Jemma asked.

Beth laughed. "Um. Lasagne?"

"Winter or summer?"

"I live in Scotland—I'm not entirely sure I've ever seen a summer," Beth joked. Of course, she'd seen a summer. It was just a Scottish one, which meant it was short and often interrupted by dreary downpours. "Is any of this relevant to the interview prep?"

"No, I'm just enjoying watching you laugh," Jemma admitted.

Beth's breath caught at the acknowledgement. She didn't want to cause any further miscommunications between them, but it was so hard. She'd thoroughly embarrassed herself when she'd very nearly kissed Jemma. Overreacting to her brother's arrival, fearful of his teasing, and then remembering exactly why she didn't get into relationships with people—they always hurt.

For some reason that Beth couldn't quite work out, Jemma seemed interested in her. At first, she thought it was simple friendliness, but now it was quite obvious that there was more to it. But it was ultimately irrelevant. Jemma was leaving soon. Not to mention the small matter that Beth was clearly very wrong for Jemma.

"Should we start?" Beth suggested, gesturing to the camera.

"We're done." Jemma stood and pressed a button on the camera atop the tripod.

Beth frowned. "Done?"

Jemma grinned at her. "I've been recording all this time. Obviously, I'll edit out the end bit, and you can see what I put together and have final approval. But I think that went really well."

Beth stood and gave Jemma a playful smack on the upper arm. "That's so sneaky!"

"It's the oldest trick in the book," Jemma replied. "And you fell for it."

Beth shook her head and tried to recall what she'd said, but it was all just a blur. Jemma seemed to pick up on her unease and put a reassuring hand on her shoulder.

"It was fine, trust me. I wouldn't allow anything to be uploaded that you're not happy with. I'll send my edit to you, and if you don't like anything, I'll take it out. If you don't like any of it, I'll not upload anything at all. You have my word."

They were so close that Beth could feel Jemma's soft breath on her lips. It would take no effort at all to lean in and finally kiss her. They remained inches away from each other for a few long, silent moments before Beth took a deep breath and stepped back. Jemma let go of her shoulder, and she let out a sigh.

"I'm sorry," Beth whispered.

"It's fine," Jemma said, though she didn't seem to believe her own words.

Beth felt guilty that she had again been giving mixed messages. "I'm not ready for..." She tried to explain, but the words died on her lips.

"For...?" Jemma encouraged.

Beth licked her lips and tried to conjure up the words that would explain how she felt. "You're going home in a couple of days," she explained. "I don't do flings."

"Neither do I. And I'm staying an extra week," Jemma replied.

"Oh." Beth struggled to process what Jemma was saying. If she wasn't interested in a casual fling, then what was this?

"I'd stay longer in a heartbeat," Jemma whispered. "Or I'd come back frequently. I...Beth, there's something between us. Don't tell me you don't feel it—I can see in your eyes that you do."

Beth was still stuck on the point that Jemma was staying an extra week, potentially longer. She tried to wrap her head around what Jemma was actually suggesting. Would she stay even longer if Beth asked? How could that even work? She travelled the globe for work—she couldn't stay at Fraser Resort forever.

Forever, she wondered, *why did I think that? Do I want her to stay forever?*

"I'm very confused," Beth admitted. "There's so much to think about."

Jemma cocked her head to one side, half a smile forming on her lips. "How about we think about all that later?"

Jemma took a step closer, reaching one hand up to cup Beth's face. She paused, giving Beth the chance to back away. Beth didn't move, her heart finally taking control over her head and wanting nothing more than to kiss Jemma, even if it would end up being a mistake. That was a problem for another day.

It felt like an eternity passed until Jemma softly smiled and brought her lips closer, brushing them against Beth's. Beth moaned, unsure whether it was one of pleasure or one cursing herself for the heartbreak that was no doubt to come. Deciding that the mistake had been made and she might as well enjoy it, she returned the kiss.

Jemma quickly leaned in to the kiss and wrapped her arms around Beth, pulling her close and holding her tightly, seemingly afraid to let her go. Beth wrapped Jemma up in a hug of her own, keeping her lips pressed to Jemma's and wishing the moment would last just a moment longer. She couldn't remember the last time she'd been kissed, and she was sure that she'd never been kissed with such depth of emotion. There *was* something between them, something unexplainable and potent.

Eventually breathing became an issue, and Beth reluctantly pulled her head back slightly to break contact and allow some much-needed oxygen into her lungs. Jemma kept her in a loose embrace.

"Wow," Jemma said through a soft breath.

A hundred questions flew through Beth's mind, swirling like a typhoon of doubt. What was next? How did Jemma feel? Had they ruined a perfectly good friendship? How could this ever work?

"I can hear you overthinking it," Jemma said, placing a light kiss on her forehead. "Do you ever relax?"

"No," Beth admitted.

"Can we talk about this properly?" Jemma asked.

"Yes, we need to," Beth replied. The sooner some of her questions were answered, the better she'd feel.

The door flew open and Cameron burst in. He stopped dead in the doorway, took in the sight before him, and then cocked his head to one side with the corniest grin Beth had ever seen. "Naaw! Look at you two, adorable," he said.

Jemma loosened her grip a little more, and Beth did the same. They let go of one another but remained close.

"Can I help you, dear brother?" Beth asked in her sweetest tone, even though at that moment she wished sincerely that she had no siblings.

"Do you *ever* knock?" Jemma asked.

Cameron held up a placating hand. "I'm sorry, ladies, really. Beth, there's an emergency online meeting being held by the board. In a few minutes."

Any thought of romance vanished from her mind and was instantly replaced by anger. "What? They can't do that!"

"They are. Literally, in a few minutes. I have it set up in my office—I need you."

Beth looked from Cameron to Jemma, and her brain stumbled for a moment, not knowing which emerging crisis to deal with first. Jemma seemed to think that Beth's mind was already made up, and she turned to start to dismantle the tripod. Beth caught a look of disappointment on Jemma's face and hated how less than a couple of minutes into whatever this was she'd already managed to hurt Jemma's feelings.

She couldn't let Jemma feel that way a second longer, even if the board were waiting for her. She caught Jemma's elbow and encouraged her to turn around. "Can we have dinner, tonight?"

Jemma's face lit up. "Yes, yes, I'd love that. I'll drop my equipment back at the hotel and will wait to hear from you."

"I'll text you," Beth said. She placed a gentle kiss on Jemma's cheek by way of a promise.

"Aww, you two are so cute," Cameron said, seemingly without judgement or ridicule.

Despite his apparently kind words, Beth glared at him, and he immediately went quiet, gesturing that he was going to his office.

"Good luck," Jemma said. "I'll see you tonight."

Beth hesitated for a moment before nodding and leaving the room. She had to hurry. If she didn't, then she'd miss the start of the impromptu meeting. Moreover, if she didn't leave her office soon, she'd be kissing Jemma again, and no meeting would stop her.

❖

Beth stepped into Cameron's office, still looking over her shoulder hoping for one last glimpse of Jemma before she was locked away in a meeting. It obviously wasn't going to happen as Jemma needed to pack away her equipment, but Beth looked nonetheless.

Cameron closed the office door and gently elbowed her in the ribs. "Wow, sis...good for you."

She felt the blush on her cheeks. "Shut up."

"I'm serious—you two look good together. I think it's a good match."

"It's a pointless match," Beth replied. She noticed he had set up two chairs behind his desk, and his laptop was set on a pile of books in preparation for the video conference. She took a seat, checking that they weren't broadcasting their conversation to anyone.

"Why pointless?" he asked.

"She's leaving soon. It's foolish to get involved. Besides, I'm me and she's…her." It sounded pathetic even to her own ears.

He sat beside her. "I don't even know what that means."

"Yes, well, it's none of your business," she told him.

He leaned forward and started to use the trackpad on the laptop to get them set up. She felt a little guilty at the tone she had used, but she was stressed and unsure what had just happened. She'd thrown caution to the wind in a way she'd never done before. Now she was thinking it was a foolish mistake, but her heart was already in too deep, and she couldn't wait to make the mistake again. She felt her resolve was slipping and knew that could lead to pain and heartbreak but almost couldn't bring herself to care. She didn't feel like herself, and that scared her. But maybe that was a good thing. Being herself had led to a very lonely life.

"Okay, here we go, game face on," Cameron muttered as he logged them in to the meeting.

It was only a couple of years ago when board meetings took place at the hotel. All the investors and board members were local businessmen, mainly university friends of Cameron's or people who had known the family for years and had worked with their grandmother.

When Beth had diversified the board to bring in more funding, she'd naturally looked further afield. Now the board comprised people from London, Manchester, and Aberdeen. Meetings were frequently held online, which made it a little harder to communicate. There were no conversations over a cup of coffee before the meeting started, no getting to know one another over lunchtime sandwiches. Just a screen filled with faces and little idea of what they were thinking. No chance to read body language, no friendly smiles before the meeting started. It set Beth on edge.

Several black squares filled the screen, and they waited for people to sign in.

Cameron muted the microphone. "I know you don't want to hear it, but Jemma's a really nice person."

"For God's sake, Cam. Not now."

"She is."

"I know she is—I kissed her, didn't I?"

"Well, just don't throw it all out of the window for no reason. I'm sure you can make it work, even if she is travelling."

"This really isn't the time," Beth pointed out. "Did they say why they had called this meeting?"

They'd both been aware that the board had been unhappy. Their reasonably new investors had gone from happy, smiling men who wanted to help the resort reach its full potential, to frowning, grumpy men who complained about everything they did.

Sudden meetings and representatives dropping by the resort without notice had started to happen more and more. Things were changing fast, and she felt as if she was losing control of the board. Beth had walked them into a trap—she was certain of it. The feeling of dread that loomed over her had been growing thicker and darker every day.

"No, but I got the impression it was urgent. They said the meeting would go ahead without us if we couldn't attend. I don't know what they could possibly talk about if we weren't there." He chuckled at his perceived ridiculousness of it all.

"Us," Beth explained. "It's about us."

The black squares on the screen came to life. One by one, stern faces filled the screen. Beth had been uneasy before, but now she felt positively panicked. It felt like an ambush.

Ivan Grey, the chair of the board, cleared his throat and began to speak. "Thank you all for coming. I'll cut right to it. A few of us have been reviewing the financial forecast, mounting debts, and management strategy of Fraser Resort, and we have grave, grave concerns."

Cameron looked like he wanted to speak out, but Beth put a warning hand on his knee. Having an argument now wouldn't help the situation. Wheels were already in motion, and there was no stopping what was coming.

"Therefore, I'd like to call for a vote of no confidence in Beth Fraser and to—if that vote is successful—call for her immediate removal from the board."

Beth's heart sank. This had always been a possibility, but it had seemed so unlikely when she'd signed the paperwork. Like taking a mortgage out on a house—you knew there was a slim possibility that the bank could take it from you, but the likelihood of that happening was so slim it never really crossed your mind. Until it happened.

"As per regulations, this meeting is to minute our intentions and to provide twenty-four hours before the vote. All those in favour?"

The entire new half of the board raised their hands, allowing the motion to carry. Beth glanced at the original board members, their friends and colleagues for many years. They all seemed unsettled, clearly aware of what had been happening but unable to stop it.

"Motion passed. The minutes will show that a vote of no confidence will take place, this time tomorrow. Attendance is mandatory."

The meeting abruptly ended, and Cameron jumped to his feet. "What the hell?"

Beth slumped. "We've said it for a while—they want me out. I'm an easy target."

Cameron paced the room. "They can't do this."

"They can. They have."

"It's our company!"

"We don't have the deciding votes, Cam," she reminded him.

"It's our name above the door." He continued to angrily pace.

"Shareholders are owners of the company, Cam. Everyone on the board is a shareholder. There are more members of the new board than of the old board. They can outvote us and do whatever they like." Having to explain it to her brother in such simple language was heartbreaking because it made Beth feel like more of a failure than she already felt. She'd allowed this to happen. There was no way out. She'd been instrumental in her own destruction, and now Cameron would remain on the board and at their mercy. Or maybe they'd push him out too. The future was too bleak to contemplate. "There are five of us—you, me, Thomas, Gregory, and Sam. There are six of them."

"So they'd all have to vote against us?" Cameron asked. "What if we managed to turn one?"

"Then it would be a split board with the chair getting the casting vote—that's Ivan, and he'll obviously vote for himself," Beth explained. "We'd need to get at least two on our side, and that's pretty much impossible."

"Can we buy them out?" Cameron asked.

"Oh, yes, sure, let me get my credit card." Beth sighed. "We brought them in because we needed money. We don't have that kind of money, not to mention that we still need them for their money. And they aren't going to want to sell now when they have us in this situation."

"This is all about money," Cameron said, sitting on the sofa, his elbows on his knees and his head in his hands.

"Yes," Beth agreed. "It's all about money. Those new rides, the spa, the water park. Most of that is borrowed, but we needed funds to show that we could repay the debts until they started to generate income. The shareholders brought that cash in."

Cameron knew all this, Beth knew. But when things got stressful, Cameron spiralled and couldn't focus. It was always up to Beth to be the calm voice of reason who explained things. Although she didn't know how much help she was being by spelling out exactly how bad the situation was.

"This is my fault," Cameron whispered. "I wanted us to be bigger and better."

"We both wanted that, Cam." She stood and walked over to the sofa, then sat beside him and leaned in to him. "We both wanted it."

"Are we going to lose the resort?" he asked.

"Maybe," she admitted. "I don't know."

Chapter Fourteen

Jemma zoomed in on the image on her laptop and sighed. Her smile still seemed a little strained, and no amount of editing would help it. She needed to take yet another selfie. She'd already had a slew of nasty comments left on her last Instagram post, where people thought she wasn't smiling enough. The cruel comments were getting worse, and Jemma's ability to push them to one side was shrinking. She knew for a fact that the commenters didn't look perfect at all times—no one did. Yet they expected her to.

It wasn't that she wasn't happy—following the kiss with Beth she was over the moon—but it was just sometimes hard to look genuine in a photograph. Especially when your mind was elsewhere.

Currently, it was on a journey of dinner plans. She wondered if they'd eat in the park and if there was a chance that Beth would show her another favourite place. Or maybe they'd go to Beth's cottage? Or maybe somewhere else entirely. Jemma was excited by the prospect, even if Beth still seemed a little unsure. Jemma was sure she could convince her that she was serious about whatever it was they had.

She'd not felt this way in a long time. In fact, she wondered if she'd *ever* felt this way. There was just something about Beth Fraser that Jemma couldn't get enough of. It had been purely physical at first, but it didn't take long for Jemma to realise there was so much more there. It was fast, but that was how Jemma made decisions. A trip, a change of schedule, a house, a relationship, it didn't matter. Jemma was blessed with the feeling of just knowing when something was right. And whatever was bubbling away between her and Beth was right.

There was a weak knock on the door, and Jemma frowned at the tired sounding tap. She hopped up off the bed and peeked through the spyhole in the door. Beth was on the other side, looking nervous and quite unwell.

Jemma opened the door. "Hey." She tried to smile, but Beth's face said that this wasn't a pleasant social call.

"Hi," Beth said solemnly. "I didn't text. I wanted to say this face to face."

Jemma held her breath, knowing what was coming simply from Beth's body language but having no idea why. What could possibly have changed in the hour since they had last seen each other?

Beth sucked in a deep gulp of air before quickly continuing, "I can't see you. I'm sorry about what happened before in my office. It was a mistake, my mistake, and for that I truly apologise. It's probably best if we try to avoid one another while you're on-site."

Beth looked absolutely broken, and Jemma got the distinct impression that this wasn't just about her. Something had happened, something terrible, and Beth was reacting to it.

"I'm sorry," Beth repeated before turning to leave.

Jemma reached out and held her arm. "Come in, let's talk. What's happened?"

Beth hesitated a moment. "I…" Jemma easily pulled Beth into the room and closed the door behind them.

"Tea?" She decided the best course of action was to just ignore what Beth had said until they'd had the chance to properly talk.

Beth looked lost and stared at Jemma in confusion.

"I'm not going to let you go that easily," Jemma said. "Something has obviously happened since I saw you an hour ago. Let's have some tea and chat about it. You look like you could use a friend."

Beth nervously looked around the room, licking her lips and obviously looking for an escape. She pointed to Jemma's laptop and paperwork strewn over the bed. "I'm interrupting your work."

"Tea?" Jemma repeated, already picking up two mugs from the

tray and placing them on the desk in preparation, giving Beth little choice but to follow her lead. Beth finally nodded and sat down on the sofa.

Jemma set about making a cup of camomile tea for Beth without even thinking about it. "So, what happened?"

"I'm about to be kicked out of the Fraser Resort," Beth said in a strange monotone voice.

"Don't you own Fraser Resort?" Jemma asked.

"Not exactly."

"Is this something to do with the board?" Jemma probed.

Beth nodded. "They're having a vote of no confidence in me tomorrow. The motion will pass, and I'll be effectively fired."

"A vote of no confidence? Why?"

"To get me out," Beth said.

Jemma wasn't entirely sure what that meant and could tell that Beth was trying to stick to short answers in an attempt to get out of there as quickly as possible by not being drawn into a conversation. Which presumably meant that Beth felt that Jemma could talk her round. Which she fully intended to do.

Jemma brought the two mugs of tea over to the sofa and placed them on the small coffee table, sitting in the armchair and looking at Beth. "Is there anything you can do?"

"No, I created this hostile board environment, and now it's my undoing. They'll kick me out and will either play Cameron like a puppet or kick him out as well. They have the deciding votes." Beth stared blankly at the table. She looked like a shell of herself.

Jemma wasn't surprised to see Beth so fragile. Fraser Resort was all Beth had in her life, and to have it forcibly removed from her was going to be a horrific shock.

"I'm sorry, I shouldn't be putting all this on you," Beth said, starting to stand. "I should go."

"Sit down," Jemma instructed softly.

Beth sat back down again, seemingly too confused to know what to do anymore.

"I know your life is kind of falling apart around your ears," Jemma said. "But I'm still here for you, if you want me to be."

"I can't ask that of you," Beth said.

"I'm offering." Jemma took a sip of tea. "My feelings haven't changed. I know you're going through hell right now, but—"

"What could you possibly see in me?" Beth interrupted. "I'm old, boring, soon to be unemployed—"

Jemma burst out laughing. "You're only just over forty, and you're certainly not boring. You're passionate, confident, sharp, and soft all at once. Stop pushing me away, Beth. I'm not going anywhere." Jemma watched as her words seemed to sink in.

Beth blinked a couple of times, her eyes glossy as she did. "I—I really don't know whether I'm coming or going."

"You're doing neither," Jemma said. "You're staying. Let's have tea, and you can tell me all about this board issue. You'll feel better for just explaining it and getting it off your chest."

❖

Jemma hadn't expected her calm but firm attitude to yield results, but it had. It seemed that Beth needed a peaceful environment where she could feel safe, and a steady hand to guide her into explaining what had happened.

It had all come flooding out. Beth's feeling that she was the only one keeping anything afloat in the resort, the poor decision of expanding the board and filling the seats with people she didn't know very well, the fear of what would come next. What kept coming up was Beth's perceived inability to connect with people, claiming that the new board members had disliked her from the start and that situation had only deteriorated as business dealings continued. As she spoke, Jemma nodded along and asked the occasional question to clarify what she was hearing.

Not long after Beth launched into the story, Jemma had taken a seat beside her on the sofa, and they sat and discussed the details of the predicament and clarified points. Jemma couldn't see a way out, but then, she wasn't exactly knowledgeable about how companies and boards worked. All she could do was be a sounding board and hope that she could relieve some of the stress that Beth was under.

"And that brings as back to square one," Beth said, explaining yet another reason why she was ultimately stuck. "I'm sorry to take up your evening with this." She looked at her watch. "Oh my, I had no idea it had gotten so late."

Jemma looked at the clock on her phone. "Dinner time." She walked over to the desk and snatched up the room service menu. "What would you like?"

"I can't intrude on your time any more than I already have," Beth said.

Jemma looked up from the menu. "You all but promised me dinner—don't make me beg."

Beth smiled for the first time in at least an hour. "Well, if you put it that way." She stood and started to walk towards Jemma, a hand out to take the menu. But she paused and held onto the back of the armchair as a wave of dizziness swept over her.

Jemma dropped the menu to the bed and came over to steady her. "Whoa, are you okay?"

"Yes, I'm fine. This just happens now and then," Beth said, but she didn't pull away from Jemma's gentle touch.

"You need to try to relax," Jemma said, knowing it was a lot easier said than done.

"You sound like my doctor." Beth chuckled.

Jemma knitted her brow. "If your doctor is telling you to relax, then you really need to."

"It's just a touch of hypertension," Beth said.

Jemma flinched and guided Beth to sit back down again. "I don't think you can say a *touch* of hypertension. What else did your doctor say?"

Beth visibly swallowed, clearly having said more than she intended to admit.

"Beth…" Jemma pressed.

"I've been having some…palpitations and dizziness. Nothing serious. My doctor said to relax, but my doctor clearly lives in a dreamworld where that would be possible."

Jemma stood up straight and mentally counted to five. Telling Beth off wasn't her place and wouldn't help. The thought of her in pain or possibly becoming more seriously ill caused Jemma's breath to briefly catch in her throat. Any notion that her feelings for Beth were a simple crush and nothing more substantial were well and truly crushed. She had feelings for Beth, deep and true. Even if it was entirely the wrong time to admit such things.

"Okay, well, that's a conversation for another day," Jemma allowed. She picked up the menu and handed it to Beth.

Beth looked at her gratefully before looking at the menu. "You know, I often overlook what an exceptional menu Fraser Hall has," Beth commented.

"It is very good," Jemma acknowledged, still a little swept up in her thoughts on Beth's health issue. She wondered how serious it was, and why Beth was obviously keeping it a secret. Probably because she was entirely ignoring her doctor's advice.

"I already know I'm having the salmon," Jemma said.

"It's good," Beth agreed. "I'll have the chicken salad—should I call down to reception?"

"No, I'll do it." Jemma took the menu, walked over to the desk, and picked up the phone.

"May I use your bathroom? I need to freshen up," Beth asked.

"Absolutely. You do own the hotel," Jemma joked.

"For now," Beth reminded her.

Beth peered at her reflection in the bathroom mirror and wondered why the lighting was so unflattering, or if it was just the source material the poor fixture was working with. She felt exhausted, more drained than she had ever felt.

She thought she had felt tired before, but that was nothing compared to the ache in her heart that she suffered now. Everything was falling apart, and the blame fell squarely on her shoulders.

The only positive thing was Jemma. Sweet, kind Jemma.

If her heart was battered by the very thought of losing her job, it was being simultaneously healed by Jemma's compassion. What she had done to deserve someone like Jemma to look at her in the way she did, Beth didn't know.

After the shock of the meeting, she'd felt with absolute certainty that she needed to end things with Jemma before they went any further. She was a mess, responsible for the end of her family legacy, a failure in business, and not suitable for someone as wonderful as Jemma.

But Jemma hadn't let her go, wouldn't let her go. She'd dragged her into the room, sat her down, served her tea, and asked to hear it all. As Beth bared her heart and soul, Jemma listened and comforted as well as she could. She didn't offer false hope or badly thought out solutions, or attempt to get Beth to look on the bright side.

She understood how much Beth was hurting and wanted to do nothing more than try to help by offering a casual smile and a shoulder to cry on.

She's not going anywhere, Beth thought. *You've spun her around so much that she'd be perfectly within her rights to go. But she's staying.*

Beth swallowed and stared at her reflection. Her fear of people leaving was as apparent as the tiredness in her eyes. Here she was, about to lose the ultimate thing in her life—the resort. And yet, she was still standing. Maybe she was stronger than she thought.

Or maybe you're stronger with Jemma in your corner?

Her plan had been to tell Jemma she was sorry for being such a failure, go home, and cry all night. It had seemed perfectly acceptable, considering her life had fallen apart so spectacularly. But Jemma's insistence she come in and sit and talk had been a valuable step in her discarding that plan and starting to feel ever so slightly better. Something she hadn't thought would be possible a couple of hours before.

Upside of being fired. You'd certainly have time to date.

While rooted in sarcasm, the thought had some credit. The more time Beth spent with Jemma, the more time she wanted to spend with her. And despite Beth's dire predictions that Jemma would never, could never, be interested in someone like her, it seemed the opposite was true. Jemma was sensitively asking to spend time with her, acknowledging that Beth was having the worst time of her life, but still wanting to be close if Beth would allow.

She's incredible, Beth thought. *No one else would ever have put up with all she's put up with and kept coming back for more. She deserves better. She deserves for you to be the best you can be.*

She drew herself up to her full height and looked herself in the mirror again. She still looked an utter mess, and yet Jemma still looked at her like she was a goddess. Beth didn't know what she had done to deserve that kind of luck, but she knew she couldn't let the opportunity go to waste.

Fluffing her hair and attempting to straighten her clothes, she exited the bathroom.

"Food's been ordered," Jemma said, looking up from writing something on her phone.

"Thank you, I really appreciate that."

"I appreciate you staying," Jemma replied with a bright smile.

Beth stepped closer to Jemma.

"I appreciate you being here for me," Beth said in a soft whisper before gently pressing a kiss to Jemma's cheek. She wasn't always great with words, but she hoped the action would show Jemma her gratitude.

"I'll be here as long as you'll have me," Jemma said breathlessly.

Beth remained close enough to breathe in Jemma's light and floral perfume. She revelled in being close to her while not having to look her directly in the eye as she asked, "How long is that, really?"

Jemma took Beth's face in her hands and looked her in the eye. "For as long as you'll have me."

"You have to work. Your work takes you away from me, from here," Beth said. "Can this really work?"

"I can make it work," Jemma promised, hope lighting up her eyes. "I'll travel less. Or maybe I'll stay in Scotland. I'll see you as much as you let me. Even if we're apart, we can always be in touch with technology. The only real question is, do you want to try?"

Jemma's thumbs gently caressed Beth's cheeks and her eyes bored into her, begging in their intensity. Any dam holding back

Beth's feelings was crushed by the earnest look. She couldn't deny Jemma, couldn't deny herself.

She nodded. "I do want to try. But I can't make any promise—"

Jemma silenced her with a soft kiss. "I'm not asking for promises. I'm asking for you to try. I don't know how we'll make this work, but I want to try. I've not felt this way about someone before, Beth. It came out of nowhere, and I'm not going to let it go. I'm not going to let you go." Jemma swallowed nervously. "Unless you ask me to, obviously."

Beth was about to reply when a knock sounded at the door. Jemma let go of her and reached for her handbag on the desk.

"If that's my brother interrupting us again, I'll—"

"It's not your brother," Jemma said, pulling a twenty pound note out of her purse.

"It can't be the food already," Beth said, looking at her watch and then to Jemma who was walking towards the door. "And that's one hell of a tip. I do pay my staff, you know."

Jemma laughed and ignored her as she opened the door. "That's amazing! Thank you so much. Here's something for all the trouble."

Beth was caught between wanting to see what was happening and wanting to stay out of sight. She didn't need the rumours to be spreading around the hotel that she was holed up in Jemma's room.

The door closed, and Jemma reappeared with a box of popcorn in her hand.

Beth stared at the treat in surprise. "How did you get that?"

"I asked. They are remarkably helpful in this hotel. I thought you might like your favourite snack as a starter before a boring chicken salad. It might make you feel a bit better."

Beth smiled. "Only if you'll share with me."

"Absolutely, I hear popcorn's best when shared."

❖

Beth smothered a yawn behind her hand, grateful that Jemma didn't seem to notice while she made some more tea. It was getting late, and technically Beth should have been heading home. But she didn't want to go back to her lonely cottage devoid of light and happiness. The idea made her feel thoroughly depressed.

From the worst afternoon of her life to a very enjoyable evening in just a few hours—Jemma had been a miracle worker. They'd shared popcorn, then dined in the room when the meal had arrived.

Once Beth had decided to leave behind the push and pull of her feelings, things had become remarkably easier and lighter. They talked about Cameron and the kids, discussed being gay in a small village, and even talked about politics. Talking to Jemma was so easy and relaxed. She understood what Beth meant without the in-depth explanations some people seemed to require.

"So, what would you say if I…stayed awhile?" Jemma asked, not so casually. Her back was to Beth as she made hot drinks.

Beth didn't know what she'd say. Probably something between jumping for joy and worrying that she was holding Jemma back.

"I'd say that had to be *your* decision," Beth admitted. "And I'd worry that your channel would suffer."

"I have some content stored," Jemma said. "Over the years, I've added a little bit of footage here and there and worked on it on the side. I have about two weeks' worth of original content that I could upload, just in case I wanted any time off, you know. I could easily stretch that out to three or even four weeks if I wanted to."

Beth felt a happy tingling in her stomach at the idea of Jemma staying for a month, but she also worried about what would happen after that.

Negative, she told herself. *You're always looking for the downside.*

"If you wanted to stay," she said, "I'd be very happy."

It was a risky statement for someone who had no idea what was happening in her life, but Beth felt that while one thing was slipping away from her it would be foolish not to hang on to something else.

Jemma handed her a mug of tea, a huge smile on her face. "Then that's what I'll do."

"I'll drink to that." Beth took a sip.

"I need to just check on my video that's been processing."

Jemma grabbed her laptop from the bed and brought it over to the sofa. She sat down and brought the device back to life.

Beth couldn't help but admire the photograph on the screen of Jemma that she seemed to be editing.

"Nice shot," Beth said.

Jemma quickly shook her head and shut down the image. "No, I haven't finished editing that yet."

"What are you going to do to it? Add some text?"

Jemma laughed. "No, I need to smooth my skin, brighten my eyes. I have this pimple on my chin that I need to brush away. I look horrible."

Beth stared at Jemma for a moment. "You don't honestly believe that, do you?"

Jemma opened the picture again and held the device up to Beth. "Horrible."

"Beautiful," Beth breathed. She took the laptop from Jemma. "You look beautiful here. It doesn't need a single thing done to it."

Jemma blushed and looked away. "No, it needs work. They all do."

Beth looked at the laptop and saw a line of similar looking selfies at the bottom of the screen. She clicked on them one at a time, looking at the larger view of each one.

"You look gorgeous in all of these. Any of these could be uploaded as is," Beth said.

Jemma shook her head again. "Definitely not. I mean, with some work, some of them might be okay. But I don't like how I look at the best of times."

To say Beth was surprised was an understatement. She thought Jemma was classically beautiful, and Beth couldn't imagine a single person ever disagreeing with her. But that wasn't the point. If Jemma felt otherwise, then it wasn't relevant what others thought.

"Well, I'll respectfully disagree and say that *I* think you're beautiful," Beth said. "But I'm sorry you don't feel that way yourself."

Jemma shrugged a shoulder. "It's the way it is. All us influencers have to present our best selves. We all try to make sure we're the best we can be. For our viewers."

Beth grimaced. "That sounds like a recipe for disaster." She gestured to Jemma's phone on the table. "Upload a picture of yourself now, no editing. Just a snapshot of you casually hanging out in a hotel room."

Jemma's eyes widened in horror. "I couldn't do that."

"Why not?" Beth suspected she knew why. Jemma felt she didn't look good enough for her hundreds of thousands of subscribers. But that path led to disastrous body issues, which Jemma seemed to already have.

"I need to do my hair. I haven't freshened up my make-up for ages. This top is a casual top, not something I'd take a selfie in." Jemma looked genuinely panicked by just the idea of uploading an image of how she currently looked. Beth's heart broke for her.

"Must you do all that to take a simple photo of yourself?"

"If it's going to be uploaded, then, yes."

Beth lowered the laptop to the coffee table, turned, and took Jemma's hands in hers. "That's all polish, Jemma. Your smile shines through. That and your beautiful eyes make you stunning. You don't have to conform to society's rules that women have to look a certain way all the time. You are allowed to just be you. Are you aware that you are enough without all that?"

Quite unexpectedly, Jemma burst into tears. Beth was shocked by the reaction and swiftly pulled Jemma into her arms and held her close.

"I hate it," Jemma confessed through tears. "I hate it. I have to look perfect all the time, and there are so many negative comments even when I try my hardest. People pick on the smallest thing. One woman said my head was abnormally large. Like, what can I even do about that?"

Beth held her tight and gently rubbed her back. The sudden outburst clearly indicated that things had been building up inside Jemma for quite some time. Beth was shocked by the reaction but not by the reason for it. She couldn't imagine being on display like that all the time, especially not for anonymous internet bullies who often took perverse pleasure in pulling people down.

"I check everything over and over again, edit things so they no longer even look like me, but not so much that it looks fake. It's exhausting. I really hate it. People are so mean, Beth. I try to brush it off, but it's so hard."

"Then stop," Beth suggested.

Jemma leaned back and looked at her as if she had lost her mind. "I can't do that. People want me to keep posting. If I have a day off, then they blow up my social media asking when the next video is."

"You don't exist to make them happy, Jemma. You have to look after you," Beth told her, feeling slightly hypocritical to be saying such things. Even in the heat of the moment, she knew she needed to take her own advice.

"But I do this," Jemma explained. "This is my *job*. I travel and I show people what I see—it's who I am."

Beth cupped Jemma's face and wiped the tears away from her cheeks with her thumbs. "That's not who you are. It's a job. And if that job makes you feel like this, then maybe you need another job."

Jemma hesitated, casting her gaze downward to avoid Beth's eyes. She shook lightly with the barely concealed sobs that were still coming. "I'm sorry, I'm just so weak."

"You're not weak," Beth stated. "You're under pressure, enormous pressure. You said yourself that you're chasing the algorithm—you're practically a prisoner to it. Always posting, replying, filming, and editing. It must be absolutely exhausting. And if you're struggling to even post a real picture of yourself, is it something that you want to be doing anyway? Is this glossy, supposedly perfect life really worth the exhaustion and the comments about your admittedly enormous head."

Jemma laughed and playfully swiped at Beth. Beth smiled, happy her little joke had landed correctly.

"I've always had self-esteem problems," Jemma confessed in a quiet voice.

"Starting a social media channel seems an odd choice for someone with self-esteem problems," Beth said.

Jemma stood and plucked some tissues from a box on the desk before sitting down again. She wiped at her tears and blew her nose.

"I didn't set out to be an influencer. Obviously, I didn't really know what one was when I started out. I just wanted to see things. Do things." Jemma sighed and leaned back against the sofa. "My parents are, well, they…"

Beth waited patiently, snuggling down into the sofa and looking at Jemma beside her.

"They love me," Jemma said, clearly keen to ensure there were no misunderstandings about that. "In their own way, they do. But when I was young, we never, ever went out and did anything together. They always said they were busy with work or resting because they had been busy with work. We honestly never went anywhere. We had the money—they just didn't want to. So we stayed home."

Jemma wiped at her eyes again before screwing up the tissue and throwing it into the bin under the desk.

"I shouldn't complain. I never wanted for anything. I was never hungry, always got everything I wanted. CDs, clothes, games consoles, everything. But we never, ever went and *did* anything as a family. No trips to the zoo, no seeing art in a gallery. We went abroad once and then sat on the beach solidly for a week."

Beth couldn't imagine never going anywhere fun as a child. She'd spent her youth with a theme park practically as her back garden. Beyond that, her grandmother took her and Cameron to tourist places all the time. When they were young it was for pleasure, and as they got older it was fun disguised as a business research trip.

"When I was old enough to go out and do things on my own, it was like a revelation. Probably because of all the pent-up enthusiasm I had and the constant denial I'd received from them. I wanted to see and do everything. And I really wanted people who couldn't go for whatever reason to see things too. I'd dabbled with social media a little, but when I started exploring places, then it really took off." Jemma let out a shaky sigh. "It became my life. And I know I'm blessed. I have no right to complain. People would give so much to be in my position, and here I am complaining about it."

Beth rested her hand over Jemma's. "You have every right to complain if you're unhappy. Which you seem to be, if you don't mind me saying."

Jemma shrugged. "How can anyone be unhappy in my shoes? I have so much freedom, money, fame. It sounds ridiculous to complain."

"You work hard for those things," Beth pointed out. "When was the last day when you didn't film?"

"For the whole day?" Jemma asked. At Beth's nod she replied, "Years. I film every single day. Even if it's just a quick Instagram Live rather than a YouTube video."

"When was the last time you spent a day without your hair and make-up being perfect?"

Jemma shook her head, clearly unable to remember.

"Maybe you need to take that break," Beth suggested. She brushed a stray lock of hair away from Jemma's wet cheek. It broke her heart to see Jemma so devastated. While Jemma was absolutely privileged, that didn't take away from the fact that she worked literally every day and was on display for the world to see all the time. Beth knew that the world could be cruel, especially social media. It was one of the reasons why she'd never really bothered with the platforms. While she knew they could be useful, she also knew of the damage they could cause. Jemma's tears were a prime example of that kind of damage.

"Maybe," Jemma said, her voice uncertain.

Beth knew it wasn't simply a matter of having a week off. It was Jemma's job, her entire career. Making changes would have huge ramifications. Not to mention the peer pressure of her nearly million subscribers who were clearly eager to see more and more of Jemma.

Jemma wiped at her tears. "I was looking at your interview before you came over—it's really good. I think you'll like it."

The subject was changed, presumably to give Jemma time to

digest what she was feeling and what had been said. Beth didn't mind. "I doubt I'll like it, but I'll be happy if you do."

"You were really funny and relaxed."

"Because you tricked me," Beth pointed out.

"Yeah. It worked, though."

"That it did." Beth nodded at the laptop. "You could show me now, before I no longer work here."

"Don't say that," Jemma chided.

Beth remained silent, but she knew what was coming and that not voicing it aloud made no difference to the situation. Soon she'd be out of a job and removed from the family business that had been her entire life. But for now, before she faced that difficulty, she wanted to spend some time with Jemma. It wasn't a perfect day, not by any means, but her mood had been turned from her darkest to her brightest in just a short space of time. She needed to hold on to that before the meeting the next day came and washed it all away.

❖

Jemma carefully moved off the bed, cautious not to wake Beth. After watching Beth's interview on the laptop, Beth had asked for more insight into what Jemma did on a daily basis. They'd sat crossed-legged on the bed, Jemma's preferred workspace, and Jemma had shown her plans, lists, schedules, videos, edits, and more.

Beth was insanely curious about how it all worked and had an understanding that a lot of planning and effort went into Jemma's channel. Many people seemed to think that content just came into being and Jemma just bumbled her way around the globe and happened to come up with great videos as she did. It couldn't be further from the truth, and the amount of work and planning often gave her headaches.

After an hour, Beth had leaned back against the headboard and promised that she was still listening before drifting off to sleep. Jemma knew that Beth was exhausted, and she had been waiting for the moment when the adrenaline would suddenly wear off and Beth could finally rest. She'd been through an incredible ordeal, and it wasn't at all surprising that she was slumbering on Jemma's bed at gone midnight.

Jemma had considered waking her but felt that Beth needed the rest. She had a big day ahead of her, and some rest would go at least some way to helping her deal with what was coming up.

She went to the sofa and plugged in her headphones. Sleep wouldn't be visiting Jemma for a while, and so she decided to keep working. She'd wanted to be a shoulder for Beth to cry on but had somehow ended up having a crying fit of her own, needing Beth to comfort her. It had been an embarrassing reversal of roles but eye-opening.

Beth had asked her if she was happy, and Jemma honestly couldn't say that she was. Her channel was nothing but gloss, smiles, and perfect days. But Jemma didn't really have perfect days. She had exhausting ones. She had days and weeks that took her away from her friends and family for long stretches at a time. She had lonely times in hotels and disingenuous online friendships with people she didn't really know. She hadn't had a relationship for so long that she'd almost forgotten what a hug felt like.

Tears threatened to spill down her face again, but she held them back. She wouldn't wake Beth, and she wouldn't allow herself to wallow in her own self-pity.

It's all fake, Jemma thought, scrolling through her channel homepage and looking at the images. *All of it is a lie.*

She thought about her younger audience, children like Abigail. They weren't mature enough to understand the art of editing, the power of lighting, or the fact that sometimes influencers just plain lied. Jemma always thought she had been relatively truthful; she didn't take bribes like some of her fellow influencers. But if she thought about it, she realised she had lied. She'd done so every single day. Every image she took was manipulated to flawlessness—it had become an art form. But was that fair if the audience didn't always know?

Jemma was in a blessed position where she could technically take time off from her channel. She had savings and an enormous back catalogue of content to live off for a while, if she chose to keep it live. Because she wasn't happy. The realisation had come out of the blue, something that had been hovering around the edges of her consciousness but never acknowledged. Not until someone directly asked her.

Her gaze flickered to Beth. She looked peaceful, but Jemma couldn't help but remember the stress that had been so clearly etched on her face lately. Unsurprisingly, it had taken some time to ease it away that evening.

Hypertension, she reminded herself. No wonder, considering the pressure Beth was under.

Jemma bit her lip. Beth had obviously not meant to mention anything about her illness, which probably meant she hadn't told anyone. Jemma knew it wasn't her place to tell people, but she couldn't help but worry.

She opened a new Instagram message to Cameron, advising him that Beth had explained the situation with the board, that she was sorry to hear of what was happening, and asking if he knew about Beth's hypertension.

She felt a little guilt at telling Beth's brother her secrets, but if it meant that Cameron would understand the seriousness of the situation and start to look after her, then it was worth it. This was one of those situations where she'd much rather ask for forgiveness than permission.

She was surprised to see an immediate reply from him. He hadn't known about Beth's condition. Jemma suspected as much but wondered if she'd done the wrong thing by telling him. It was done now, and her reasons were pure.

Jemma replied to say that she was worried about Beth and suggested that they both look out for her. She didn't have to wait long for a reply. Cameron agreed and said he was trying to find a solution. He was reading through all the paperwork he could find in order to save Beth's spot on the board.

Jemma read his message a few times. Beth had already looked at the problem from every angle, and she couldn't find a way out, so Jemma wondered if Cameron would really manage it. The fact that he was trying to was great, but his chance of success wasn't something Jemma held out much hope for.

What Beth would need was support if the worst did happen and she was removed from Fraser Resort. She'd need something to fall back on, something to give her hope when everything else looked grim.

An idea suddenly occurred to her. Her fingers poised over the keyboard, she considered how best to ask Cameron for help with a rather unusual project.

Chapter Fifteen

The moment Beth woke up, she knew something was very different about that morning. She felt different in herself, the bed felt unusual, the morning light streaming through the window was coming from the other side of the room, and there was the sound of someone else quietly tiptoeing around her.

Her eyes shot open and she sat up. Confusion hit hard. She was fully dressed, and in a hotel room.

"Good morning."

She looked at Jemma in surprise, trying to piece the series of events together that ended with her waking up in Jemma's room.

"I ordered some breakfast—I was starving," Jemma said. She was busying herself around the room, tidying up and towel-drying her wet hair. Her preoccupation meant she thankfully didn't see Beth's brain scramble to catch up.

She rubbed at her eyes and focused on controlling her breathing. There was clearly a logical explanation—she was just too disorientated to find it. Slowly, a memory of the board meeting came to mind. Her heart sank at the recollection that she was about to lose everything.

Then she recalled coming to Jemma's room with the intention of breaking everything off, only to eventually decide to do the exact opposite. Talk of trying and Jemma staying whizzed through her brain at light speed, and she tried to catch on to the fragments of conversation.

Mortification that she had overstayed her welcome and fallen asleep on the bed won out over all the other emotions whirring around her.

"I fell asleep," she said pointlessly.

"You did." Jemma continued to rub the towel over her hair. "It was adorable. You were chatting away and then, boom, asleep."

"I am so sorry." Beth stood and tried to smooth out her clothes.

"Don't be—you were exhausted."

"I outstayed my welcome," Beth corrected. She looked around the room. "Where, um, where did you sleep?"

Jemma pointed to the sofa.

Beth winced. She'd come over and cried on Jemma's shoulder, fallen asleep, and denied her a comfortable night's sleep.

Jemma noticed her reaction, tossed the towel on the back of a chair, and swept Beth into a hug. "The sofa was super comfortable, and I wouldn't have slept much anyway, I had a lot to think about after our chat."

Beth was still putting the jigsaw pieces of the previous evening together. So far she had done all the edges, but the middle was a confusing mystery. She'd never been great at waking up in the morning, and doing so in a strange location, completely exhausted, made everything worse.

"I feel so guilty for kicking you out of your bed," Beth admitted.

"You didn't," Jemma said. "It's big enough—I could have slept on the other side. I just had a lot to think about."

Jemma pressed a soft kiss to Beth's cheek and went to walk away. Beth softly grasped her hand and pulled her close, placing a kiss on her lips. "What were you thinking about?"

"My career," Jemma said, leaning in and kissing Beth lightly again.

Beth smiled and allowed a few moments of gentle kisses. She wanted to get to the bottom of what they had discussed and what had caused a sleepless night for Jemma. She also wanted more deliciously soft kisses that seemed to short-circuit her brain with how much care and tenderness they held. Things started to ratchet up, and Beth took hold of Jemma's upper arms and softly held her back, a big smile on her face as she did. "What about your career?"

Jemma rolled her eyes playfully at being denied the opportunity to carry on kissing. She stepped away and grabbed her hairbrush, looking in the mirror above the desk as she tamed her damp hair.

"Sorry about all the tears last night. I don't know where it all came from," Jemma said.

It came back with a flash. Jemma had broken down in her arms. Beth crossed the room and stood behind her.

"There's nothing to apologise for. We both had a terrible evening in some ways." Beth plucked the hairbrush out of Jemma's hand and directed her to sit. When she did, Beth gently brushed through Jemma's hair. "Did you come to any conclusions?"

"That being scared to post an unedited photo of myself is really unhealthy," Jemma said, her voice soft as her eyes met Beth's in the mirror.

"It is," Beth agreed.

"And I can't change what I look like."

"Nor do you need to," Beth added.

"So maybe I need to take a break. Or change the direction of my channel."

Beth's heart fluttered happily. "What kind of change?" she asked. If Jemma no longer ran a travel channel, then maybe there was a chance she'd stay. Not that she wanted Jemma to sacrifice her career for her.

"I'm not sure yet."

Beth paused brushing Jemma's hair and regarded her reflection. She wasn't sure how she could tell, but she knew Jemma was lying. She strongly suspected that she did have an idea, but she just wasn't settled on it yet.

"Don't stop," Jemma whispered.

Beth continued brushing, knowing in that moment that it would be hard to deny Jemma anything.

"I think you do know," Beth guessed.

Jemma eyes clouded with nervousness. "I'm thinking it through. It's a big step."

Beth knew not to pry. Jemma would talk about it when she was ready. The crying fit from the previous evening had taken them both by surprise. It would take a while to process and plan for next steps. But Beth suspected that Jemma had done a lot of soul-searching the night before. She had switched from depressed to pensive, which presumably meant she had at least part of a plan in place. Beth would be there if and when Jemma needed her.

"I have decided one thing, though," Jemma said.

"Oh yes?" Beth continued to brush, enjoying the feel of being so intimate and yet so innocent. Connecting with people other than her family had been increasingly rare over the years. Being able to touch Jemma in this way was a gift.

"I know it's fast, like, really fast," Jemma said. "But I'm serious about you."

Beth held her breath. She felt the same way. Something had clicked between them. Something she couldn't quite understand but inherently knew was right. In the same way that she could look at a new hire and immediately know if they were going to work hard for the company or be a problem, she'd looked at Jemma and she just knew. But she still wasn't quite ready to dive in, for Jemma's sake if not hers.

"You hardly know me," Beth said, focusing on the hairbrush.

"I like everything I do know." Jemma gazed at her reflection, and Beth swallowed hard.

A sharp rap on the door caused them both to jump.

"That will be breakfast," Jemma said. "I'll get it."

Jemma got up, and Beth looked at her reflection and started to fluff up her hair. She looked a mess. Her eyes clearly showed how emotional and exhausted she was. Her clothes were crumpled from a night of sleep. It certainly wasn't her best look.

"Good morning!"

Beth spun around at the sound of Cameron's voice. Before she had time to hide in the wardrobe, he was wheeling in the breakfast trolley. Heat surged in her face, and she wanted to hide. She absolutely couldn't deal with her brother's suggestive comments and winking right then.

Before she had a chance to threaten him with certain death, he enveloped her in a hug.

"Jemma and I were messaging last night—she mentioned you had fallen asleep here. I wanted to check that you were okay," he explained. "I had Mrs. Halton babysit the kids last night. I tried everything. I've read every single piece of paper in the office. I can't see a way out."

He stepped back and started to set up the breakfast table. It was only then that Beth realised that he was also wearing the same clothes he wore yesterday. He also looked an exhausted mess.

Beth didn't have to read every single piece of paper in the office to know there was no way out. She'd already read every contract, disclosure, share form, and more. She knew she was screwed. But she appreciated her brother's efforts, nonetheless.

Jemma stood beside her and whispered, "Sorry to tell him, but he was worried about you and was going to call you. I didn't want him to wake you, so I said you were here. Sorry if that was the wrong thing to do."

Beth shook her head. "Not at all, I appreciated the rest."

Cameron expertly set up two chairs, took the hot food out of the warming cupboard on the trolley, and set everything up. Beth was a little surprised that her brother knew how to do such a thing, but then he did spend a lot of time at the hotel speaking with the staff.

"Are you joining us?" Beth asked.

Cameron looked uncertain and looked from Beth to Jemma. Jemma picked up a chair from beside the desk and dragged it to the trolley. "Please, stay—I think you two have a lot to talk about. I ordered extra in case you did stay."

Beth smiled at the forethought.

"Thank you, I will," he said, making eye contact with Beth to ensure that he was welcome. She smiled and nodded to him.

A few moments later, everything was set up, and they were sitting and sharing breakfast as if it was the most normal thing in the world. But Beth couldn't shake the feeling that it was like her last meal before execution. She shuddered at the thought, reminding herself that it was a job and not her life. Even if it felt like it was so much more than just a job.

Jemma noticed the shudder and rubbed her upper arm comfortingly.

"I appreciate you working through the night," Beth said to her brother. "But I think we have to conclude that I made this bed and now I must sleep in it. I always knew it was a risk that I'd be pushed out. It's happened, and that's that."

Cameron didn't look happy about the fact as he grumpily chewed on a slice of toast. Beth knew he'd take a while to settle into the idea, but he had to realise that he'd soon be going it alone. She felt like someone was staring at her and turned to see Jemma looking at her in slack-jawed shock.

"You can't just give up," Jemma said.

"The contracts are clear, if a vote—" Beth started.

"That doesn't mean you don't *fight*. You explain to the board that you are the best person for the job. You fight for your right to be there."

Beth smiled at Jemma's innocent outlook. "It doesn't work like that."

"Yes, it does," Jemma insisted. "It's a vote, right?"

"Yep," Cameron said, his interested clearly now piqued.

"Then you sway them to your side. You convince them that no one can run the park like you can, that you're the lifeblood behind it—no offence, Cameron—and that they need you."

"None taken," Cameron said and turned to Beth. "Could that work? Legally, I mean."

Beth huffed. "Well, technically. The vote is today, this afternoon. If the majority side with us, then I won't be removed from the board. But we have a hostile board, need I remind you both?"

"But they're all businesspeople, right?" Jemma asked. "They want successful businesses that make money. What if you convince them that you, and only you, can do that?"

"Then, technically, I could win a vote. But I think you're underestimating how much they dislike me and how bad I am with people."

"And you're underestimating how good I am at influencing

people," Jemma replied. "I can teach you how to convince them. If you're willing to try."

Beth looked from her brother to her...girlfriend? That would take some getting used to. She briefly closed her eyes to refocus her mind. They were both looking at her with such hope on their faces.

"I'll try," Beth agreed. "But this is a real long shot—you both need to know that. Convincing these men won't be easy."

Jemma smiled from ear to ear. "It won't, but I have a few tricks up my sleeve. It's a vote. You're asking people to vote yes or no. How many do we need to convince to change?"

"Two," Beth said.

Jemma clapped her hands with obvious glee. "We can do this."

Beth didn't feel so sure. But if there was anyone who could help her give a really good speech, it had to be Jemma Johnson. The woman had made a successful living out of influencing people and guiding them to whatever she wanted them to do. Positivity was Jemma's watchword—a bit of that, and maybe Beth could convince even the hardest of business investors.

"If we get over this hurdle," Cameron said, "then we need to bring in new investors, loyal to us, to make sure this doesn't happen again. The last time we needed to do this, I left it to you, and I shouldn't have. It just seemed like such hard work to know all the figures and go out and beg people for money." He looked genuinely angry at himself for leaving Beth with all the hard work. "I'm sorry, this is on me."

Beth placed her hand on his. "We both made mistakes. We are where we are."

"I've been researching some of my contacts, and their contacts. I know a guy from the golf club I used to be a member of in Edinburgh. He has been supporting Scottish businesses for a while. I think it's worth chatting to him," he explained.

"If, and it's a big if, we get over this hurdle, we'll talk to him together," Beth promised.

"Let's eat breakfast, and then I'm going to teach you how to influence someone's socks off," Jemma said.

Cameron and Jemma clinked a toast with their glasses of orange juice. Beth smiled at them, but deep down she had no idea if she was capable of influencing anyone. She needed to change the minds of two people, and that felt like a mountain to climb. She'd try her best but wondered if she'd be letting down everyone.

❖

Jemma held the takeaway mug in her hands and leaned on the handrail, watching as the waterfall flowed in front of her. After a few hours in the room talking about influencing and tactics, Jemma had decided the best way to spend the time before the meeting was in one of Beth's favourite places in the nature reserve.

Beth had jumped at the opportunity to return to her secret retreat. They'd grabbed a quick takeaway lunch, which they had eaten while strolling around the reserve, and then they'd ended up in the quiet backstage area.

"It's so peaceful here," Jemma whispered, not wanting to break the silence but not being able to hold back any longer.

"It is," Beth agreed.

Jemma watched as Beth stared at the water churning below the waterfall effect. As the day had gone on, Beth had become quieter. Jemma couldn't blame her as she was about to have one of the biggest meetings of her life, and there was a very real chance that she'd lose everything.

They'd talked about what Beth would say, how she would say it, best phrases to use, things to avoid. Jemma had imparted every single piece of advice she could think of. She had no idea what the board members were like or what they would listen to, so Beth would have to judge that for herself.

"Come to dinner tonight?" Beth asked. "Whatever happens. Commiserations or celebrations."

Jemma smiled. "I'd love that."

"I'll have to get some shopping in," Beth mused, suddenly lost in thought at the logistics of planning a meal.

"Think about that later. We can order in if we need to."

Beth chuckled. "You're not in London any more, sweetheart."

The word fell from Beth's lips without her seeming to notice, which just made Jemma smile all the more. They had both leaned in to their feelings rather than attempting to fight them, agreeing that things could be ironed out as and when they arrived, rather than being blindsided by the logistics up front.

Jemma had looked at the rental cost of apartments in the next nearest town the previous evening. She hadn't told Beth as much, not wishing to sound too eager. She figured she could rent something for a six-month term and see what happened.

"Then we'll bring something from the park. Or eat a tin of peas. We'll figure it all out later," Jemma said brightly. Her new mission was to tap into some of her own positivity and channel it into making Beth feel better, or at least taking some of the pressure off her.

"This might be the last time I stand here," Beth said.

Jemma couldn't deny the claim. If Beth was voted from the board, she was effectively fired and could easily be banned from the park if they so chose. Judging from what Beth had told her about Ivan, it was something he'd happily do.

"I'm glad it's with you," Beth added, approaching Jemma and kissing her cheek with incredible tenderness. "I have to go."

Jemma licked her dry lips and pulled her phone out of her pocket. "Before you do, can you quickly read this post before I film and upload it?"

Beth frowned in confusion but took the phone from her shaky hand. She read the text and her eyes widened. She looked back at Jemma. "Are you sure?"

"I'm going to film it live in a couple of minutes. Read the rest of it," Jemma requested.

Beth returned her attention to the device, her keen eyes quickly swiping across each line of text. A minute later, she handed the device back and offered a tight smile. "I'm incredibly proud of you."

"I've been living a lie for years. There's nothing to be proud of," Jemma stated with a shrug.

"You have to look forward, not back," Beth said, pulling her into a quick but firm hug.

Jemma closed her eyes and drew every bit of strength she could from Beth before the embrace ended. "You too," Jemma replied. "Good luck."

"Thank you, I'll need it," Beth said. "Feel free to stay here for a while if you like. Just close the gate behind you."

"I'll stay a bit, thank you."

Beth pressed a quick kiss to Jemma's lips before disappearing around the corner. Jemma touched her lips and wished things were calmer so she could enjoy the kisses more. But it wasn't the right time. Beth was stressed and so was she. When things settled, there would be time for more intimacy. But right now, they were each living in her own state of flux.

Speaking of which, it was time for Jemma to light the ignition paper on her career. She had no idea what the outcome of her next upload would be. Either she was setting fire to her career, or she was starting something new and exciting. Whatever happened, she knew she was about to disappoint a lot of people.

She stepped away from the waterfall to ensure the noise wasn't picked up on her phone microphone and she'd be easily heard by anyone watching her live stream. She held up her phone and opened the camera. She hadn't put on a full application of make-up that morning, and while her hair was clean, it wasn't styled. Ordinarily, she'd never allow herself to be seen in public the way she currently looked. Realising that she had set unrealistic standards for herself simply to be out in public, she'd rebelled that day and had done the bare minimum she was comfortable with.

And now, she was going to broadcast live to however many people would be willing to tune in. After that, her video would be processed and accessible to anyone on YouTube, including her almost one million subscribers.

She sucked in a deep breath and hit the necessary buttons to start live-streaming, then opened up her notes app to see her prepared speech.

"Hey, guys!" she said. "So, I'm going live from Fraser Resort, as you can see. I'll just wait a few minutes for people to join us, and then I have a couple of things to say. How are you all?"

She flipped back to YouTube and could see the number of viewers steadily climbing with each second that went by. The chat box was filling up already with people telling her that she looked great and wishing her a good morning.

Reading through the comments aloud, she replied to a few questions and greeted everyone who was saying hello. Her nerves jangled as she saw the number of viewers going into the high tens of thousands. Ordinarily she'd be loving the high number, but this wasn't a normal live stream. This was going to be very different. She almost didn't want the pressure of such high viewing figures there and then.

She flipped back over to her notes and sucked in a deep breath.

"Okay, so, first things first, some of you have probably noticed that I look a little different. I don't have all my usual make-up on, and I haven't done my hair as I normally would for you guys. The thing is, I've been doing a lot of soul-searching lately, and the truth is that I'm not happy with some of the content I put on the channel."

She took a breath and was relieved that she couldn't see the comments in the chat. She could imagine that right now her most ardent of fans would be posting nothing but positive comments, and while that was lovely, it didn't help the fact that she needed to remain strong and stick to her script.

"Very little of what I show you is realistic. Very little of what you see on YouTube at all is realistic. And that's okay, as long as you know about it. But I'm beginning to think that a lot of you guys might not know, and that's a problem. You see, I spend a long time preparing for videos on this channel. Not to mention the pictures I post on Instagram. All my social channels are very polished. It's not accurate, it's not realistic, and I don't feel that's fair. On you, or on me."

She started walking, unable to stay still.

"I get a lot of hate online for how I look. Always have. I don't know a single YouTuber who doesn't. There's a lot of people who are trying to be mean, and a lot who don't know that their comments come across as hurtful. But it's made me become really picky about my looks. I realised just yesterday that the thought of posting a selfie without any make-up on scared me so much that I felt sick. And that's not right. Being an influencer has made me too frightened to look at an image of myself without all the editing tools at my disposal.

"I know I'm really blessed to have my channel. I love you all, and I appreciate your support and you taking the time and the effort to spend time with me. But I'm going to have to change my content up, and I really hope you'll join me in this. I want to be more honest. I don't know what that means yet. It does mean I won't be spending an hour taking pictures and editing them for one post on Instagram. And it does mean that I'm going to take some time off, starting now."

She sighed. "I know a lot of you will be unhappy with that, and I'm sorry. But this is something I have to do for me. And I'm probably going to film a series about the behind-the-scenes of influencers, and a series on online bullying. I have a few friends who have said they'll help me, and I think this is an important step towards honesty and transparency for my industry."

She realised she hadn't really been looking at the camera, almost too ashamed to do so. She looked back at the glass lens and smiled.

"So, there you have it, a new direction. A new me. Less of me. Thank you to everyone who has supported me so far. I know some of you are here for travel and advice, and you'll probably unsubscribe now, and that's fine. I appreciate the support you gave, and I wish you all the best in your journey. For those who stay, I hope we can have some real conversations about this mad online world. Thank you all, I appreciate each and every one of you.

"Have…" She hesitated and then laughed. "Have a perfect day, if you can."

She ended the stream and quickly turned off her phone. Her

notifications, emails, and texts were about to blow up, and she didn't feel emotionally strong enough to deal with it all yet.

Thankfully, she had a project to keep her busy. She reached into her pocket and picked out the keys that Cameron had subtly delivered to her earlier. She had no idea what the future would bring, but right now she was going to fix something from the past.

CHAPTER SIXTEEN

B eth had never worn the same outfit to work two days in a row, but if there was ever going to be a time when she would, this was it. Usually, she was fastidious about wearing freshly pressed clothes. Having her entire life turned upside down had put a quick stop to that.

Priorities were shifting. Fast.

"I'm sorry," Cameron said, for the umpteenth time.

They had met up again in the lobby of Fraser Hall and were walking over to the park together through the gardens. Cameron still wore the expression of a lost little boy who had no idea what to do next. She couldn't blame him; he'd never been equipped to deal with anything like this.

Their grandmother had allowed him to be a dreamer and live on another plane of reality while Beth had been moulded into the leader of the pair. Lillian Fraser was from a school of thought that considered boys untrainable, which had ultimately led to Cameron playing with action figures and creating fantasy worlds in his mind, while Beth got extra maths homework.

Anytime Beth showed an aptitude for something, her grandmother had insisted that she leaned in to it. As a child it was basic decision making and logic puzzles. As a teenager it was financial management.

Now, the two of them were products of their grandmother's hard, if uneven, work.

"It's not your fault," Beth said back for the umpteenth time.

"I should have supported you more. I just never thought anything like this could happen. I can't believe I was so naive."

Beth stopped walking, and Cameron abruptly did the same, looking at her in confusion.

"You and I always had roles, Cam. We've been pushed into this since we were children. Because you were a boy and you appeared to not be academically minded, you were left to play. You're a product of our upbringing, not naive."

"I want to change." He dug his hands into his trouser pockets, his head down and his eyes peeking through his uncombed fringe.

Beth knew that circumstances meant that he would have to change, like it or not. It was clear that the shock of the situation had done what Beth had never been able to do with her repeated warnings and predictions of doom. Cameron could now see the dangers ahead.

"I appreciate that," she told him sincerely. She looped her hand through his arm and held on tight. "I'll always be here for you, Cam. Even if I can't be right here in the resort."

They continued walking, each of them taking a little more time to enjoy a sibling stroll through the garden than they had in the past.

❖

Beth's leg twitched nervously. They were just a couple of minutes from the virtual board meeting starting, and she was rapidly forgetting everything that she'd talked about with Jemma. She wasn't quite sure if that mattered, though, as she was very convinced that she wasn't going to be much of an influencer, no matter how much knowledge Jemma imparted.

Beth believed that being an influencer, or being good at negotiations or sales, was just something that someone was born with. You were either a master at connecting with people and speaking with them, or you weren't.

And she was in the latter camp.

The screen flickered to life, and she sat a little taller in her seat. Cameron and Beth had decided to sit in their separate offices.

It looked more professional, and it meant that Beth could be on her own and not distracted by her brother's nerves, which came off him in waves.

One by one, like a nightmare version of *The Brady Bunch*, her fellow board members appeared. Each looked as stern as the next. She didn't know if she was being paranoid, but it looked like Ivan had a twinkle in his eye as he opened the meeting.

As was usual practice, everyone was muted. Beth pressed the button on the conference software that allowed her to virtually raise her hand, indicating to the chair that she wished to speak.

Ivan kept speaking, talking of the vote they were about to have, and for one terrible moment Beth wondered if he would ignore her. Was it possible that her whole career would slip down the drain because she was on mute?

"I see that Miss Fraser is asking to speak," Ivan finally said. "I shall unmute her in a moment, but I must point out that in these situations and with the time constraints that some of us have, I can only allow you five minutes."

Five minutes to save your career and the park, Beth thought. It seemed ludicrous and impossible, but she knew she had to try.

The icon on her screen changed, and she was given permission to speak. She took a quick breath and attempted to lower her shoulders and relax into what she was about to say.

"Thank you for allowing me the opportunity to speak, Ivan," Beth said, remembering Jemma's advice on being courteous and giving praise. It pained her to be kind to the man who was stabbing her in the back, but she knew that graciousness would look good to the other board members, who were not as emotionally injured as she was.

Jemma had also said to lead with a story. Beth hadn't been sure if that would be the best thing to do, thinking that it would be a waste of time when she should be defending her previous decisions by backing them up with facts and figures. But Beth had promised that she'd follow Jemma's advice.

"You all know my long and detailed history with Fraser Resort. I think of it as my home—in fact, I spend more time here than I do in my home. I remember seeing my grandmother burning the midnight oil evening after evening and not quite understanding why. I asked her once, why did she work so hard? She told me that even though she had a team of people, they needed a leader. And that leader had to be the one with the vision. She held my hand and told me that vision was always the key to success. Just looking back at the extraordinary history of Fraser Park, and more recently Fraser Resort, I don't need to tell you all how important vision and leadership are."

Beth shifted a little uncomfortably.

"I've not always been the best leader I could be. And I know I have rubbed many of you the wrong way with my demands and with my attitude. I can't apologise for that because it's who I am, and it's born out of a desire for Fraser Resort to be the absolute best it can be. I know that's something that we all desire. Our goals are aligned. We all want to see Fraser Resort grow into what we know it can be—the best theme park resort, spa, hotel, and water park in Scotland. Hell, in the United Kingdom. And even in Europe."

Beth couldn't tell if her speech was working, but she knew she was ticking off all the bases Jemma had suggested. *Find common ground, don't criticise or complain, acknowledge your own mistakes.* It was a little like a masterclass in manipulation, but right now Beth didn't care.

"When my brother and I took over Fraser Resort, we had big plans. Some of them were our own, and some of them were a part of the ongoing business plan that our grandmother and great-grandmother had laid out. All of them were founded in our knowledge of the industry and decades of speaking with guests and knowing what it was they wanted from us.

"I have that knowledge, and I'm probably one of the very few people who do. Yes, you could take Fraser Resort and make it into a replica of another resort. I'm even certain that you could churn money from it for a while before it started to go stale in the eyes of the guests. I know all of you are expert investors—you know a good balance sheet when you see one. And I know that Fraser Resort's balance sheet right now looks a little unbalanced. It doesn't help that we're so far away, and it becomes difficult for you to see the vision we have and talk to us about why we have it."

Beth leaned a little closer to the camera, attempting to show them the raw emotion on her face, because this was going beyond influencing and into just sharing her heart and soul.

"But I promise you, if you allow us to stay on course, we will prevail. We will build the Fraser vision. When Cameron and I took over, we increased profit margins by thirty-two percent in three years without any impact to our guest satisfaction scores. We know this business—we know our guests. Most importantly, we know our competition. The growing pains we are going through right now are essential. At the end of this process comes a resort like no other, one that will attract the lucrative Japanese and Chinese markets. But it requires someone with a solid understanding of the market, someone who has lived and breathed this resort since they could walk.

"Please, don't think I'm blindsided by emotion. While I love this business with all my heart, I know what it takes to build it up to the vision we all collectively have. I'm not afraid to make the hard decisions. Doing so is why many of you may have heard negative things about me. I'm the person who cuts staff when ticket sales are low. I'm the person who sits here and tells you that we're over budget because it *had* to be done. And I do it happily because I know it's the right thing to do, and it will, ultimately, make the park what we all want it to be."

Beth glanced at the clock. Her time was nearly up, and not a single expression had changed. She had no idea if she had just poured her emotions onto a platter for no reason.

"I know it's been proposed that getting rid of me will be a way to save money, increase profits, and take control. And it will do those things, in the short term. In the long term, it will destroy a unique resort that has an unmistakable soul that guests respond to. A soul that I can inject into every single new project we complete as we strive to grow this resort. I know that you are long-term investors, looking for growth and opportunity that will nourish you and your families for years to come, rather than a short burst in the short term. With that in mind, I respectfully request that you do not vote me out of a job that I was literally born to do. Thank you."

Beth clasped her shaking hands in her lap. She had done everything she could possibly do, and now it was in the hands of board. She couldn't read their faces, had no idea if she had done enough. Fear bubbled within her, and she could hear rushing in her ears. She promised herself that whatever happened next, she would seek medical help on the hypertension issue. She owed that much to Jemma and Cameron, not to mention to herself. She'd been frightened before and operating on autopilot, but now things had to change.

She couldn't take it any more. She excused herself from the call and hung up. If she sat and watched the votes come in, there was a strong chance that she'd pass out. Cameron was on the call, and he could manage whatever was needed and tell her the outcome.

Standing on shaky feet, she walked over to the window and watched guests walking in through the front gates. Some were smiling happily and making their way somewhere, some stood with mouths open as they took everything in, some were crying in joy at being back in a place they worshipped. She'd miss watching these different expressions. It wasn't an easy job, but it certainly was a rewarding one. She had no idea how long she'd been standing at the window and jumped when the door burst open and Cameron rushed in.

"You did it, you bloody did it!" He pulled her into a hug, lifted her off the ground, and spun her around.

"What? What happened?"

Cameron lowered her down, an enormous smile on his face. "So, you left, and Ivan was all like, blah, blah, let's vote. And then all our side voted for you to stay, and then we get to Aaron, and he says that he sees no reason to vote out the brains of the business. Ivan's face was a picture. Then Marcus, same thing. He said he could tell that you were sincere and authentic, and he wanted you to stay on. It all fell apart, Beth. Ivan didn't have a leg to stand on."

"I'm...staying?" Beth asked, still too shocked to really understand what was being said.

"You are, and there's more."

"More?" She could hardly believe she was staying, never mind there being any more.

"Ivan's gone."

Beth blinked. "What do you mean?"

"His people turned against him. He got angry and then said he'd stand down unless they voted with him. Like, instantly rolled out the ultimatum big guns. No one liked that. He had no choice—he had to stand down. He's gone."

Beth sagged in relief. Cameron caught her before she fell and guided her to the sofa.

"He's gone?" She double-checked.

"Gone. You were voted as new chair of the board."

Beth couldn't understand what had happened. In just ten minutes her life had turned around, again. "I don't understand."

"You made people *believe* in you," Cameron explained softly. "That speech was epic. Authentic, they said. They were right. You showed them that you could do something that no one else could."

Beth leaned in to his chest, and he wrapped her in a hug.

"I wanna get someone in to help us with things," Cameron said. "Someone with experience, maybe someone from a European park. Take the load off, help us with the management and forward planning. I was looking at the financials, and I think we can cut a few little things here and there and get them in shape. Then the three of us can manage things going forward. It will take some of the pressure off you, and we'd not get into so much conflict between the two of us. We'd have a third experienced voice."

Beth sighed in relief. Having a businessperson in would mean more clout when she suggested they do or shouldn't do something. And she'd have someone to bounce ideas off, rather than being alone with her theories and stressing over them for hours on end.

"I'd like that," she admitted.

"Good. And we need to talk about the fact you have hypertension and never told me."

Beth sat up straight and stared at him. She couldn't comprehend for a second how he could possibly know. But then it became clear. "Jemma told you?"

"Yeah, because she was worried about you. And I'm glad she did because I can't lose you too, Beth." His eyes filled with unshed tears and she tugged him into a hug.

"You won't lose me. I didn't tell you because I didn't want you to worry."

"I would have worried when you dropped down dead from a heart attack from all the stress you're carrying around," he pointed out.

Beth didn't argue, just held him tighter.

"Jemma told me because she really cares about you," Cameron said. "I don't know what you did, but the girl is head over heels."

"Hush," she whispered.

"Seriously. You need to hold on to her," he said.

Beth loosened her hug and sat back again. "I intend to," she said seriously. "I know it's quick—"

He laughed. "Diane and I met and moved in together in four weeks, remember? Sometimes you just know. Maybe it's a gene thing. We make really good decisions really fast."

Beth scrunched up her nose. "I don't know about that. Remember the time you thought you'd be a pop star?"

"Oh wow, ouch." He chuckled. "Anyway, grab your coat. We need to get back to yours."

"Mine? Why?"

Cameron was already on his feet, taking her suit jacket from the coat stand and holding it out for her. "It's a surprise, come on."

CHAPTER SEVENTEEN

Jemma worried her lip and hoped that she was doing the right thing. It felt like it was the right thing, but only time would tell. Any nerves she had were irrelevant because there was absolutely no going back now.

During a little free time that morning when Beth was checking her emails and making some phone calls, Jemma had stepped out under the guise of doing some filming. In truth, she had a list of tradespeople Cameron had recommended, who she was going to beg to come to help her with an urgent project.

If Jemma knew one thing, it was how to motivate someone to help. She'd cleared her idea with Cameron via messages the night before. He was in full agreement that no matter what happened with the business, Beth needed the cottage garden to be repaired.

Jemma had seen how soul-destroying Beth found it to live with such devastation on her doorstep. It was clear that nothing could be done to fix the problem without heavy duty equipment and a small army of people willing to help.

There had been some reticence and a little pushback from a couple of tradespeople, but by the third call Jemma had found someone willing to help. The first task was clearance, getting the fallen trees, mud, bricks, and more out of the area so the actual garden underneath could be rediscovered.

Beth had enough on her plate to worry about, and so Jemma and Cameron decided to keep it a secret from her, so it would either be something to cheer her up following bad news or an additional thing to celebrate if there was good news. Jemma stood in the doorway with a mug of tea in her hand and watched as the large digger easily scooped up a pile of mud that would take the average person half a day to clear.

Cameron had passed her his spare key to Beth's place and reassured her that Beth would be fine with it. Jemma wondered how sensible it had been to listen to his guidance, considering what she knew of his usual reading of Beth's needs and wants, but she'd done it now.

In truth, watching them clear the garden was the exact distraction she needed. She'd turned her phone off after her live broadcast and needed something to occupy her. While she wanted to turn the phone on and get a reading on what her audience thought of her announcement, she also didn't want to know. Even if the overwhelming number of people were supportive, there would still be some who wouldn't be. It was the way things worked; you couldn't please everyone all the time.

So she watched as the builders set about the hard task of land clearing. It was satisfying to watch, especially as she knew just how long the devastation had been niggling Beth.

"Err, she's here," Patrick, the head builder, told her, having obviously just hurried around from the front of the house to the back.

Patrick had been a little reluctant to take the job, only caving after some cajoling from Jemma and a promise that Beth would be ecstatic to see the work happening. He'd heard rumours that Beth was impossible to please, and Jemma had done her best to convince him that wasn't the case at all.

Now she hoped that she was right.

She smiled at Patrick in an indication that she wasn't at all worried, hoping that her nerves didn't show through. She pulled on the big pair of work boots that one of the builders had lent her so she wouldn't ruin her own shoes as they showed her around. Placing the—also borrowed—hard hat on her head, she headed out and walked around the cottage to meet Beth and Cameron.

When she got to the front, Beth was getting out of the car and looking around in utter bafflement at all the equipment and workers milling around the front of the property. When she saw Jemma, she blinked in confusion and gestured to the hard hat.

"What's happening?" Beth asked, looking from Jemma to Cameron with concern.

Before she could worry any more, Jemma took her hand and led her to the side gate. From there, they could view what was happening, but Beth wouldn't be knee-deep in mud.

"Your garden is being fixed," Jemma whispered in her ear.

Beth's eyes widened as she watched the digger scoop up mud, bricks, and sawn-up logs and move it to one side for removal.

"But...how?" Beth whispered.

"I made some phone calls. My treat. Cameron helped a little."

Beth looked at Jemma in astonishment. "I can't accept this as a gift, but I can thank you for getting someone to come and help me." She placed a soft kiss on Jemma's lips, clearly mindful that her brother and half a dozen builders were surrounding them.

Jemma beamed at the acknowledgement that Beth was happy with her surprise.

"So, what happened?" Jemma asked, eager to know more.

"I texted you," Beth said.

"My phone's been off."

"She smashed it," Cameron said, standing next to them and looking into the garden with interest. "Best speech they'd ever heard. They even voted her to be chair."

"And Ivan left," Beth added. "Don't forget the best bit."

Jemma looked between them in surprise. "Left?"

"Hard to stay when you tried to organise a coup and it backfired," Cameron explained. "Do you think they'll let me have a crack at scooping something? I've always wanted to drive one of them."

Cameron was already wading into the garden, not a care in the world about his smart shoes and suit trousers being covered in mud. Beth ignored him, seemingly used to her brother's antics.

"I did everything you told me," Beth said. "And, somehow, it worked. I can never thank you enough. I couldn't have done it without you. And now you've done this for me as well."

Jemma playfully nudged her. "I'm sure we can work out the details of a payment plan."

Beth grinned. "Oh, you think so?"

"I hope so," Jemma admitted.

Beth cupped her cheek and dived in for another kiss. This one wasn't sweet and chaste like the previous kiss—this one was fuelled by emotion. Jemma didn't hesitate to take full advantage. Within moments, she was breathless, having been taken by surprise by the intensity of Beth's kiss. Reluctantly, she pulled away.

Beth smiled coyly and then indicated the builders with a nod of her head. "I'll get my boots on and then go and say hello and thank you to the workforce you rustled up. However did you manage it?"

"I'm an influencer," Jemma said with a wink.

"Are you still?" Beth asked seriously, clearly remembering the notes Jemma had asked her to read earlier.

"I'm not sure what I am," Jemma admitted. "I'm figuring it out."

"With your phone off?"

"Yeah. I needed some space. I'm a little worried about what people will say."

Beth ran a comforting hand up and down Jemma's arm. "If you want, we can look at the replies together."

Jemma nodded. "I'd really like that."

She'd been avoiding it, but with someone else there to hold her hand and maybe even read some of the comments to her, she felt like she could cope with whatever lurked in her inbox.

"Excellent. Let me get changed, and then we can have a chat with the builders. Oh, Cameron asked if he and the children could come over for dinner. I automatically said yes, forgetting I already had dinner plans with you. It's all a bit new—I usually don't have plans."

"A family dinner sounds like a lovely idea. We can celebrate together," Jemma said.

"Are you sure? I can tell him we'll do it another day," Beth offered. It was a genuine suggestion, but Jemma suspected Beth wanted her family around her that evening.

"We'll have lots of opportunity to have dinner just the two of us," Jemma promised. "It will be nice to have everyone together."

Beth's warm smile was all the reward Jemma needed. It wouldn't be a hardship to share Beth with her family that evening. In fact, Jemma looked forward to joining the Fraser clan.

❖

Beth looked at the piles of building material and covered equipment in her back garden. It looked a mess, but a good mess. It was the start of something new, the opportunity to move in the right direction rather than stagnating.

In the kitchen she could hear the sound of Cameron plating up the takeaway fish and chips he had picked up after collecting the children from the babysitter he sometimes used. Jemma was in an animated conversation with Abigail, hearing all the latest about her three best friends and which of them would be allowed to be a part of her upcoming science project that only allowed pairs to work together. Beth smiled to herself as Jemma made all the right noises and asked Abigail questions about what she would do with such a tricky situation.

"When will the builders be back?" Luke asked, coming to stand next to her to look out of the window at the garden.

"Tomorrow," Beth said. "They think it will take a few days to clear everything, and then we'll go from there about what to do."

"Are you going to try to make it like Grandma's garden, or start fresh?" Luke asked.

Beth didn't know. She'd not exactly had time to think about it. Her immediate reaction had been to attempt to recreate what had been there before, but she wondered if a splash of something new would allow her to put her own mark on the place.

"I'm not sure. What do you think?" she asked him.

"I think it's big enough for a football pitch, and you should build that," Luke said, a cheeky grin on his face.

"Do you know anyone who might get some use out of that?" Beth asked, reaching for his side and tickling him.

He tried to pretend he wasn't fazed by her movements but quickly gave in, being as ticklish as his father was. After a couple of screams of mercy, she let him go.

"Stop bullying my son," Cameron said playfully. "Dinner's served."

In the dining room, a place was saved between Abigail and Jemma, both of them patting the seat for Beth to come and sit down. She did, marvelling at how quickly Jemma had integrated herself into the family dynamic.

Cameron and Luke took their seats, and everyone started to eat.

"I saw your video," Luke said to Jemma.

Jemma paused, a forkful of food nearly at her mouth. She looked nervously at him.

"I thought it was cool," Luke said, not noticing Jemma's near panic.

"You did?" Jemma asked.

"What video?" Cameron asked.

"Jemma's taking some time off because her job is really hard sometimes," Abigail explained to her father. "She did a live video about it this afternoon. We saw it at Missy's."

"She's going to show things more honestly," Luke added. "Like, not editing things as much. Because it's all a bit fake, and if people don't know, then that might not be fair."

Abigail nodded in agreement. "And people online are bullies, so she's going to talk about that. Missy said it's really brave, and I agree."

Beth put a hand on Jemma's thigh and gave it a little squeeze. "I agree too."

"Well, so do I," Cameron said. "It looks like a lot of hard work, and you post every day—you deserve a break. There's a lovely little hotel up the road. Fraser Hall, I think it's called? You should have a break and stay there for a while. They do a lovely breakfast."

Beth kicked her brother under the table. She turned to Jemma. "Ignore him—there's no pressure."

"I've already been looking at short-term leases in Stirling," Jemma admitted.

Beth felt light-headed. Stirling was a short drive away. While she'd hoped that Jemma would visit or at least stay close, she hadn't allowed herself to believe it would actually happen.

"If that's okay?" Jemma added, clearly worried about Beth's prolonged silence.

"Very okay," Beth said quickly. "Extremely okay."

"It's a shame you were thinking of taking a break," Cameron said. "I had a wee idea."

Beth frowned at him. She couldn't believe that mere hours after they'd had a heart-to-heart and had agreed to run everything by each other, Cameron was already slipping into his old ways.

"What idea is that?" Jemma asked.

"I think we need a brand ambassador at Fraser Resort, someone who takes control of our social media and promotes the park properly. Lord only knows the two of us don't know what we're doing, and the small marketing team we have aren't really cut out for such a thing. I wouldn't know how to hire one, either. I thought you'd be a good fit. I didn't say anything to Beth because she'd get all worried about"—Cameron looked the kids—"perceived conflicts of interest. But I'm looking at this as a businessman, not a brother. I think we need the role to be filled, and I think you're the right person for it. Of course, if you wanted to remain off camera, that would still work for us. Better really, more focus on the resort."

Beth opened and then closed her mouth. On one hand she was annoyed that he hadn't said anything to her, but on the other hand she absolutely understood why. This was a business decision and one that she was too close to.

Marketing was a problem for the park, and a brand ambassador was a good decision as it would bolster their failing social media channels. Jemma was the perfect candidate for such a role. But Beth couldn't possibly have offered the role to Jemma herself. Cameron had been thinking of the business and snatching up an opportunity. Pushing her out of the decision-making process was actually the right thing to do on this occasion.

Jemma looked at Beth. "Well, I'd have to know what you thought about that."

Beth swallowed. She didn't know what to say. The idea of having Jemma with her at the park set her heart aflutter, but was that asking for too much too soon?

"I think you're the right woman for the job," Beth admitted.

"If you're interested, we could start with a six-month rolling contract," Cameron suggested, "so we could see how things go. Obviously, we wouldn't hold you to anything if you had another job to go to. But I do think you'd end up staying." He smiled and winked at Beth before shovelling another forkful of food into his mouth.

Jemma looked intently at Beth, seemingly trying to read her mind.

Beth loved her niece and nephew dearly, but for once wished they weren't present. The whole abstract and partially silent conversation the three adults were having would have been so much easier if they weren't there. Then again, Beth considered that maybe it was best that the children were nearby. With no opportunity to dissect the potential flaws in the plan, they could take the leap together and see what happened.

Beth grinned and slowly nodded. Jemma beamed and turned to look at Cameron.

"That sounds like a wonderful idea. It will help me keep in the influencer business, while focusing on a single product and location, rather than myself. It sounds like a really good fit."

"You're staying?" Abigail screeched happily.

"I am," Jemma confirmed. "You're going to have to show me absolutely everything. After school, of course." She turned to Luke. "I may need some help from my number one cameraman, if you have some time."

Both the kids eagerly nodded their agreement and immediately started discussing things Jemma needed to see and shots they thought would be great on social media. Jemma tilted her gaze to Beth and offered her a smile.

Beth couldn't help but beam in return.

Chapter Eighteen

Jemma revelled in the feel of Beth's hand in hers, as Beth gently guided them through the semi-darkness of the park. The family dinner had been wonderful, so easy and full of life and laughter. Jemma couldn't remember the last time she'd sat at a busy family dining table and let the sound of loved ones wash over her.

Soon after they'd finished eating, Cameron had made his excuses to leave. He had claimed that it was nearly the children's bedtime, as Abigail loudly proclaimed that it was nowhere near that time. Regardless, he hurried them out the door with a wide grin on his face at the two of them left behind.

It could have been awkward, but it wasn't. Something had changed in Beth's mood, some of the stress had floated away, and a sense of almost exhilaration seemed to have taken its place.

Beth had asked if Jemma was ready to turn her phone on and see what the fallout had been from her announcement, but she wasn't. A glance at her watch and Beth had declared they were going on an adventure.

After borrowing some clothes to wrap up warm for a slightly chilly evening, Jemma had gotten into the car and waited to be told of the upcoming adventure. Beth wouldn't divulge any details other than to say they were heading to the park, not a surprise for Jemma and not a problem, either. Fraser Park was Beth's home away from home, and Jemma wanted to learn every single thing there was to know about it.

Once through the gates, Beth had taken Jemma's hand and led her through shortcuts, shops, and quiet pathways. They entered a shop that Jemma had been in a couple of times, themed to mythical creatures, where she'd bought a cuddly toy of a unicorn as a giveaway for her channel.

Her channel.

She sighed but wasn't able to dwell too much on that as Beth gently pulled her in the direction of a large fibreglass dragon. Behind it was a door that Beth opened with her key card.

"Are we going to make out behind a dragon?" Jemma teased.

"Maybe, if you play your cards right." Beth winked. She opened the door and started to climb the spiral staircase. Jemma followed, intrigued by this behind-the-scenes glimpse of the park. Within a couple of minutes, they were on a dark roof, the murmur of guests below them. It was so dark that Jemma could hardly see, and she tentatively stepped forward with her hand out.

"I've got you," Beth said, guiding her into position.

"Where are we?" Jemma asked. "I can't see a thing."

"We're in the best place in the park. The absolute best view of the show, front and centre and not a tall person or balloon to interrupt your view of everything," Beth said, her voice a soft whisper in Jemma's ear.

Jemma felt goosebumps run down her arms at the breath wisping around her. "Ah, do you take all the girls here?" she joked.

"I've never brought anyone here," Beth said. "I watch the show from here nearly every night. People know I'm here, but they know to not disturb me. They think I'm watching the show out of some kind of act of quality control, but I'm actually watching it because I find it beautiful. I want you to see it how I see it."

Jemma couldn't help but feel blessed that Beth had chosen to share such a sacred space and experience with her. She could only see an outline of Beth, but it was enough to pull her into an embrace and press her lips to Beth's. Beth quickly responded, wrapping her hands up around Jemma's neck as she had done a few times before. It was all encompassing and a little possessive, and Jemma couldn't help but enjoy the little thrill she got as a result.

Jemma melted into the kiss. She couldn't get over how right it felt. She'd once heard someone say that falling in love happened when least expected, that your entire life could be turned upside down, and you'd just know in your heart that you'd found someone special.

Jemma felt that with Beth. She couldn't explain it, couldn't justify it, it was just there. Her life had been turned upside down, a long overdue change that came about partly because of Beth's curiosity and honesty about the influencer business Jemma called her career. The floodgates had opened, and Jemma felt as if she could see more clearly once she was no longer treading water and chasing the elusive algorithm.

She didn't know if Beth knew just how big an impact she'd had on her life, but she was determined to do everything she could to thank and repay her.

Beth ended the kiss. "You didn't feel pressured into staying, did you?"

Jemma chuckled. "Not at all. Do you feel pressured?"

"Not at all." Beth laughed. "I have no idea what I'm doing, but it feels so right. It's never felt this right."

"I know what you mean." Jemma reached for Beth's hand and placed a kiss on her palm. "I want to stay. I want to get to know you. And figure out how to be a brand ambassador. I love this resort, and I already have some ideas for things to do to promote it."

"And what if this doesn't work? Between us, I mean?" Beth asked, her voice a whisper.

"We'll approach that bridge when we come to it," Jemma said. "I'm on a six-month contract, and I'm eager to impress the boss."

Beth laughed again. "I hear she's a bit of a taskmaster."

"I do hope so," Jemma whispered, nuzzling Beth's neck and peppering her skin with kisses.

The ambient music changed, and Beth stood to attention, pulling away. "The show's starting."

Jemma smiled. It appeared that not much would come between Beth Fraser and the night-time show. She liked that about Beth. It was like a little secret that only she had been allowed to discover.

Beth was passionate about sharing popcorn with a loved one and enjoying the best evening show in Scotland on a quiet rooftop. Jemma couldn't wait to discover what else made Beth Fraser tick.

The lights and lasers from the show lit up the park, and when a crash of music sounded, she glanced to her side, and her breath caught in her chest at how beautiful Beth was, illuminated by the glow and staring at the show with ageless wonder.

She positioned herself behind Beth, wrapping her arms around her waist and resting her chin on Beth's shoulder so she could watch the show in comfort.

Now, *this* was a perfect day, Jemma thought.

Epilogue

Jemma sat in the meeting room and scrolled through the Fraser Park Instagram account on her phone. She'd been in her new role for two weeks and had created a marketing plan to present to Cameron and Beth. Opportunities were rife in a company that had only half-heartedly used social media up until that point.

Cameron entered the meeting room and smiled at her. "Morning!"

"Hey, boss," Jemma joked.

Cameron flopped down into a chair and grinned. "Have you figured out a way to make us the number one tourist attraction in Europe yet?"

Jemma patted the papers in front of her. "Yep, all in here."

Beth entered the room, and Jemma couldn't help the fact that her heart started beating a little quicker. It had been two weeks since she'd thrown in the towel on her influencer career and started to work at Fraser Resort. She'd be lying if she didn't admit to herself that a big part of that decision was to spend more time with Beth, something she was absolutely thrilled to have done. Especially as things were going extremely well between them.

Romantic dinners and midnight walks through the park had led to much conversation and an understanding that their quick attraction to one another was just the start of so much more. Jemma didn't know if she believed in things like love at first sight, but a part of her had become caught on Beth. Something about the woman had caused Jemma to pause, and just a few weeks later her entire life had been turned upside down in the best possible way.

Beth glanced at her but quickly looked away, cheeks reddening as she did. Jemma assumed that she was thinking about their morning in bed together, neither wanting to get up and start the day. Eventually, Jemma had gotten up and explained to Beth how she had a meeting with her hot boss that morning. She'd also mentioned that she struggled to concentrate in meetings with her boss as she spent most of her time mentally undressing her.

Jemma thought it was adorable how Beth attempted to draw a distinct line between work and private life. It was impossible to completely separate the two, and Beth did work with her brother on a daily basis.

"Sorry I'm late," Beth said, taking a seat beside Cameron.

"Jemma is going to make us the number one tourist attraction in Europe," Cameron said.

"Oh, excellent, I need a new car," Beth said.

"What is the number one tourist attraction in Europe?" Cameron asked.

"Depends how you calculate it," Jemma replied. "Either the Eiffel Tower or the Colosseum in Rome."

"Pfft. Neither of them have waffles on a stick," Cameron said.

Jemma shook her head in disagreement. "Actually, you can get waffles on a stick by the—"

"Can we be serious for a moment?" Beth asked.

Cameron sat up a little straighter. "Of course, sorry."

Jemma smiled to herself. Cameron's behaviour had changed considerably recently. The shock of nearly losing the park and seeing the stressed mess his sister had become had been the catalyst for him to turn a corner. That and Jemma's gentle guidance on the things he probably ought to do and definitely should not do.

He was still the carefree man he was before, but now with a little more consideration for all the work his sister did. Slowly, things were being taken from Beth's inbox and being placed in Cameron's. And, to Beth's surprise, he was coping admirably.

Jemma handed each of them a copy of her report. "I've done some analysis on the social media accounts for the park, what's working and what I think could be improved upon."

She paused at a knock on the door. Mary, one of the financial controllers, popped her head around the door.

"I'm sorry to interrupt. Cameron. James Milton is returning your call. He said it was urgent," Mary said.

Cameron looked apologetically to Beth. "This is about the payment glitch from last week— I'll need to take this. I'll only be a couple of minutes."

Beth nodded, and Cameron jumped up and left the meeting room.

"Dinner at mine tonight?" Beth asked, flipping casually through Jemma's report.

She didn't really need to ask. They met up every evening without fail. They either went back to Beth's, travelled the short distance to Jemma's, or hung around in the park. Every time Jemma thought that Beth had finally shown her every single secret corner of Fraser Park, she was surprised to be introduced to yet another one.

"I'd love to," Jemma said. "Are the kids coming by this afternoon?"

Beth nodded. "Join us for a couple of rides?" Beth looked up.

"Absolutely." Jemma smiled.

"Not regretting your decisions yet?" Beth asked.

Beth asked that question every other day, seemingly convinced that Jemma would one day get the itch to travel again. And every time Jemma reassured her that she absolutely did not regret her decisions. Leaving her influencer lifestyle behind had been the biggest load off her shoulders. Working at Fraser Park was like a dream with fun and discovery around each corner and a wonderful family to share every moment with.

"Definitely no regrets," Jemma said. She grinned. "Except allowing you to get out of bed this morning."

Beth blushed and looked towards the door. "Shh, he'll be back soon."

"I think he knows what we get up to," Jemma pointed out.

Beth shook her head. "No, I refuse to go there. Thank you very much."

The door opened and Cameron took his seat again. "I'm sorry about that. All sorted. Right, you have my full attention, Jemma. What does the future hold?"

About the Author

Amanda Radley had no desire to be a writer but accidentally turned into an award-winning, best-selling author. Residing in the UK with her wife and pets, she loves to travel. She gave up her marketing career in order to make stuff up for a living instead. She claims the similarities are startling.

Books Available From Bold Strokes Books

A Turn of Fate by Ronica Black. Will Nev and Kinsley finally face their painful past and relent to their powerful, forbidden attraction? Or will facing their past be too much to fight through? (978-1-63555-930-9)

Desires After Dark by MJ Williamz. When her human lover falls deathly ill, Alex, a vampire, must decide which is worse, letting her go or condemning her to everlasting life. (978-1-63555-940-8)

Her Consigliere by Carsen Taite. FBI agent Royal Scott swore an oath to uphold the law, and criminal defense attorney Siobhan Collins pledged her loyalty to the only family she's ever known, but will their love be stronger than the bonds they've vowed to others, or will their competing allegiances tear them apart? (978-1-63555-924-8)

In Our Words: Queer Stories from Black, Indigenous, and People of Color Writers. Stories Selected by Anne Shade and Edited by Victoria Villaseñor. Comprising both the renowned and emerging voices of Black, Indigenous, and People of Color authors, this thoughtfully curated collection of short stories explores the intersection of racial and queer identity. (978-1-63555-936-1)

Measure of Devotion by CF Frizzell. Disguised as her late twin brother, Catherine Samson enters the Civil War to defend the Constitution as a Union soldier, never expecting her life to be altered by a Gettysburg farmer's daughter. (978-1-63555-951-4)

Not Guilty by Brit Ryder. Claire Weaver and Emery Pearson's day jobs clash, even as their desire for each other burns, and a discreet sex-only arrangement is the only option. (978-1-63555-896-8)

Opposites Attract: Butch/Femme Romances by Meghan O'Brien, Aurora Rey & Angie Williams. Sometimes opposites really do attract. Fall in love with these butch/femme romance novellas. (978-1-63555-784-8)

Swift Vengeance by Jean Copeland, Jackie D & Erin Zak. A journalist becomes the subject of her own investigation when sudden strange, violent visions summon her to a summer retreat and into the arms of a killer's possible next victim. (978-1-63555-880-7)

Under Her Influence by Amanda Radley. On their path to #truelove, will Beth and Jemma discover that reality is even better than illusion? (978-1-63555-963-7)

Wasteland by Kristin Keppler & Allisa Bahney. Danielle Clark is fighting against the National Armed Forces and finds peace as a scavenger, until the NAF general's daughter, Katelyn Turner, shows up on her doorstep and brings the fight right back to her. (978-1-63555-935-4)

When In Doubt by VK Powell. Police officer Jeri Wylder thinks she committed a crime in the line of duty but can't remember, until details emerge pointing to a cover-up by those close to her. (978-1-63555-955-2)

A Woman to Treasure by Ali Vali. An ancient scroll isn't the only treasure Levi Montbard finds as she starts her hunt for the truth—all she has to do is prove to Yasmine Hassani that there's more to her than an adventurous soul. (978-1-63555-890-6)

Before. After. Always. by Morgan Lee Miller. Still reeling from her tragic past, Eliza Walsh has sworn off taking risks, until Blake Navarro turns her world right-side up, making her question if falling in love again is worth it. (978-1-63555-845-6)

Bet the Farm by Fiona Riley. Lauren Calloway's luxury real estate sale of the century comes to a screeching halt when dairy farm heiress, and one-night stand, Thea Boudreaux calls her bluff. (978-1-63555-731-2)

Cowgirl by Nance Sparks. The last thing Aren expects is to fall for Carol. Sharing her home is one thing, but sharing her heart means sharing the demons in her past and risking everything to keep Carol safe. (978-1-63555-877-7)

Give In to Me by Elle Spencer. Gabriela Talbot never expected to sleep with her favorite author—certainly not after the scathing review she'd given Whitney Ainsworth's latest book. (978-1-63555-910-1)

Hidden Dreams by Shelley Thrasher. A lethal virus and its resulting vision send Texan Barbara Allan and her lovely guide, Dara, on a journey up Cambodia's Mekong River in search of Barbara's mother's mystifying past. (978-1-63555-856-2)

In the Spotlight by Lesley Davis. For actresses Cole Calder and Eris Whyte, their chance at love runs out fast when a fan's adoration turns to obsession. (978-1-63555-926-2)

Origins by Jen Jensen. Jamis Bachman is pulled into a dangerous mystery that becomes personal when she learns the truth of her origins as a ghost hunter. (978-1-63555-837-1)

Unrivaled by Radclyffe. Zoey Cohen will never accept second place in matters of the heart, even when her rival is a career, and Declan Black has nothing left to give of herself or her heart. (978-1-63679-013-8)

A Fae Tale by Genevieve McCluer. Dovana comes to terms with her changing feelings for her lifelong best friend and fae, Roze. (978-1-63555-918-7)

Accidental Desperados by Lee Lynch. Life is clobbering Berry, Jaudon, and their long romance. The arrival of directionless baby dyke MJ doesn't help. Can they find their passion again—and keep it? (978-1-63555-482-3)

Always Believe by Aimée. Greyson Walsden is pursuing ordination as an Anglican priest. Angela Arlingham doesn't believe in God. Do they follow their vocation or their hearts? (978-1-63555-912-5)

Courage by Jesse J. Thoma. No matter how often Natasha Parsons and Tommy Finch clash on the job, an undeniable attraction simmers just beneath the surface. Can they find the courage to change so love has room to grow? (978-1-63555-802-9)

I Am Chris by R Kent. There's one saving grace to losing everything and moving away. Nobody knows her as Chrissy Taylor. Now Chris can live who he truly is. (978-1-63555-904-0)

The Princess and the Odium by Sam Ledel. Jastyn and Princess Aurelia return to Venostes and join their families in a battle against the dark force to take back their homeland for a chance at a better tomorrow. (978-1-63555-894-4)

The Queen Has a Cold by Jane Kolven. What happens when the heir to the throne isn't a prince or a princess? (978-1-63555-878-4)